TWO LIKE
ME AND YOU

Borne Back Books
West Egg, New York

Copyright © 2019 by Chad Alan Gibbs

All rights reserved, including the right to repdocue this book or portions thereof in any form whatsoever.

First Borne Back Books trade paperback edition May 2019

Cover Design: Damonza.com
Interior Illustrations: Wes Molebash (wesmolebash.com)
Author Photo: Selfie

Manufactured in the United States of America

Publisher's Cataloging-in-Publication Data
provided by Five Rainbows Cataloging Services

Names: Gibbs, Chad Alan, author.
Title: Two like me and you / Chad Alan Gibbs.
Description: Auburn, AL : Borne Back Books, 2019.
Identifiers: LCCN 2019901372 | ISBN 978-0-9857165-3-0 (paperback) | ISBN 978-0-9857165-4-7 (ebook) | ISBN 978-0-9857165-5-4 (audiobook)
Subjects: LCSH: Bildungsromans. | CYAC: Teenagers--Fiction. | Fame--Fiction. | Love--Fiction. | Veterans--Fiction. | France--Fiction. | Young adult fiction. | BISAC: YOUNG ADULT FICTION / Coming of Age. | YOUNG ADULT FICTION / Social Themes / Emotions & Feelings. | YOUNG ADULT FICTION / Social Themes / Friendship.
Classification: LCC PZ7.1.G4991 Tw 2019 (print) | LCC PZ7.1.G4991 (ebook) | DDC [Fic]--dc23.

TWO LIKE ME AND YOU

A NOVEL

CHAD ALAN GIBBS

BORNE BACK BOOKS

For Tricia,
je t'aime à la folie.

One world was not enough for two like me and you.
—Oscar Wilde, "Her Voice"

Saint-Lô was bombed out of existence in one night.
—Samuel Beckett, "The Capital of the Ruins"

TWO LIKE
ME AND YOU

Chapter One

In which our hero complains about his assigned seat.

You can't make this shit up.

That's what Garland Lenox would say about this story—my story—the story of how I tried to win back Sadie Evans, my super famous ex-girlfriend. Of course, Garland said that a lot. It was his go-to reply anytime anyone raised so much as a skeptical eyebrow at one of the more outrageous details of his own life story. Details like …

"Scientists said they'd never heard of a Great White that far up the Mississippi River, but when they pulled its tooth from my leg they had to rewrite their little science books."

Or …

"Saddam Hussein never could remember all the rules to chess. He'd move pawns backward and he wouldn't even touch his bishops because he said they were papists."

Or …

"The Super Bowl is faker than professional wrestling. I know the fella in Bakersfield who used to write scripts for the NFL. Why'd you think they take two weeks off before the big game? It's so the players can rehearse."

1

Garland would watch you while he told his tales, and if he saw even a shadow of disbelief he'd pounce: "Son, you can't make this shit up."

In the week I knew the old man he said those words to me approximately sixty-three times, though for the record I'm not his son. Garland called everyone son, even Parker sometimes, though I'm pretty sure he knew she was a girl. Also for the record, I never once accused Garland of making up anything, though I usually had my doubts, and sometimes my face would betray me. But in my defense, you'd likely catch a raised eyebrow at the final table of the World Series of Poker after Garland said something like, "NASA built a space station on the dark side of the moon and they've been sending teams up there twice a week since 1974. I went there once in the eighties and trust me, it's boring as hell. Just a bunch of nerds playing Atari."

But I'm getting ahead of myself. This story—my story—began on a Monday, April 13th, which coincidentally was a year to the day from Black Saturday (the day I lost Sadie Evans), and not so coincidentally the day I met Garland Lenox. I was a junior then, at J. P. Hornby High school in Hornby, Alabama, a little town east of Birmingham named after Josiah Prescott Hornby, a former Alabama governor known best for keeping a passel of pet possums in the governor's mansion.

"He was also a self-taught dentist," our history teacher, Mr. Graham, said when one of my classmates broached the subject of our collective embarrassment, but we told him that only made it worse.

On that fateful morning I walked into Mr. Graham's first period class and groaned when the realization I was about to spend five straight days in that abyss of despair manifested itself in a stabbing pain behind my left eye. Like boy bands, each class at J. P. Hornby was awful in its own way, but I hated Mr. Graham's class in particular because of our alphabetically assigned seats, something he claimed sped up the attendance-taking process.

Of course there were shouts of protest when he arranged us on day one, because everyone knows last names are too arbitrary of a way to assign seats. Mr. Graham's alphabetical reign of terror was particularly unkind to me. My last name is Green, because my ancestors had green teeth or began recycling way before it was cool. And because of this, in a cruel twist of surname fate, I had to spend sixty minutes each morning sitting behind Tyler Godfrey, who hadn't cut or washed his hair since getting into Lord of the Rings cosplay in eighth grade, and in front of Parker Haddaway, the terrifying new girl who'd spoken exactly two words to me since her January arrival.

"Hi, I'm Edwin."

"Don't. Care."

That said, I thought pretty much everyone at J. P. Hornby was a dick slap, so in reality every seat was an assigned seat between two people who'd serve time if mouth breathing were ever declared illegal. But even I'd have enjoyed a change of scenery once in a while.

Monday was our first day back at school from spring break, and I sat there between Parker and Tyler's gross hair, rubbing my head and trying not to listen to the what and where of everyone's vacations, when Mr. Graham walked in and all conversation slid to a stop.

"It's April 13th," he shouted, slamming both hands hard on his desk, "and that means we only have five weeks left together. So we're going to spend the next four of them learning about World War II, and then we'll cram the last sixty years of US history into one week because the people in Montgomery who created your curriculum are imbeciles."

A murmur of excitement passed over the room, but only because wars sound like a departure from the doldrums of history, when in fact they're no more exciting to study than the Teapot

Dome Scandal. Mr. Graham drove this point home over the next fifty minutes as he droned on about the end of World War I and the Treaty of Versailles and the League of Nations. He didn't even mention Hitler until the last five minutes or so, and only to tell us he'd written a book called *Mein Kampf.*

Then, only a few minutes before the bell freed us, Mr. Graham closed his notes and said, "You're all going to hate me, but for the next four weeks you will have an outside assignment. In teams of two you will interview someone who lived through World War II. Correction— someone who lived through and remembers World War II. If your great aunt Myrtle was born in 1944, that's not going to cut it. I will provide a question each Monday, and on Fridays you will report back what your eyewitness to history had to say. This will bring history to life in a way this outdated textbook …" And here he held aloft his copy of *US History 1866–2009* before dropping it to the ground with a thud. "… could never do."

Groans of dissent rose from around the room but Mr. Graham silenced us with a raised hand. "As for teams," he said, "you have sixty seconds to find a partner or I will assign one for you. Ready, go." I watched as three dozen juniors calmly began pairing up by social status with alarming efficiency. I didn't move. There was no need to. Soon Tyler Godfrey would turn around and say, "I'm glad to be partners with you, Edwin Green … here at the end of all things," and I'd say, "Yeah, sure, whatever." I counted to five in my head, and on cue Tyler turned around and began to speak, but a voice behind me said, "Forget it, Frodo. Edwin Green is mine."

Tyler's eyes widened, and my eyes widened, and he quickly turned around leaving me to face the terror behind me alone. I took a deep breath, then four more, and turned around to acknowledge my partner, but she had earbuds in and appeared to be sleeping. What the hell?

4

Mr. Graham spent the last minute of class extolling the academic benefits of his assignment over a rising crescendo of objections, and as always he kept going after the bell rang because he liked to shout his final words of the day over the bustle of closing books and zipping backpacks. "Remember," he shouted, "to know nothing of what happened before you were born is to forever remain a child. Ten points if anyone knows who said that. Anyone? No one?"

It was class tradition for someone to answer "Beyoncé" to Mr. Graham's extra point question, but that day everyone shuffled out in silence, pissed off about this new time consuming assignment. Seemed we all believed we had better things to do than drive around town interviewing geriatrics about world wars. Well, everyone except for Parker Haddaway, who was still asleep at her desk when I left the room. Sooner or later I'd have to talk to her about the assignment, but I figured it could wait until after lunch. I'd skipped breakfast, and she was not the sort of person you could talk to on an empty stomach. So I went to my locker and grabbed my shorts for second period gym.

Chapter Two

In which our hero and his best friend discuss religion and human sexuality with a cavalcade of morons.

"People say she's a lesbian."

Coach Cowden only required strenuous exercise from the J. P. Hornby football team during gym class, while the "civilians", as he called the rest of us, were left to loiter around the track for sixty minutes as he sat in his office and daydreamed of parlaying his current job into one with the Crimson Tide. Never mind he'd led the J. P. Hornby Possums to three consecutive winless seasons, the man was eternally optimistic, and I admired that. That day, like every other, I walked around the track with Fitz Lee, my best friend since third grade, and the only person at school I purposely spoke to. Fitz's parents divorced three years ago on account of his dad being gay, which made the Lees a hot topic of the Hornby grapevine. It also left Fitz and me with an understanding, and we never discussed his folks or Black Saturday, though jokes were never off limits.

"Not that it matters Green, but I'm pretty sure she's not a lesbian," Fitz said. "A bunch of dumb jocks only started saying that after she turned down a date with Buzz Booker."

"No offense, but your family isn't known to have the most accurate gaydar."

Hornby Martial Arts had named Fitz their top student for twelve consecutive years—he was practically a ninja—and had anyone else in school said this he would have sent them to the hospital with a dislocated trachea, but all I got was a bruising punch to the arm.

"She turned down the date with Buzz Booker," I said, rubbing my arm, "because she's into girls."

"Or because she's not into meathead linebackers who read on a second-grade level."

"How dare you. Buzz Booker is a gentleman and a scholar," I said, and Fitz laughed.

But it wasn't just Buzz Booker. In the first five days of her midyear arrival, Parker Haddaway declined dates with no less than a dozen of J. P. Hornby's most eligible bachelors. Actually, declined might not be a strong enough word to describe the voracity with which Parker rejected her potential suitors, since she told half to consume feces and die, and the other half to go have sexual relations with themselves. After seeing our top guns crash and burn in such spectacular fashion, the rest of the guys at school pretty much left her alone, though her multitude of early admirers gives you some idea of Parker's allure, even if most days she wore jeans and an old army surplus jacket. A week later the rumors began, and before long Buzz Booker et al. began propagating a revisionist history where they repelled Parker's unwanted advances, although never within her earshot, since she scared even our scariest football players.

"Are you guys talking about Parker Haddaway?"

Our conversation had drawn the attention of a passing gaggle of senior girls all wearing the same teal running shorts and last year's prom T-shirt, "Enchantment Under the See." Yes, the senior class misspelled half the words on their prom T-shirts, and yes, the senior class was full of morons.

"Yeah," Fitz said, before I could say no. "Green has to interview old people with her for history class."

"I heard she's a lesbian," the tallest of the three girls said between smacks of gum.

I gave Fitz a knowing look and he asked the girl, "And whom did you hear that from?"

"Buzz Booker," the girl said, and Fitz returned my look.

"Don't you think it's possible someone might not want to date Buzz Booker?" Fitz asked, but the girls all shook their heads no.

"Maybe she's asexual," the shortest girl said.

"Yeah, like a fern," the middle girl agreed.

"Are y'all talking about Parker Haddaway?"

Now a couple of sophomore guys had stopped to join the conversation.

"Yeah," the shortest girl said, "She and Edwin have to interview old people about lesbians for history class."

"That's not exactly—"

"I don't think she's a lesbian," one of the guys said. "We live down the street from her and her aunt. My mom said they're Jewish, and Jews can't date outside their religion because of the Holocaust and all."

"What is Buzz Booker?" the shortest girl asked.

"Sith," Fitz said, but only I laughed.

"You're thinking of Muslims," the other guy said. "Jews can date whoever they want because odds are that person was Jewish in a past life."

"You're thinking of Hindus," I said.

"But she doesn't have one of those dots on her forehead," the tallest girl said.

"I'm not saying Parker is Hindu. Hindus believe in—never mind."

"She's a cop." Jeff Parker, our school's most notorious pothead had stopped to join the conversation.

"She's not a cop," Fitz said.

"Like you'd know, gay-dad," Jeff said, then flinched and backed away when Fitz halfheartedly karate chopped in his direction. Shaken, Jeff the stoner continued, "These cops try and pass themselves off as students but they're easy to spot. She says she's seventeen, but that girl is twenty-two, at least."

"Makes sense," the tallest girl said. "I heard she hooks up with that Todd dude who sells iPhone cases in the mall, and he's like twenty-nine. If she were really seventeen they'd arrest him."

"I thought she was a lesbian," I said.

"And lesbians don't want free iPhone cases?" the middle girl shot back.

"Exactly," Jeff said. "And why do you think she misses so much school and never gets in trouble? It's because she's in meetings down at the precinct."

"So has she tried to buy drugs from you?" I asked.

"I don't sell drugs," Jeff said with a scowl, then conceded, "but no, she hasn't. I tried to talk to her once in the hall and she stared at me until I walked away."

"Me too," the shortest girl said.

Then they all stood there silent for a moment, having exhausted J. P. Hornby's second favorite topic of gossip, before turning to their favorite.

"So Edwin," the tallest girl finally said, "have you talked to Sadie lately?"

Everyone turned their attention to me, and I was about to tell them to go play in traffic, but Coach Cowden bellowed from his office window, "This isn't social hour, ladies, get moving!"

"Come on," I said to Fitz, and we resumed our slow orbit around the track, leaving the rest of them to discuss me and the dating practices of reincarnated Jewish lesbian narcs.

Chapter Three

In which our dumbfounded hero is kissed.

For the rest of the day I halfheartedly looked for Parker between classes but never saw her. However I did calculate what my final grade would be if I skipped the team assignment, and it wasn't pretty, so I'd have to talk to her eventually, though it could wait until tomorrow, or maybe even Wednesday. But as I stood at my locker before last-period English literature, someone tapped me on the shoulder and whispered, "I know where they keep the old people."

I turned around to see Parker Haddaway smiling at me, and I laughed out loud because (1) Parker Haddaway didn't smile, ever, and (2) Parker Haddaway only spoke to people if they spoke to her first, and only to tell them she was not interested in speaking with them any further and would they kindly go to hell, and (3) I laugh when I'm terrified.

"You what?" I asked, and laughed again before somewhat composing myself.

"The old people. I know where they keep them."

"You know where they keep the old people," I repeated, but

Parker put her hand over my mouth and shushed me. "Yes," she whispered in my ear, "but we've got to get there first to make sure we get the best one."

"The best old person?" I asked after she took her hand off my mouth, but Parker didn't hear me. She was staring at one of the security cameras the school installed after some vandals broke in over Christmas and spray painted a penis on every locker in the school. That's four hundred and seventy-six penises if you're keeping score at home, not counting a long one that ran the length of the trophy case. I cleared my throat and she turned back and peered into my locker, raising an eyebrow at the old picture of Sadie taped inside. I quickly closed the door and tried to steer the conversation back toward old people. "You said something about making sure we get the best old person," I whispered. I wasn't sure why I was whispering.

She moved in closer and I realized she was at least an inch taller than me, maybe more. I backed away until I hit the lockers, but she kept inching closer and said, "You drive that old Jetta, right?"

"Uh ... yeah," I said, and glanced down at her mismatched pink and white Chuck Taylors, because it was hard to look her in the eyes for more than a second or two.

"I thought so." She was so close now our legs were touching. "I'll meet you at your car after school. Oh, and Edwin Green?"

"Yeah?"

"Stop telling people I'm a lesbian." Then she smiled again, and before I had time to say anything she grabbed my face with both hands and kissed me. The girl, who before that morning had literally only said two words to me, kissed me. She kissed me right on the mouth. Kissed me right on the mouth for six seconds, or maybe half an hour, it was all a bit of a blur. Dumbfounded, I just stood there and watched her walk away.

I stood there until the bell rang and I was late for class.

11

Chapter Four

In which our hero recalls the events of the preceding chapter in alarmingly poor detail.

Fitz once told me scientists believe the more times our brain recalls a memory, the more unreliable that memory becomes. They say when we pull a file from our subconscious it will inevitably have an error or two, and the next time we recall that event we actually recall the new, slightly incorrect version, subsequently adding more errors to it in the process. It's like our brain is playing the telephone game with itself, and in the end, our most treasured memories become our most unreliable ones.

If true, this would make my memory of Parker telling me she knew where they kept the old people my least trustworthy memory, because halfway through literature class I'd already replayed it a hundred times. And maybe the scientists are right, because now when I picture her leaning in to kiss me we're not always standing in the hall at school. Sometimes we're knee-deep in a sea of yellow flowers, and sometimes we're atop a hill, looking down on a city below. I know she must have worn the same thing she always wore—jeans, her old army jacket, and a thrift store T-shirt, this one with a faded Carter-Mondale '80 logo on the front. But when I think of us in the hall she's wearing a green dress, and she's paralyzing me with impossibly blue eyes. But she'd never wear a dress to school, and her eyes were brown, I think. I don't know anymore. I just know there was a strand of red hair falling from her knit cap, and when she leaned in close she smelled like perfume and coffee, and in that moment I remembered there were indeed other girls in the world, and with just a smile they could reduce you to fear and trembling.

"Mr. Green?"

"Huh?"

Mrs. Clayton and the rest of the class stared at me.

"Mr. Green, please do not 'huh' me. We are waiting for your interpretation of the green light at the end of the first chapter of *The Great Gatsby*. You have read the first chapter of *The Great Gatsby*, haven't you, Mr. Green?"

I shrugged and shook my head and Mrs. Clayton said to see her after class.

Before Black Saturday I was on pace to be our class salutatorian (no one was catching Fitz for top honors), but now I was ranked a little lower, okay, a lot lower, okay, I was tied with Buzz Booker. A few teachers, like Mrs. Clayton, had expressed some concern over my rapidly plummeting GPA. And while I admit for the last year there'd been a complete lack of effort on my part, I'd honestly intended to read the first chapter of *The Great Gatsby* the night before, but got freaked out by the short bio of F. Scott Fitzgerald in the opening pages.

You should know I was obsessed with becoming famous, but not for the reasons most people want to become famous, e.g., cruising the Mediterranean on a gold-plated yacht accompanied by four supermodels and a pet tiger. No, I wanted to be famous because, well, because my ex-girlfriend, Sadie Evans, was famous. She was easily the most famous of the three famous people from Hornby, a list that went (3) Carl Bowers, a 1969 graduate who played wide receiver at Auburn and now sold insurance, (2) Becca Stuckey, the 1984 homecoming queen who posed in *Playboy* and later married then divorced Carl Bowers, and (1) Sadie Evans, who became famous on Black Saturday by—you know what, I'd rather not talk about it right now. But Sadie wasn't just famous by Hornby standards, she was cover-of-every-tabloid-at-the-grocery-store famous. She was one of *People's* 25 Most Beautiful People, and *Time's* 30 Most Influential People, and *Maxim's* 35 People We Want to See Naked, the latter issue pulled from shelves once attorneys reminded the folks at *Maxim* that Sadie was only sixteen. So while I should have been reading F. Scott's classic, I spent another night of my younger and more vulnerable years fretting over fame.

What freaked me out about Fitzgerald was that he didn't die famous. In fact, when he drank himself to death in 1940, *The Great Gatsby* had only sold about twenty thousand copies, and there were still unsold stacks in his publisher's warehouse. By comparison, Snooki, of *Jersey Shore* fame, has sold over forty thousand copies of her novel, *A Shore Thing*, since 2011. Granted most people purchased that book as a gag gift, but still, for someone desperately seeking fame it's more than a little discouraging to think you could write the Great American Novel and die believing yourself a forgotten failure.

For me this begs an interesting question. Would you rather die in relative obscurity only to become famous once you're gone, or die famous only to slip from the public consciousness in a generation or two? In the former category you've got people like Vincent Van Gogh, Emily Dickinson, Edgar Allan Poe, and Johann Sebastian Bach, and in the latter you've got, well, they're not famous anymore so who knows? It may be shortsighted, but when it comes to fame I'll take the fleeting variety all day, because seriously what good is fame when you're dead? Sure you won't leave a lasting legacy, but the sun will explode in four billion years, so no one does really.

I didn't mention any of this to Mrs. Clayton after class. Instead I told her I'd left my copy of *Gatsby* in my locker and didn't have a chance to read it the night before.

"Late for class. Unprepared. This has been happening all year."

"I know," I said, "It's just—"

"Edwin, we all know the last year hasn't been easy for you, but this is your future we're talking about. You can't let this one thing define the rest of your life, okay?"

"I know. I'm going to try harder."

She stared at me for a moment, then smiled and motioned for me to go on, but as I reached the door she said, "By the way, have you spoken to Sadie lately?"

"Go drink antifreeze, Mrs. Clayton," didn't seem like an appropriate response, so I turned and walked out before saying something I'd get suspended for.

Chapter Five

In which our hero displays an encyclopedic memory of Dutch cyclists and later defends his tabloid fetish.

Spring in Alabama is a mixed bag. Most days the weather is heavenly, particularly compared to the oppressive summer soon to follow. However, once a week the sky turns a spooky shade of green, spins itself into a mile-wide funnel, and sucks entire towns into oblivion. When school let out that afternoon a line of apocalyptic thunderstorms was passing over Birmingham, and the quickening wind swirled trash and leaves around J. P. Hornby's rapidly emptying parking lot. This only added to the anxiety I felt about seeing Parker Haddaway again. I'd only had sixty minutes to process the fact she'd (1) smiled at me, and she'd (2) talked to me, and she'd (3) freaking kissed me, and I estimated these things would take at least seven years to properly digest. But I didn't see her waiting by my car, which was somehow both relieving and disappointing.

I planned to wait a few minutes to see if she'd show up, but when I opened my door I found her fully reclined in the passenger seat, reading my March 29th issue of *Celebrity Digest*, the one with the cover story on celebrities who had moles removed.

My muscles involuntarily froze at the sight of her, and my mind began listing people I could have more easily imagined finding in my car—Norwegian Prime Minister Erna Solberg, 1980 Tour de France winner Joop Zoetemelk, Korean pop sensation HyunA—and I would have stood there listing people forever but she looked at me and said, "Edwin Green, you should lock your doors. Someone might steal your magazine."

"I … uh … that's my mom's," I lied.

She flipped back to the address label and said, "Your mom's name is Edwin Green too? Weird. I've read about villages in Côte d'Ivoire where boys share their mother's names, but I wouldn't have pegged you as Ivorian. Shows what I know."

I wasn't sure how to respond to that so I got in the car and tossed a couple Burger King bags into the backseat and tried to change the subject by apologizing for the mess.

"Don't apologize to me for your squalor, Edwin Green. They say a messy desk is a sign of genius. I'm sure Einstein's Volkswagen was knee-deep in Taco Bell sacks." Then she mumbled something about my, "raggedy ass Jetta."

"What?"

"Ol' Dirty Bastard."

I shook my head in confusion and she shook hers in apparent disappointment, and it dawned on me I'd never considered the possibility she didn't talk to people because she was weird as hell, but that was my new working theory.

"So where do they keep these old people?" I asked, cranking my car.

"Turn right out of the parking lot," she said, adding, "So you really read this trash?"

"I … no. I told you, that's my mom's," I said, then trying to change the subject again, added, "Can you believe Mr. Graham gave us this assignment?"

"It's been on the syllabus since January," Parker said. "Left at the stop sign. I mean, even if Taylor Swift is having Kanye's

17

baby, why's that any of your … mom's business?"

"I don't know. She likes to read about famous people, I guess." Parker turned the page and I asked, "Aren't you interested in celebrities?"

"No, I'm interested in everyone else. Left here."

"Okay, then why are you reading my magazine?"

"Because it's the only one in your car. Straight at the light. But you get what I'm saying, right? Just because you or your mom or whoever can pay $4.99 for this magazine doesn't make it any of your business that Sadie Evans is dating Chris Hemsworth."

"Wait, what?" I said, louder than I meant to, and Parker laughed out loud. "That was a joke, Edwin Green," she said, and I forced a smile. "There it is, ahead on the right."

Chapter Six

In which a nonagenarian threatens our hero before telling a story that has nothing to do with the explosion of an illegal fireworks factory in Benton, TN

We pulled into the parking lot of a nursing home called Morningview Arbor. It was, in fact, the only nursing home in Hornby, so it's not like Parker was privy to the whereabouts of some geriatric hiding place. But she did act like she'd been there before, so I followed her down a long hallway to a nurse's station where a woman in scrubs said, "Well hello, Miss Parker, I don't believe your aunt is working today."

"Oh I know, but we're supposed to interview someone who …" She looked back at me for help.

"Remembers World War II," I said.

"Remembers World War II," Parker repeated, "for history class."

The nurse smiled. "I'm sure a few of our older residents remember World War II."

"If they remember anything," another nurse added and laughed at her own joke.

"I was thinking about Mr. Lenox," Parker said.

"Oh he'd love that," the nurse said. "He should be down in the big room."

The storm had arrived and I could hear rain falling hard on the roof as I followed Parker down what had to be the most depressing hallway in the history of hallways. There were colorful yet terrifying clown paintings hanging on the walls, and each room we passed contained one or two moaning or babbling or shouting old people lying helplessly in their beds. The urge to turn and run out the way we came in was strong, but I fought it.

"Do you come here a lot?" I asked, trying to breathe through my mouth because the place smelt like old eggs and cat piss.

"Almost every day," Parker said. "My aunt works here. But I'd come here even if she didn't. Old people are the best."

"Yeah," I said, unconvincingly.

At the end of the hallway we entered what I suppose they call the recreation room at Morningview Arbor. There were nine or ten residents in wheelchairs lined up in front of an old wooden console television watching *Family Feud*. Another woman worked on a jigsaw puzzle at a large round table. And two men at the table next to her had fallen asleep while playing checkers. It wasn't the happiest place on Earth, but it beat the hallway of despair. I followed Parker toward the back corner of the room where a short, white-haired man sat sleeping on a couch with a copy of *The Da Vinci Code* in his lap.

"Garland," Parker said softly, but the old man did not stir. I thought for a moment he might be dead, but Parker shook him by the shoulder and Garland Lenox jolted awake shouting, "Bogie at four o'clock!"

I took a step back but Parker kept patting his shoulder saying, "It's okay Garland, you're here, at Morningview Arbor."

"Dammit, I can smell where I am," Garland said with the voice of a man who smoked his first cigarette in third grade. He rubbed his eyes and woke himself up, then looked at me and said, "but I don't know who the hell that is."

"Be nice, Garland, this is Edwin Green, my friend from school."

"Oh, so this is the boy I'm gonna have to whip to win your affection? You didn't say he was a featherweight. You had me worried."

Wait, had Parker been telling elderly men I was her boyfriend? Was that why she kissed me?

"I said be nice, Garland."

"I am being nice. I plan to kill him quickly."

I extended my hand and tried to introduce myself. "It's nice to meet you, Mr. Lenox," I said, but Garland just looked at my hand and said, "I knew a man named Green in Hong Kong. Biggest pervert in the Eastern Hemisphere."

"I give up," Parker said.

"He was a pervert," Garland protested, "but I'm sure this boy is perfectly nice."

Parker finally laughed and said, "So how's the book?"

"Damn nonsense," Garland said. "This Brown fool thinks Jesus Christ has grandchildren running around France. At least the chapters are short." He tossed the book on the table next to him and asked, "Now exactly why did you two wake me up again?"

"We need to interview you for history class," Parker said.

"If it's about the Charlie's Angels rumor, I can go ahead and tell you it's not true." Then he winked at me and added, "At least not all three at once."

"Now who's being a pervert," Parker said, and slapped him on the wrist.

"Son, you can't make this—"

"Don't say it," Parker interrupted. "We need to interview you about World War II, if you don't mind talking about it."

"I don't mind talking about anything except my damn prostate," Garland said loud enough for everyone in the room to hear. "Hell, I'll even tell you about that if you really want to know. But Parker, hon, you know I didn't do jack shit during the war."

"Then I guess we could talk to Dick Walker," Parker said, teasing him.

"I did more than Dick Walker," Garland growled. "That man spent the whole damn war conducting air raid drills in Oklahoma. So unless you want to learn about the Battle of Tulsa, I suggest you talk to me."

"Okay, calm down," Parker said, patting him on the knee, "we're going to interview you." She turned to me and asked, "What was this week's question?"

"We're supposed to ask you about the first time you heard the name Adolf Hitler."

"Who?"

"Adolf Hitler."

"Doesn't ring a bell."

I looked at Parker for help and Garland laughed at me. "We're not all crazy in here, son," he said, then with a twinkle in his eyes, he locked his fingers together and brought them up to his mouth before launching into the first of many incredible life stories he'd tell that week. "Now Parker knows all my stories already," he said, "but when I was nine or ten my parents began listening to this preacher out of Nebraska named Raymond Pirkle. He'd just founded the Omaha Prophetic Presbyterian Church, and he had a radio show that—"

"Wait, Mr. Lenox, do you mind if I record this?" I asked, holding up my phone.

"Knock yourself out, son," he said, then turned to Parker and asked, "Where was I?"

"Raymond Pirkle."

"Right, Ol' Ray said the world was gonna end in 1936, and some German fella named Adolf Hitler was the anti-Christ. My parents, bless their hearts, tossed all rational thought aside and moved us into a cabin in the mountains east of Chattanooga, and there we waited for the world to end. Every morning Mama would say, "Now you enjoy that breakfast Garland because this will probably be the day the world ends." Garland grew quiet for a second before chuckling to himself and saying, "Kind of a strange childhood, come to think of it."

"Anyway," he continued, "as they've no doubt taught you in school, the world did not end in 1936, so Raymond updated his prediction to 1942, and my parents stayed in the woods six more years. My dad farmed and hunted, and Mama taught me to read the King James Bible and what little math she knew. I was an only child, thank God, and I was sixteen when the Japanese bombed Pearl Harbor. Of course my folks didn't tell me about Pearl Harbor, or what was going on in Europe. They just said the entire world was at war, but not to worry about that because the world was 'bout to end anyhow."

Lightning crashed outside and I flinched at the thunderclap. Garland laughed at me then pointed toward the television, which was now showing black and white snow. "Damn zombies. They'll sit there and watch that fuzz until someone moves 'em."

"Should we turn the TV off?" Parker asked.

"Doesn't matter. They seem to enjoy that just as much as the *Feud*." The old man looked at the television again and shook his head before continuing his story. "Looking back," he said, "my folks must have anticipated a January end of the world, because by February '42 we were low on everything. So I went with my dad on one of his infrequent trips to Benton, and while I waited for him outside the general store I found an old newspaper and I hid it in my coat pocket."

Then the story got sideways, as Garland's stories tended to do.

"There was a big illegal firework plant explosion in Benton a few years back that killed a bunch of people. One poor guy was mowing grass outside and the blast threw him seventy yards over the top of a nearby house. Seventy yards, can you imagine?"

Garland stopped, as if he'd finished the story, and Parker tried to prod him along, "So the first time you heard the name Adolf Hitler was in a preacher's end-of-the-world prediction?"

"I suppose so. And I learned more about him in the newspaper I found. I took it home and hid it under my bed and whenever I had a chance I'd read stories about the war. The entire country was getting ready to fight in Europe and the Pacific, and I thought, the damn world ain't gonna end if we can go whip this Hitler fella. And then I saw a recruitment flyer. The famous one with the finger-pointing Uncle Sam. The 'I Want You for the US Army' one. At the bottom it said to contact your local recruitment office.

"Now Mama always said when the world ended Jesus would take us up to heaven, and there we'd sing songs to him all day, every day, forever and ever, amen. I suppose that beats the alternative of burning in a lake of fire all day, every day, forever and ever, but still it didn't sound like a whole lot of fun to me. So I wrote my parents a note and told 'em I was going to join the army and fight the anti-Christ so the world wouldn't have to end just yet, and that night I set off walking to Benton. I waited outside the post office, and when the postmaster came in I told him I wanted to enlist. He said all right, told me to take a seat, and when the delivery truck came I hitched a ride to the recruitment office in downtown Chattanooga."

"So you joined the Army to—"

"I didn't join the Army," Garland said. "I joined the United States Army Air Forces. I walked into that recruitment office with this other fella from Chattanooga whose dad worked on planes out at Lovell Field. The recruiter knew him and figured he'd make a good mechanic. Later I learned if you volunteered you could choose your branch of the service, but the recruiter signed me up for the Air Force without asking. Guess he thought me and that other guy were buddies since we walked in together."

I tried again, "So you joined the Air Force to fight the anti-Christ and keep from going to heaven and singing songs to Jesus all day?"

Garland scowled at me. "No son, I joined the Air Force because I love my country."

"Sorry," I mumbled.

"Hell, now I'm wondering why you didn't enlist after 9/11."

"Because he was two, Garland," Parker said, coming to my aid. "Now leave poor Edwin alone and finish your story."

Garland laughed and winked at me and said, "Son, I joined the Air Force to get out of the damn woods and see the world. To be honest, I never believed all those things my parents told me. Well, I believed some of it, but I knew Raymond Pirkle was crazier than bat shit when I was twelve, and I never understood why my parents couldn't see it. That newspaper was my first glimpse of the outside world, and I wanted to see more of it. Joining the war was a chance to get away, so I took it, and it changed my life."

The old man let out a long sigh, leaned in toward me, and said, "You might get one chance like that in your life, son, and you damn well better be ready to take it or it'll haunt you forever."

Chapter Seven

In which our hero expresses an unpopular opinion of Americans born between 1900 and 1924.

The rain had stopped by the time Garland finished his story, and the windows around Morningview Arbor's recreation room grew brighter as the line of storms moved off to the east. I thanked the old man for his time and he managed a grunt in my direction. Parker told him she'd be back to see him soon and he smiled. Then we left him there, sitting on the couch with *The Da Vinci Code* in his lap. He was asleep before we reached the door.

"I love that old man," Parker said on the drive back to school.

"I'm not sure he liked me," I said.

"Oh, he didn't," Parker assured me. "But you shouldn't take it personally, he doesn't like anyone at first. He'll warm up to you though. Probably."

Parker picked up my tabloid again and said, "I could talk to him all day. People from his generation are just … I don't know." She held up an article entitled "When Boob Jobs Go Horribly Wrong," "They're just better."

I never bought the whole Greatest Generation crap. I mean everyone pretty much agrees the Baby Boomers are the worst, so how can the Greatest Generation be so great if they're universally acknowledged as terrible parents. Maybe the Greatest Generation's parents are the real greatest generation, except they caused the Great Depression and fixed a World Series and outlawed alcohol, which only bolsters my theory that all generations suck in their own way. I didn't mention this to Parker though, because I try not to argue with people who scare me. "So is that why you never talk to anyone at school?" I asked instead. "Because we're not in our nineties?"

"I talk to people at school."

"No you don't. You'd never even talked to me before today." She'd never kissed me before today either, but I wasn't sure how to broach that subject, and so far she'd acted like it never happened. And maybe it hadn't. We did have sloppy joes for lunch, and at J. P. Hornby those can cause hallucinations.

Parker thought for a moment and said, "Well it's not like you talk to people at school either."

"Fair enough," I said. "But I have my reasons."

"You and me both, kid," she said, then patted me on the head like a puppy, "but I'll try to remember to talk to you tomorrow."

I smiled and said, "That's very generous of you."

Parker's rusty green moped was the only vehicle left at school, and I pulled up next to it and let her out, but no sooner had she closed the door than she opened it right back and asked, "You take French for foreign language, right?"

"Yeah," I said, wondering how she knew that. "This is my second year."

"And you're fluent?"

"I won the Excellence in French award last year on Award's Day," I said. Technically this wasn't the same as being fluent. In fact, it only meant I could conjugate verbs on a multiple choice test, but I wanted to impress her.

"Perfect," she said, "I'll see and speak to you tomorrow, Edwin Green."

Then she smiled and walked away before I had a chance to say anything else.

Chapter Eight

In which Slovenian salutations are referenced.

I couldn't sleep that night—getting randomly kissed by Parker Haddaway will do that to you—so instead I lay in bed and replayed my memory of the kiss over and over again, making it a little less trustworthy each time. And though I'm functionally illiterate at reading the opposite sex, what really kept me up was the sneaking suspicion that Parker wanted something from me, and that something probably wasn't more kisses. Which was fine, I guess. I didn't want more kisses either. I mean, it's not the worst thing in the world for the hottest girl in school to walk up and lay one on you, but I wasn't looking for a girlfriend, you know? I did want to know why she kissed me though, and since calling her was out of the question because it was two a.m. and I didn't know her number, I went to my desk and began writing down possible reasons for the unexpected smooch, applying Vegas-style odds to each one.

She mistook me for Todd the iPhone case salesman: 15-1.

She was from Slovenia and that's how they greeted assignment partners in the motherland: 39-1.

She was playing Truth or Dare and rather than admit to killing a drifter she chose the dare: 4-1.

She has a fetish for scrawny guys who can recite long passages from Monty Python films: 50-1.

She wanted to make Buzz Booker's head explode: 5-2.

The list wasn't very helpful, so I crawled back into bed and fell asleep an hour before my alarm went off. And here we are, at the end of the first day of the craziest week of my life, and you might be thinking nothing much happened, because maybe you're the sort of person who's always being indiscriminately kissed, but I was not that kind of person. I was, well, boring. I was neither a vampire, nor a werewolf, and I was not involved in a love triangle with two people who were. I was not a boy wizard, though if I had been, the Sorting Hat would have sent me to Hufflepuff. I didn't live in a dystopian future where the government chose random children to fight to the death on live television. I lived outside of Birmingham, in a double-mortgaged, three-bedroom rancher with my mom and stepdad. And I wasn't, to my knowledge, divergent, whatever that means. I was not a memorable person, and apart from Black Saturday, nothing memorable had ever happened to me. That's why people at school, if they called me anything, called me Sadie's ex-boyfriend. She was the only thing people knew about me. This, however, was about to change.

Chapter Nine

In which #RaymondPirkle isn't trending, yet.

"Is that a lot of views?"

"Yeah. Well, no. Not really. But it's a lot for one of my videos."

The Monday before last Thanksgiving I was reading a *Newsweek* article on the Thirty Most Influential Teens in my dentist's waiting room. Wait, that makes it sound like the thirty most influential teens were in my dentist's waiting room. They were not. It was just me and a lady with two screaming kids. The list was pretty standard—a couple of actors, some singers, a few athletes, Will Smith's son, President Obama's daughters, that Pakistani girl the Taliban shot just for going to school, and my ex-girlfriend—but what caught my eye was a girl about my age who was earning $1.1 million a year just from making YouTube videos. Five years ago she went shopping, and when she got home she posted a video of all the stuff she'd bought, and five years later 11 million people had subscribed to her channel. She has her own clothing line at Target, she released an album that randomly enough peaked at number six on the Portuguese Top 40 chart, she was a guest judge on *Line Dancing with the Stars*, and she even appeared on that reality show where they stick a bunch of B-list celebrities on a deserted island and make them eat bugs, all because she had a coupon for free mascara and made a video about it in her bedroom. What a time to be alive.

Intrigued, I went home and discovered dozens of people my age with insanely popular YouTube channels. A lot of them made more money than doctors, and they were all famous. Not Taylor Swift famous, but if two million people care enough to watch a video of you eating Lucky Charms, you're famous, and I wanted to be famous too, so that night I made my first video, and I've made a new video almost every night since.

Typically I talk about my day for three or four minutes, then upload the video to YouTube where it is thoroughly ignored by the internet at large. My channel had recently peaked at seven subscribers—three appeared to be Russian spammers, one was almost certainly my mother, one was Fitz, and I wasn't sure about the last two. On average my videos got between three and six views, which is, by almost any measure, pathetic. And sure, I could have found some sad level of fame had I talked about Sadie on my videos. I could have taken my rightful place as king of her fanboys. But even if I did manage to get her attention that way she'd only feel sorry for me, and her pity wasn't exactly what I was shooting for.

In 1968 Andy Warhol predicted in the future everyone would be famous for fifteen minutes, but 147 videos later *Newsweek* wasn't any closer to naming me one of the Thirty Most Influential Teens—in the world or in my dentist's waiting room—because my video blog, it seemed, remained destined to stay hidden in the darkest corners of the World Wide Web. But then I uploaded the video of Garland Lenox telling the story of how he joined the Air Force to fight the anti-Christ, and I tagged it with words like #veteran, #WWII, #Hitler, and #RaymondPirkle, and when I checked the video the next morning before school, it had, drumroll please, three hundred and fifty-two views. There was even a comment, my first, from a member of the Omaha Prophetic Presbyterian Church, threatening a lawsuit if I didn't edit out the part where Garland called their founder batshit crazy. It wasn't overnight fame, but you've got to start somewhere, right?

"I've been posting videos every night since November," I said to Fitz, "and this is the first one to get more than twenty views."

Fitz wasn't impressed, but he tried to be kind, "Good work Green, but more importantly, what's Parker Haddaway like?"

"She's nice," I said, opting not to tell Fitz about the kiss, because (1) my chivalry knows no bounds, and (2) I hadn't ruled out a sloppy-joe induced hallucination, and (3) Parker might cut my tongue out if I told anyone.

"She's nice?" Fitz asked. "We're talking about the same person, right? Parker Haddaway. Tall, redheaded girl with all the charm of Pol Pot?"

"Yeah, I know, but she's pretty cool once she stops giving you the death stare. Weird, but cool."

Fitz shook his head and said, "What's her voice like? I always imagined it as a cross between James Earl Jones and a dental drill."

"What would that even sound like?" I asked, and Fitz gave an admirable impression.

"I don't know," I said, realizing I hadn't paid any attention to Parker's voice. "It sounds like any other girl's voice, I guess. She said she'd talk to me at school, but she didn't show up for first period."

"You sound disappointed."

"No, it's just …"

"Don't get your hopes up man, I heard she's a lesbian."

I tried to punch Fitz on the arm but missed on account of him being a ninja. "My hopes aren't up. It's just that she …" I stopped to let yesterday's gaggle of senior girls walk by, then finished in a lower voice, "… she couldn't care less about Sadie, and it would be nice, no offense, to find at least one other person at school I could talk to who wouldn't spend the entire conversation asking questions about my ex-damn-girlfriend."

"None taken, dicknose."

I laughed and said, "I mean, she was actually interested in me as a person."

"How so?"

"Like, she wanted to know if I'm fluent in French."

"Are you?"

"No. But I told her I was."

Fitz raised an eyebrow. "Dude, you're totally smitten."

"Smitten? Who says smitten? Are you my grandmother?"

"You're smitten … with the strangest girl in school."

"Shut it, asshat."

I wasn't smitten. I was, I don't know, curious, which is understandable considering everything that happened on Monday. But what I told Fitz was true. After making fun of my tabloid fetish Parker didn't mention Sadie Evans again, and consequently the hour I spent with her was the longest I'd gone without thinking about my ex-girlfriend in a year. That evening, after posting Garland's video, I still went through my sad ritual of scanning all Sadie's social media accounts, but I stopped after a few minutes and spent even more time looking for Parker online, without any luck. Fitz was right about one thing, though. I was disappointed Parker didn't show up for first-period history. I wanted to talk to her more. But more than that I wanted Sadie to know there was another girl I wanted to talk to, and I really wanted her to know that girl kissed me, and I suppose that goes to show that even though I went a whole sixty minutes without thinking about her, I was still as obsessed over Sadie Evans as ever.

Chapter Ten

In which there is a Sir Mix-a-Lot reference.

I'd gone a little, okay, a lot, out of my way to look for Parker at her locker between classes, which, if he'd known, would only have strengthened Fitz's smitten theory. She wasn't there though, so I walked on to algebra, mentally preparing myself for the scholastic equivalent of the Bataan Death March.

Class began like always. Mr. Strane asked us to take out our homework and called out the number of a random problem, then we copied that problem on a separate sheet of paper and turned it in. The homework component equaled one quarter of our final grade, and more than half the time I'd turned in a blank sheet of paper. Thankfully, Mr. Strane didn't take much interest in individual students, so he never stopped me after class to discuss my perilously close to failing grade and/or if I'd spoken to Sadie Evans lately.

After homework check—which I actually passed but only because I could see Emma Bower's paper and copied her answer while she wasn't looking—Mr. Strane began solving the previous night's homework on the blackboard. He did this every day, and it was mind numbing. Sometimes we'd try and ask random questions to get him off track but he was relentless. The man would only stop solving algebra problems one minute before the bell rang, and only to assign more algebra problems. Looking back I think he may have been some sort of math robot the state purchased in an attempt to save money on teacher pensions.

We were ten minutes and six problems into class and Mr. Strane stood before his blackboard droning on about coefficients and constants while I stared at the clock trying to break my personal record for breath holding (one minute and thirty-seven seconds), when we heard a loud knock at the door. Mr. Strane looked perturbed and set down his chalk, and in his robotic voice said, "Enter," and in stepped Parker Haddaway wearing a tight T-shirt that read "God hates T-shirts."

We all stared at her for what felt like an eternity, before Mr. Strane finally said, "Yes?"

Parker scanned the room until she saw me and smiled, then she held up a slip of paper and said, "Principal Denham needs to see Edwin Green in her office."

Mr. Strane looked at me, and the rest of the class looked at me, then he turned back to his blackboard and resumed the problem he'd been working on. I took this as my sign to leave, so I packed my books and nearly tripped on my way toward the door where Parker winked before handing me the slip of paper.

On it she'd written the lyrics to "Baby Got Back."

Chapter Eleven

*In which our hero boasts of his excessive cautiousness,
despite evidence to the contrary.*

"What is this," I whispered, once we were both in the hall.

Parker took the note from me and examined it for a moment before saying, "This is a rap. By Sir Mix-a-Lot. He likes big butts, and he's incapable of telling lies. Although I'm not sure if he tells the truth about everything, or only concerning his fondness of the large ass. I'm thinking the latter though. I mean, I doubt he was actually knighted, you know?"

I didn't know. I was terribly confused and wasn't even sure what to ask next. The transition from algebra on the blackboard to Parker and Sir Mix-a-Lot in the hallway happened way too fast. I wondered if I had the bends.

"We can discuss it later," she said, grabbing me by the wrist. "Garland needs to see you right now."

"In the principal's office?"

"What? No. I made that up. He needs to see you at Morningview Arbor. It's very important."

"Oh shit. Did that church from Omaha contact him? The prophetic one?"

"What? No. I don't think so. Wait, what did you do?"

"Shit. I didn't mean to get him in trouble. I can delete it … the library, come on, let's go to the library. Mrs. Davis will let me use a computer and I can—"

Reminding me that she could kick my ass if she wanted, Parker grabbed me by both shoulders, slammed me hard against the puke green lockers, and said, "Edwin Green, stop talking."

I stopped talking. In part because she'd told me to, but mostly because I found it impossible to look her in the eyes and form coherent sentences.

"Garland needs to see you right now," she said, loosening her grip on my shoulders. "And if you've stirred up the Omaha Prophetic Presbyterians, we don't have a second to lose." She let one hand slide down from my shoulder to my wrist and added, "Now come on, let's go."

I didn't move. "Wait, we're going to see him now? Like, we're just walking out of school?"

"Yes."

"We can't do that. Can we do that? I don't think we can do that."

"Garland needs to see you. Do you think I would sneak into school to sneak you out if it wasn't important?"

I was a cautious teenager. And caution, if it is a virtue, is not one often associated with teenage boys. On the whole we make rash decisions without giving much thought to the consequences, either intended or unintended. You know how most products have absurd warning labels like, "Do not attempt to cut your hair with the Poulan 38cc 2-Cycle Gas-Powered Chain Saw" or "Never insert Black Cat Silver Fox Triple Whistle Bottle Rockets into your nostrils"? Lawyers placed those warning labels there because of teenage boys. My mom was an emergency room nurse, and in what I suppose was an attempt to make sure I lived to see my eighteenth birthday she spent a great deal of my childhood regaling me with tales of kids who'd jumped off cliffs into what they thought were deep waters, only to break their backs. Or kids who thought the speed limit on a particular curvy road was merely a suggestion, only to learn the front windshield is not the preferable way to exit a car. These stories, and by this time I'd heard hundreds of them, made me perhaps the most cautious teenager of all time. Rarely did I make a decision, any decision, without thinking two or three steps ahead and considering all possible negative outcomes. A girl in our class once told me I thought like a grown-up, and I don't think she meant it as a compliment. But when you think the way I do, you don't put much stock in the opinions of sixteen-year-olds. I never understood the point of those countless peer pressure lectures we had to endure. I'd always look around and think, "These morons are not my peers."

What I'm trying to say is I didn't take the decision to skip school with Parker lightly, but then again, it didn't even feel like a decision. I began slipping toward some unknown future the moment she told me she knew where they kept the old people. Theologians talk about free will, but I couldn't have told her no if I'd wanted to.

"Okay," I said, "let's go."

Chapter Twelve

*In which our hero learns of his leadership position
in an imaginary student organization.*

I'd be lying if I said it wasn't exhilarating to just walk out of school, but as we left J. P. Hornby's parking lot my excitement mutated into oh-dear-lord-what-had-I-done regret. My anxiety only grew when Parker refused to divulge any more information on the short drive to the nursing home, saying she'd promised Garland he could explain it all to me in person. Then she put in her earbuds to discourage any follow-up questions.

"Okay," I said loud enough for her to hear me over her music, "he can explain it, but at least talk to me. I'm starting to freak out here."

Parker removed her earbuds and said, "And what shall we discuss, Edwin Green?"

I glanced over and have no doubt she saw my eyes drift from her eyes down to her absurdly tight T-shirt before darting back to the road. "Uh ... where'd you get your shirt?" I asked.

"I made it," she said. "Where'd you get your shirt?"

"I'm not sure," I said, looking down at my polo. "Target maybe? My mom bought it."

An awkward silence followed, and I remembered I found talking to her difficult and wished she'd just put her earbuds back in, but when I dared to look over again she was still staring at me, waiting for me to make conversation. "I don't even really know you," I said. "Like, what are you into?"

"The collected works of Oscar Wilde," she said, "and '90s hip-hop."

Of course, I thought, and when I didn't reply to this bizarre pair of interests she asked, "And what are you into, Edwin Green?"

I took note of Parker's voice in case Fitz required further proof she'd spoken to me. It was soft and low, lower than Sadie's at least, but not low like a guy's. Her voice was, I don't know, honeyed, and teasing, but her words were so matter-of-fact I was never sure when her jokes were for my benefit, or at my expense, or even jokes at all. Parker had a voice that, once you'd heard it, was all you ever wanted to hear. In the end I decided not to mention any of this to Fitz, since such overanalysis would only encourage his smitten theory.

"I like playing Xbox," I said, and after some thought added, "and stuff."

"Quite the Renaissance man," she said and I tried to laugh but it came out more like a cough.

"Edwin Green, are you always this nervous?" Parker asked.

"No," I said, then after a moment added, "yes." This time Parker laughed and I relaxed a bit. I felt like the best version of myself whenever I made her laugh.

"Okay," I said, "What are you listening to?"

"I'm listening to the New Pornographers," she said. "Do you like them?"

"Uh … yeah," I said, though I'd never heard of them.

"You've never heard of them, have you?" Parker said.

"No."

"My dad loved them," Parker said. "I'm only listening to Canadian supergroups this month." I didn't know what to say to that, so I didn't say anything. "Here," she said, "this is my favorite," and she stuck an earbud in my ear, and while Neko Case told me to come with her and go places in one ear, Parker sang along in the other. We drove like that the rest of the way to the nursing home. It was only three minutes, but it was the best three minutes I'd had in twelve months.

Morningview Arbor was no less depressing in the morning, though at least the freshly mopped floors masked some of the smell. A nurse saw us enter and waved from down the hall. Parker whispered, "That's my aunt. Just go along with whatever I say."

"Sure, but what are we—shit!"

Parker's bony elbow caught me hard in the ribs and I shut up just as we reached her aunt.

"Aunt Marcy, this is Edwin Green from school."

Aunt Marcy was tall and thin and a little older than I would have imagined. She smiled and said, "Nice to meet you, Edwin. Are you part of the Geriatric Outreach Program as well?"

"I …"

"He's our treasurer," Parker said. "We're thinking about having a checkers tournament in the big room this morning."

"Oh how fun. But keep an eye on Dick Walker. He cheats."

I laughed and Aunt Marcy said, "Seriously, he cheats. Six months ago we had a brawl on casino night after someone caught him counting cards."

"We'll keep an eye on him," Parker said, "but first we need to ask Mr. Lenox a few more questions for our history assignment."

"Well I know Garland will love seeing you both. I believe he's still in his room this morning."

Parker told her aunt thanks and began pushing me down the hallway of despair toward Garland's room. "It was nice to meet you, Edwin," Aunt Marcy said, and I looked back and returned the sentiment before whispering to Parker, "Geriatric Outreach Program?"

"Yeah, I told her I'm the president of a program that lets me leave school and spend time with elderly people in Hornby."

"Wait, you are?"

"No."

"So all those days you don't show up at school, you're hanging out in a nursing home?"

We stopped in front of room 31 and Parker smiled at me and said, "Yeah, but don't tell anyone, okay? It's more fun if people think I'm a cop." Then she knocked softly on the door and Garland shouted, "Come in, dammit."

Chapter Thirteen

In which our hero cannot recall the name of The Villages,
Florida's friendliest hometown.

"Is he okay?"

"Yeah he's okay," Garland growled. "He lays there in bed all day drooling and mumbling gibberish about fried okra, but turn that television off Animal Planet and you'll see just how okay he is. Ol' boy loves him some meerkats."

The sign above Garland's roommate's bed said his name was Hershel Thomas, but introductions were not in order—I'm not sure Hershel knew the world was still spinning. By contrast Garland sat neatly dressed on the edge of his bed, and I wondered why he lived in this place and not that town in Florida comprised entirely of old people who golf and rollerblade all day. I tried to think of a delicate way to ask but Garland said, "Y'all pull up those chairs," and our meeting came to order.

"Now, son," the old man said, with such an infinitely friendlier tone than the day before I wondered if he was off his medication, "has Parker told you why you're here?"

"No, she just snuck me out of school and brought me here. She said it was important."

Garland nodded. "She's right, it is important. Parker here tells me you're fluent in French."

I glanced at Parker, betrayed she'd passed on my half-truth to someone else. "I, uh, yeah. I'm pretty fluent."

"And you can drive a car?"

"I can," I said, not knowing where this could possibly be going.

"Well, son, I've got a big favor to ask of you. Parker dear, will you shut that door?"

Parker obliged and when she sat back down, Garland continued, "A big favor. And if you can help me out, I'll give you twenty-five thousand dollars."

I've always wanted to take a big sip of water just before someone says something this preposterous so I could spit it out like they do on sitcoms, but I hadn't just taken a big sip of water, so instead I laughed out loud. How could I not? "Twenty-five thousand dollars," I repeated, and laughed again because it somehow sounded even more ridiculous when I said it. I stood up and said, "I've got to get back to school. This is—" Garland tossed something toward me and I caught it and looked down to see a thick roll of hundred-dollar bills. I sat back down.

"Son, that's ten thousand dollars. Consider it a down payment. You'll get the rest after you help me out."

After two summers of mowing lawns I'd paid four thousand dollars cash for my Jetta, and that was, by far, the most money I'd ever held at one time. I looked down at the money again, then at Parker, then back at Garland. If this was a practical joke I was about to fall hard. "Okay," I said, "what do you need me to do?"

Garland smiled, leaned in, and whispered, "Son, I need you to bust me out of here and take me to Paris."

Chapter Fourteen

In which our hero says no a dozen times, before finally saying maybe.

"I'm sorry, what?"

"I need you to take me to Paris. The City of Light. *La Ville Lumière.*"

"Yeah ... no."

Garland smiled. "Son, you didn't even think about it."

"I don't need to think about it. It's insane." I tossed the money back on Garland's bed and said, "If you offered me $25,000 to paint myself blue and run around Hornby naked I wouldn't need to think about that either."

"Not a great visual," Parker said, and I shot her a dirty look for bringing me to this half-baked intervention.

"Thirty thousand."

"What? No."

He glanced at Parker and she gave a little nod. "You drive a hard bargain, son. Fifty thousand it is."

"No!"

Garland shushed me. "Keep it down. There's no need to get all upset, we're negotiating here."

"We're not negotiating," I whispered. "I'm not taking you to Paris for any amount of money."

"One million dollars."

"No—wait, really?"

"No, not really. But we've determined you do have a price."

"I'm not taking you to Paris," I repeated.

"And why not?" Parker said, like Garland had only asked for a ride to his urologist.

"Because," I said, mentally scanning through my Rolodex of a thousand and one good reasons, "my mom and stepdad would flip out if I even asked them if I could go to Paris. Besides, I barely know you, and I don't know him at all, and no offense, but this is how people get sold to warlords. Also, I'm pretty sure it's illegal. He'd go to prison for kidnapping us, or we'd go to prison for old-person napping him. Someone would go to prison, probably all three of us, and look at me, I'm not cut out for prison."

"Stop being dramatic, Edwin Green," Parker said. "No one's going to prison."

"And I don't even know any warlords anymore," Garland added.

I ignored the old man and said to Parker, "Then why don't you take him yourself?"

"I'm going with you," she said, "but I don't speak French, and I don't know how to drive a car. We need you."

"We need you, son," Garland echoed.

I let out a sigh. It dawned on me if Garland and Parker couldn't understand why I was hesitant to bust an old man out of a nursing home and take him to Europe they both might be as far gone as everyone else in Morningview Arbor. I wondered if I turned the TV to the test pattern how long they'd stare at it.

There was a long silence before Garland resumed going over his plan in a paranoid whisper. "We can leave as soon as you're ready, though at my age the sooner the better."

"I can't take you to France," I said again, louder than I meant to, and Garland held a finger to his mouth. I continued a little softer, "I've got school, and track practice, and my—"

"So you're a runner? I should have known from those bird legs. Did you know I won bronze in the 400 meters at the 1944 Olympics? The medal is in my closet. It's yours if you help me out."

"There wasn't a 1944 Olympics," I said.

"Well no, not officially …"

It felt wrong to call a war veteran a liar to his face, so I just let out another long sigh and rubbed my eyes and Garland continued like I'd already agreed to help him. "Of course I'll pay for the flights and everything else once we're there. It's just I can't see to drive anymore, and Parker never learned how, so we'll need you to drive us around."

"And translate," Parker added.

"Mr. Lenox, I'm not taking you to France."

"But you haven't even heard why he—" Parker started but I cut her off.

"There's nothing he could say to change my mind."

Garland took a deep breath and sat back defeated, but a moment later rallied and asked, "Did you know in 1942 the Nazis destroyed thousands of paintings in a bonfire outside the Jeu de Paume in Paris?"

"No," I said. "I mean it's not surprising. The Nazis were sort of dicks."

Garland chuckled. "They were sort of dicks. But what if I told you someone saved a painting from the bonfire? A Picasso, worth at least a hundred million dollars today. And what if I told you that painting is still hidden in a little French village, just waiting for someone to come back and retrieve it, sell it, and oh, I don't know, share the proceeds with the young man who helped recover the lost treasure? If I told you that, would it change your mind?"

"Maybe, but you're not going to tell me that, are you?"

"Hell no," the old man sighed and said, "I sold that painting for a song in 1948." I rolled my eyes and Garland said, "But trust me, son, something even more valuable to me is in France, and I need you to help me find it."

"What?" I asked, then regretted playing along because it would only give him false hope.

"A girl," Garland said. "Well, she'd be an old woman now. That's her, on the right."

The old man handed me what looked like a page he'd torn out of a book with a photograph of a young nun and an even younger woman standing beside her. The caption read, "Irish Hospital, Saint-Lô, March 1946."

"I met her during the war, and all this time I thought she was dead, but a couple weeks ago I was flipping through one of Parker's books about the war and there she was. My girl. She was alive. She was alive after they told me she was dead. And son, if she's still alive, I've got to find her."

"Mr. Lenox, I—"

"And I've got to find her soon, because if you're not familiar with nursing homes, they don't send you here because you have a long and fruitful life ahead. I don't have much time left, son. I've got to get to France and find my girl."

"Mr. Lenox I just don't think—"

"Son, have you ever been in love?"

I stared at Garland for a moment, not wanting to have this conversation with him. "I ... I don't see what—"

"And if you lost that love, wouldn't you do anything to get her back?"

Looking at Garland Lenox you wouldn't peg him as a master manipulator, but he'd set a hook, and I think he knew it.

"Mr. Lenox, I'm not—"

"Son, will you just think about it?"

I took a deep breath and studied the pattern on the cloudy yellow linoleum. I hated to disappoint people, especially to their face, so I couldn't say no again. Not with Parker and Garland both fighting back tears. So I said I'd think about it, though I didn't intend to, and he thanked me like I'd said yes.

Chapter Fifteen

In which a New Coke reference will likely be lost on younger readers.

Hornby wasn't big enough for a Starbucks, or any coffee shop for that matter, so Parker and I sat in a booth at McDonald's waiting for the fourth-period bell at J. P. Hornby when we could slip back in to school unnoticed. Neither of us had said much since leaving Morningview Arbor. Parker sipped her coffee and tapped her nails on the table, and I stared at a Coke I didn't want and checked the time on my phone every two minutes or so.

"When do you think you'll have an answer?" Parker finally asked.

I took a deep breath and said, "I already have one, I'm just trying to think of a word that means the same as 'no' since you and Garland both have trouble taking no for an answer."

"You promised Garland you'd think about it," she snapped.

"I have thought about it. It's the worst idea in the history of bad ideas. New Coke, Jar Jar Binks, only having twenty lifeboats on the Titanic—those all look brilliant compared to this. Look, I'm sure he's promised you a bunch of money or something, but I don't think that man is in his right mind."

"Oh I wish you could have seen him," Parker said, apparently changing the conversation midstream. "I've been researching Garland's time in the Army, for a good deed I'm working on, and he found one of the books I'd been reading in my backpack. He started flipping through it, and he came across that photograph of the woman he knew, and he just lost it. He tore the page out and started crying and saying, 'That's her, Parker, that's her. They told me she died but that's her.' He hasn't stopped talking about going to France ever since. We've got to help him."

I sighed and said, "Look, it's sweet and all, but his family put him in that nursing home for a reason. If you sneak him out you could get in a lot of trouble."

"He doesn't have any family," Parker said, "if that's all you're worried about."

"That's one of an infinite number of things I'm worried about."

Now Parker looked pissed off again, and I braced myself for whatever verbal or physical assault she was about to unleash, but instead she rubbed her eyes. Was she crying? Surely not. Not Parker Haddaway. I cursed under my breath. I didn't want to upset her, but if helping her sneak an old man out of the country was my only alternative she'd just have to be mad at me. I tried reasoning with her. "Look, you don't need me at all. People who don't speak French go to France every day. I've seen this app you can download that translates anything you say into like forty different languages. It even has a weird talking mouth you can hold over your real mouth. French people will love it. And you don't even need a car. Take trains, or hire someone to drive you around with some of that money Garland promised me."

Parker wiped her eyes and looked at me. "It won't work," she said. "We've got to be so quick and discreet once we get there. When Garland's lawyer finds out he's gone he'll have half of France looking for us."

"So his lawyer wouldn't want him to go?"

"No."

"Another good reason for us not to take him."

Parker picked up her coffee, shook the empty cup, and abruptly changed tactics again. "Edwin Green," she said, her eyes bright and smiling again, "I can tell you're all about the Benjamins."

"You can?"

"Fifty thousand dollars. Don't tell me you couldn't find a way to spend it."

Garland wanted me to keep his ten thousand dollars while I thought things over, but I refused, since holding that much money would have definitely influenced my thinking. I'd be lying if I said I hadn't considered it though. My mom was a nurse, and my stepdad just lost his job at a nonprofit in Birmingham, and though they never talked about their finances in front of me, I knew we weren't exactly flush with cash. More than once I'd overheard one of them say to the other, "… and then we've got to somehow pay for college," to which the other would let out a defeated sigh. Fifty thousand dollars would be life-changing, but then again so would going to prison for the international laws we'd certainly be breaking.

"He really would give you the money," Parker said.

"I'm sure he would," I said. "Come on, let's get back to school."

Chapter Sixteen

In which there is a hint of foreshadowing.

I tried to apologize to Parker in the car—because I apologize for everything, even when it's not my fault—but she was mad, and the only thing she said was to take her to her aunt's apartment. I felt bad about upsetting her, but the longer I thought about the absurd situation she'd put me in the more pissed off I became. It was obvious she'd only talked to me, only been nice to me, only kissed me, so I'd help her and that crazy old man get to Paris. I wondered what he'd promised her in return. We drove in silence and I parked in front of the apartment complex, but before she could get out I said, "Why didn't you ever talk to me before yesterday?"

My fragile confidence would only let me talk to her or look at her, but not both at the same time, so I don't know how she reacted to my question. She didn't say anything though, so I kept going. "I sat in front of you all year and you've never said a word to me, but one day you need something and suddenly we're best friends."

"That's not—"

"Right. Whatever. It's just a coincidence you ignored me right up to the point that you needed my help."

She frowned and said, "It's ... it's complicated."

"Try me."

Parker took a deep breath and said, "Okay, for starters I've gone to seven schools in the last four years. Seven. And I've found it's easier not to make friends because I'll have to leave them anyway, and besides, they always find out about ..."

"... About what?"

"Nothing. Just ... nothing, okay?"

I waited for Parker to get out of the car but she didn't move. After a moment she said, "It's not like I didn't want to talk to you. You seem like a nice guy, and you're cute, in a Harry Potter sort of way."

It's hard to stay mad at someone when they say you're cute, albeit in the nerdiest way possible, but I tried. "Whatever," I said, "you thought if you kissed me I'd throw away my future and help you smuggle an old man out of the country just because you're hot."

I hadn't meant to call her hot, but I couldn't think of any way to pull the words out of the atmosphere and stuff them back into my stupid mouth, so we sat there in the silent car until I found the courage to glance over at her, and when I did she flashed a mischievous grin.

"What?"

"I'm sorry," she said. "I haven't played fair, and one should always play fairly when one has the winning cards."

"What are you talking about?"

"Oscar Wilde said that," Parker said, and I shook my head in confusion.

"The fake tears at McDonald's," she said. "That was wrong."

"Wait, those were fake?"

"Edwin Green, you don't have it in you to make me cry. But you're stronger than I thought."

"Thanks," I said. "I guess."

"I was never mad at you either," Parker said, "because you're going to help me take Garland to France."

"I am?" I asked, and wondered if this was a Jedi mind trick.

"Of course. You've got as much to gain from this trip as Garland."

"I know," I said, and let out a sigh. "But my parents probably have some college savings plan I don't even know about. And even if they don't, there's always student loans or whatever."

Parker spun toward me and grabbed my hand. "Not the stupid money. Haven't you even thought about what would happen if you help Garland find this woman?"

"Yes! That's why I keep telling you both no over and over."

"But you're only thinking of the negative repercussions."

"Right, because those are the repercussions that lead to prison time."

She smiled and squeezed my hand because she was six moves ahead and could see the checkmate. "Okay, Edwin Green, think about this sentence. A high school student helps a D-Day veteran escape from his nursing home and carries him to France to find the long lost love of his life."

I thought about it and said, "It sounds like the plot of a book I wouldn't read."

"Sure," Parker said, "but what else?"

"I don't know. It's a sweet story, I guess."

"Not a sweet story. The sweetest story. And when people hear it …"

My mind got there just before she said it.

"… you'll be famous. Instantly famous. *The Today Show, Good Morning America*, Jimmy Fallon, they'd all want to talk to you. Every talk show on every network would beg to hear this story because it's the feel-good story of the year, and you'd be at the center of it."

Parker let go of my hand and climbed out of the car, then leaned back in the open window.

"I … I hadn't thought about it that way."

"What would you do without me, Edwin Green?"

"I'm … I'm going to think about it."

"I know you are," she said. "Now hand me your phone." I did, and she programmed her number into my contacts. "I won't be at school tomorrow—big meeting down at the precinct—so call me tonight when you're willing to admit this is a terrific plan and you're lucky I let you be a part of it." Then she turned and walked away before I had a chance to say anything else.

She did that a lot.

Chapter Seventeen

*In which our hero laments the loneliness of the
ninth-fastest long-distance runner.*

I didn't go back to school for fourth period. I needed to think, and contrary to popular belief, school just isn't the place for that. Instead I spent the rest of the afternoon driving aimlessly around Hornby. Well, not entirely aimlessly, because after a few minutes I ended up on Sadie's old street. Her house looked like it did the day she moved—rumor was her parents still owned it—and I was wondering who mowed their lawn when I noticed the old lady across the street watching me from her kitchen window. I wasn't sure if skipping school and/or driving down the same road sixteen consecutive times was illegal, but decided either way it was best to move on before she called the cops. But by now I was running low on gas, and I was always running low on gas money, so I stopped at Sadie's father's old church, Hornby Christian Fellowship, and sat in the parking lot and tried to process the morning.

Parker was right. The media would eat this story up. Fame was a certainty, and fame was my goal, because Black Saturday left me painfully aware of the giant chasm between my world and the world of the famous. I mean, anyone can call Chris Martin of Martin's 24-Hour Plumbing in Fort Worth, but it's a little harder to call the lead singer of Coldplay. So I decided to become famous, and it didn't matter what for, so long as it was legal. Famous and imprisoned wasn't going to do me much good. My first plan was to just wait for it, because it seemed to me for at least half the famous people out there fame just fell on their heads like bird shit. That's what happened to Sadie. Why not me? But that plan was too passive, so instead I began searching for something I was great at, knowing once I found that something it would lead to instant celebrity. I know that sounds a little naive, but I was sixteen, and sixteen-year-olds are predisposed to daily delusions of grandeur. Anyway, as you've likely guessed, finding something I was great at proved difficult.

I didn't have the looks for modeling, or the words for writing, or the rhythm for music, or the money to be famous just for being rich. This left sports, which was a problem in itself, because most people who find fame through athletics possess a combination of (1) size, which at 5 9″ and 140 pounds I sorely lacked, and (2) strength, something I regretted not having more of whenever I asked my mother to open a jar for me, and (3) coordination, that hard to define quality that blesses some people with the graceful movement of a gazelle, while I stumble around like a drunken giraffe.

I wasn't lying to Garland. I was currently a member of J. P. Hornby's track team, but wished I were not. Not long after Black Saturday my stepdad, who is not licensed to practice psychiatry in Alabama or anywhere else, diagnosed me with situational depression and prescribed either exercise or an hour a week with our school's guidance counselor. I chose exercise and started running in the evenings, and actually loved it because the sensation of rubbing alcohol in my lungs, a sharp knife in my side, and a thousand needles in my shins made it hard for me to think about Sadie Evans or anything else except how much running sucked. I even started to look forward to the pain, but much to my annoyance my endurance increased, so I had to start running faster and farther to get Sadie off my mind. It was like a drug for someone who was too scared to take actual drugs. In the spring I even joined the track team because I'd seen this movie where a kid was winning a cross-country race only to stop at the finish line and walk away to prove a point about something or other. I figured if I could do that at the Alabama State Championships they might show it on SportsCenter, but after one day of practice I realized I was at best the ninth-fastest guy at J. P. Hornby, and unless plantar fasciitis conveniently struck the eight guys in front of me, I wasn't even going to run at the State Championships, let alone win a race with only a few steps to go. I would have quit, but my stepdad had this stupid rule about not quitting things once you've started them, so I was stuck on the team until school ended in May.

I was wondering if our coach would even notice I'd skipped practice that afternoon when a knock on my window scared the shit out of me.

I looked up, and smiling down at me with blinding white teeth was the pastor of Hornby Christian Fellowship. I'd forgotten his name. They called him Brother something. Brother Dale? Brother Rick? I rolled down my window and he said, "May I help … oh, Edwin Green, we haven't seen you around here in ages. How are you, son?"

"I'm good," I said, and wasn't sure what to say next—not that I once made out with his associate pastor's daughter in the baptismal pool and worried sometimes I might have condemned my soul to hell, though that thought did cross my mind every time I drove past a church.

"Well can I help you with anything? Is your car giving you trouble?"

"No sir. I had some time to kill before track practice. Stopped here to read for a few minutes."

Brother What's-His-Name smiled and said, "Well stay as long as you like. All are welcome in God's house … and His parking lot."

He laughed at his own joke and I faked a smile and he started walking toward his car, but he stopped and asked, "By the way, do you still hear from Sadie?"

I'm sure it's a sin to tell a pastor to go to hell, so I just said no, and he left me alone with my thoughts.

Chapter Eighteen

In which our hero watches HGTV before making the biggest decision of his life.

"You're being awfully quiet Edwin."

I shrugged. My mom said this every night during dinner, which made it untrue. She should have said, "You're being awfully normal Edwin," and only worried if I'd had a lot to say. I did not tell her this, because I was being quiet, as usual.

We were in the living room eating dinner, frozen pizza, and watching *House Hunters International* on the TV. A couple from San Diego wanted to move their family of six to a farmhouse in the middle of nowhere France, and I kept picturing myself driving those same country roads with Parker and Garland, hunting a woman who may have died years ago. I did not tell my mom this either.

"You look like something's bothering you," Mom said. She said this every night too.

"I'm worried about this family. They don't look like farmers. If the winter is harsh I'm afraid they'll starve."

Mom didn't laugh. She never knew when I was joking. "But you're okay?" she persisted.

"Yes, I'm okay!"

"Don't yell at your mother," my stepdad said. He said this every night when my mom's interrogation reached peak annoyance.

"Sorry," I muttered.

"That's okay, dear," my mom said. "By the way, I read today Sadie might be starring in that remake of *The Breakfast Club*. They want her for the Molly Ringwald role."

"Alice, do you think the boy wants to hear about his ex-girlfriend every night," my stepdad said. He said this every night when mom inevitably brought up Sadie Evans. Mom was Sadie's biggest fan in Hornby, which, considering the town's obsession, was saying something.

"But he's still friends with Sadie," my mom said. "You two still Facebook, don't you dear?"

"Facebook isn't a verb," I said, and my stepdad shot me a look. "I haven't heard from her in a few weeks," I said.

A long silence followed before my stepdad asked, "How was track practice?" He asked this every night. My real dad died when I was two—brain aneurysm—and Mom married Carl five years ago. He's not a bad guy, all things considered. Sort of strict, but nice enough. He's not comfortable talking to me about things a father would typically talk to his son about though. Like Sadie, he's never known what to say to me about her, so he never said anything. I think it was a relief when I joined the track team and he had at least one non-Sadie question to ask each night.

"Fine," I said, like I said every other night, even though I'd skipped it.

The family on *House Hunters* made their decision, and six months later it appeared they had indeed survived their first winter, and I excused myself to my room to do homework.

"But you promise you're okay?" my mom asked again as I left the room.

"Yeah." I skipped school for the first time in my life today because I'm strongly considering helping a crazy girl bust a ninety-year-old man out of his nursing home so we can take him to France against his attorney's wishes to find a woman he met during World War II, all in the hope of becoming famous and winning back my ex-girlfriend. "I'm fine. I promise."

I checked my homework assignments online, and debated whether I should read the third chapter of *The Great Gatsby* or attempt three dozen algebra problems first, before deciding to do neither and instead lay in bed and played out Parker's scenario in my head. It made sense. As long as we made it to France it would be the feel-good story of the year. Sure we might get into some trouble, but we'd be famous, and famous people never really get into trouble. However if we were somehow stopped before we made it out of the country things could turn ugly. But the more I thought about it, the risk was worth the reward.

I pulled up Sadie's Facebook page. She'd changed her profile picture. It was her and Trevor, the guy with the third worst haircut from that terrible new British boy band, sitting next to each other at the Grammys. Then I looked at her name in my contacts. She'd changed her number months ago, but I couldn't bring myself to delete the old one. I clicked her name and saw a year's worth of text messages, starting with the last nearly twelve months ago.

SADIE: Edwin this is Pastor Mark. Sadie regrets that she can no longer be your girlfriend. God Bless.

I called Fitz.

"This better be important, Green. *American Ninja Warrior* is on."

"I'll make it quick," I said. "So hypothetically, if someone had an opportunity to win back the love of his life, an opportunity of, let's call it, questionable legality, should he take it?"

Fitz hesitated. "This doesn't sound very hypothetical."

"If you say so."

Fitz hesitated again. "If you——"

"Not me."

"Right. If someone takes this opportunity of ... what'd you call it?"

"Questionable legality."

"This opportunity of questionable legality, could other people get hurt? Or would it be a victimless crime, like shoplifting?"

"I'm pretty sure there's a victim in shoplifting," I said.

"You know what I mean."

I didn't really, but said, "No, in this purely hypothetical situation, if the person takes this opportunity of questionable legality, no one would get hurt."

"Yeah, you should totally take it."

"Not me."

"Right, someone should totally take it."

I hung up and remembered I hadn't checked Garland's video since that morning. I pulled it up and thought I was on the wrong page. The video had 4,134 views, and over forty comments, all between an angry atheist and a few Omaha Prophetic Presbyterians. This was more views than every other video I'd ever posted combined, and it confirmed what I already suspected. As unlikely as it seemed, Garland Lenox was my ticket to fame.

What the hell, I thought, and grabbed my phone off the old green blanket I'd been sleeping under since kindergarten, but it took me a while to call Parker because she'd entered her name in my contacts as "She-Ra: Princess of Power."

"Hello," she said, "this is She-Ra: Princess of Power."

"Hey, it's Edwin."

"Well, hello Edwin Green. Calling to admit I'm a genius with a terrific plan and you're lucky I even asked you to be a part of it?"

"Yeah … pretty much."

I could hear her smile over the phone. "I knew you'd get there sooner or later. I've already told Garland you're in. We're leaving in the morning. Pack light."

Chapter Nineteen

In which thirteen lies and a couple half-truths are told.

As instructed I arrived at Morningview Arbor at eight a.m. the next morning and promptly began lying through my teeth. This was phase one of the plan Parker revealed to me the night before. A shitty plan that in retrospect makes the Bay of Pigs Invasion look like *Ocean's 11*.

"A field trip to where now?" A nurse I recognized from Monday afternoon asked as Parker, Garland, and I stood before her at the nurse's station.

"The National Medal of Honor Museum," Parker said.

The nurse frowned and said, "Parker honey, I don't know the first thing about this."

"Aunt Marcy knows," Parker lied. "I was here when she spoke to Mr. Lenox's attorney yesterday."

"Old Lucian faxed my release form," Garland said. "I'm sure Marcy left it lying 'round here somewhere."

The nurse began looking for the imaginary lost form and asked, "Where's this museum again?"

"In Chattanooga," I said, then added, "Tennessee. Chattanooga, Tennessee. Not some other Chattanooga in Europe or somewhere." Parker stepped on my toes and applied pressure until I shut up.

"Mr. Graham thinks taking a veteran with us will bring the history to life," Parker said, and the nurse nodded enthusiastically. "We're taking one of the school buses, and we'll be back by four this afternoon because the baseball team has a game tonight. We're playing Rome. Win and we're in the play-offs!" None of this was true, but Parker operated under the impression the more details you could add to a lie the more believable it became.

"Okay, just let me call Marcy real quick to——"

"Oh please don't wake her," Parker said, and the nurse took her hand off the phone. "She worked a double shift yesterday and she'd just fallen asleep when I left the apartment."

It could have gone either way, but Garland smiled and said, "Don't you worry, Nurse Duncan, I'm in good hands with these two. I'll be back in time for the early bird supper. It's Salisbury steak night, and you and I both know I wouldn't miss that."

The nurse bit her lip and thought for an eternity before finally saying, "Okay, y'all have fun." We turned and walked toward the exit, but only made it a few feet before the nurse noticed Garland rolling his suitcase. "Mr. Lenox," she said, "are you planning on spending the night at the museum?"

I stiffened, but Garland didn't skip a beat. "I figured that museum might have some use for my old flight suits," the old man said, then patted his stomach and added, "they don't fit me like they used to." The man could tell a lie.

The nurse smiled and said, "How thoughtful of you." Minutes later we were in my Jetta, barreling down I-20 toward Atlanta.

Chapter Twenty

In which the last P is not that simple.

"What I don't understand," I said, as my back was Shiatsued into submission, "is why they even sell massage chairs in an airport." It was five hours and a thorough pat down from a less than friendly TSA officer later, and the three of us were killing time before our flight by testing out obscenely expensive massage chairs in Brookstone. I needed a massage too, after my first experience driving in Atlanta traffic, something I now believe should require NASCAR experience. Never mind the added stress of thinking we were followed.

"Son, no one's following us," Garland shouted six or seven times during the trip. "Keep your eyes on the damn road."

He had a point. No one from Morningview Arbor had any reason to suspect we weren't on a school bus headed toward Chattanooga. But still I kept envisioning men in an unmarked nursing home security van pulling us over and jumping out with guns drawn. I mentioned this and Garland said, "Morningview Arbor has one security guard. His name is Hank and he's older than me and drives a golf cart. I think we'll be okay son, but if I spot him I'll be sure to let you know." Garland was right, and now we were safely inside the airport having our backs turned to Jell-O.

"I don't care why they sell them," Parker said, her voice shaking as the chair switched to karate chop mode, "I'm just ha-ha-happy they d-d-do."

"By the way," I said to Garland, "I can't believe you paid twenty-eight thousand dollars for our tickets."

"Twenty-eight thousand six hundred and thirty-seven dollars," Garland said, "but who's counting?"

"We should have flown coach," Parker said.

"The hell we should've. I intend to leave just enough money for Lucian to bury me in a pine box. No need flying coach at this point in life. I might even buy one of these chairs when we get back."

I laughed and said, "Okay, maybe old men spending their life's savings are the target market. But seriously, who buys this stuff? Can you imagine stepping off a plane and saying, 'Oh thank God, I really needed to grab a pair of crystal candlesticks from Schweiger's during this layover.'"

"Damn Nazi sympathizers," Garland growled loud enough that a woman standing nearby grabbed her child and left the store in a hurry. "You know they had me in Austria after the war hunting war criminals, and I actually ran into Josef Schweiger at a pub in Wattens. He wasn't on my list, but I broke his nose anyway and barely made it out of there alive. Not my finest moment—he was ninety years old at the time—but I can't say I wouldn't do it again. You haven't lived until you've punched a Nazi in the face."

He said stuff like this all the time, and I was never sure how to respond, so the three of us sat there in relative silence, only grunting when the massage rollers passed over our shoulder blades. "So," Garland finally said, "Parker tells me you've stirred up the Prophetic Presbyterians."

"Yeah," I said, "who knew they were still around?"

"Everyone knows they're still around, son," Garland said.

"You seriously don't know about that church?" Parker asked. "They're on the news like once a week." I shrugged and she said, "In the early nineties they transitioned from a predict-the-end-of-the-world cult to a we-really-hate-gay-people cult. Now they picket funerals and bully people online and are basically a horde of bigots who wouldn't be missed at all if a small asteroid took out Omaha. Best part is, they sometimes call themselves OPP and have no idea why people think it's funny."

I laughed and said, "You know me."

"Wait, why is that funny?" Garland asked.

"OPP?" Parker asked. "Hmm, Edwin Green, how can I explain it?"

We both laughed and Garland waved a hand at us and mumbled, "Weird-ass kids."

The chairs were back on our shoulders and for a moment we were again reduced to grunting, then Garland said, "Alright son, tell me 'bout the girl."

"What girl?"

"What girl? You know damn well what girl. Parker told me the only reason you agreed to help us was to impress some girl."

"I agreed to help you for fifty thousand dollars," I said.

"Now wait one minute, I only remember offering twenty-five."

I looked over and he grinned, and I got the feeling if I let on I didn't want to talk about Sadie he'd only want to talk about her more, so I said, "Her name is Sadie, and she was my girlfriend, but she moved away."

"I'm sorry to hear it, son. How long were you two an item?"

Parker sat up in her chair to hear me better.

"Little over a year," I said, because I'd learned it made people uncomfortable when I said one year, two months, six days, four hours, and seventeen minutes.

"You keep in touch with this old girlfriend of yours?"

"She emails me sometimes," I said, "but I haven't spoken to her in months." Again, vague lengths of time were more socially acceptable than saying eleven months, twenty-two days, eleven hours, and sixteen minutes. "I did see her aunt in the mall last week—she remembered me from Sadie's sixteenth birthday party. I asked her how Sadie was and she just shrugged. Said she hadn't heard from any of them since they left."

"Her family join a cult?" Garland asked.

"Sort of," I said, and left it at that.

The Grand Inquisitor was thinking of a follow-up question when Parker threw me a lifeline and said, "Edwin Green, let's go for a walk."

"Okay," I said, and pried myself from my chair.

"Go on," Garland said. "I don't want to walk with the two of you anyway. Think I'll run in the Montblanc store and buy me a thousand-dollar fountain pen. We'll need 'em to fill out our landing cards in Paris."

I laughed, but he bought three and gave us each one.

Chapter Twenty-One

*In which our hero realizes his best friend may have been right,
then calls him an assface.*

Parker and I walked into the duty-free shop where a man was
arguing with the cashier over the five-carton-per-person limit on
cigarettes. We watched them argue for a moment before Parker
began, what I can only describe as, aggressively sampling perfume. "Would you like a bottle?" I asked through a haze of fra-
grance. "I'm about to have fifty thousand dollars in the bank."

She smiled and said, "I can afford my own, thank you," then
she sprayed me with the pink bottle in her hand and I almost
knocked over a table full of tax-free liquor trying to get out of
the way. Parker laughed and moved on to look at the purses. I
followed.

"So did Garland offer you money to help him get to Paris
too?" I asked.

She looked up and said, "That's kind of a personal question,
don't you think?"

"No," I said. "You know what he's giving me."

Parker considered this for a moment, then said, "He's giving
me a new life."

She moved again, on to the watches, and again I followed. "A new life? What does that mean?"

"Whatever you want it to mean," she said, this time without looking at me, and for some reason it pissed me off.

"Look, if you're going to be all weird and mysterious the entire trip it's going to get old quick."

Now she looked at me, and for a moment I understood how a gazelle feels when it makes eye contact with a lion across the Serengeti, but her face softened and she smiled and said, "Oh Edwin Green, like you don't have your secrets."

"Like what?"

"Like what really happened between you and Sadie Evans."

"Oh God, not you too." I walked away and this time Parker followed me.

"Edwin Green."

I kept walking.

"Wait. What is wrong with you?"

I stopped and turned around and said, "Can no one talk to me for ten minutes without asking about Sadie Evans?"

Parker laughed.

"It's not funny," I said.

She laughed some more, and when I turned to walk away again she grabbed me by the arm and said, "Edwin Green, please believe me when I say I don't give a shit about Sadie Evans. Not a single, solitary shit, I swear. I don't care who she's dating, or what she wore to the Grammys, or when her next movie is coming out. But I do care about you, and helping you with this Sadie thing is, I don't know, sort of my good deed. So if you can lower your defenses for a moment and talk to me like a friend, maybe I can help."

I wanted to tell her I didn't want her help with Sadie, not because I didn't want her help, but because I'd (1) convinced myself Parker sort of liked me. I mean, I was 67% sure she'd kissed me in the hallway two days earlier, and (2) I liked thinking that she liked me. Obviously I still wanted Sadie back—that's why I was about to fly to Paris—but if my plan didn't work it was nice to think I had options. Hot redheaded options. And though I'd gone twelve months without even acknowledging the existence of other girls, this meant (3) Fitz might have been on to something with his smitten theory. I hated when he was right. The assface.

"Sorry," I said. "It's a reflex at this point. You can't imagine what it's like for people to constantly want to talk about the one thing in your life you don't want to talk about."

"Oh I could imagine," Parker said. "So you really haven't spoken to her in months?"

"No. I haven't actually spoken to her since a few days before we broke up."

"Wait, how did you not talk to her when you broke up?" Parker asked.

I looked at my shoes and let her figure it out on her own.

"Whoa, hold on, she dumped you by text, didn't she? You dated for a year and she dumped you by text and you haven't spoken to her since?"

I nodded and Parker said, "Tell me again why you're trying to win this girl back?"

I started to answer but Parker wasn't finished. "I'm just saying, if it were me, and I'd let some guy pay for a year's worth of dinners and movies, I'd at least have the decency to dump him in person. Maybe over the phone if he'd been a dick."

She was joking and trying to prove a point at the same time but she didn't know what she was talking about. "That's where you're wrong," I said, "we never had an actual date."

"Wait, what?"

I sighed. I hadn't talked about Sadie Evans to anyone since Black Saturday, but not because I didn't want to talk about her, not entirely at least. It was just that she felt so far away, and I thought talking about her would make her seem even farther away. But that was before I had a plan. Now Sadie seemed so close I could hardly fail to grasp her. (Sorry, I'd read some *Gatsby* the night before to make up for the fact I wasn't going to school the rest of the week). Besides, Parker wanted to know about Sadie because she wanted to help me, not out of some tabloid curiosity. "Sadie moved to Hornby in first grade," I said. "You know her dad was a preacher, right? At Hornby Christian Fellowship? Do I have to tell you all this? I'm sure they've got her autobiography in the book store. You can read about her on the flight."

"I'm going to sleep on the flight. I need to hear this right now."

"Okay, but let's talk somewhere else," I said. "All this perfume is making me sick."

Chapter Twenty-Two

In which Parker Haddaway defends a respected physician before causing a scene.

"Sadie couldn't play with Barbie dolls."

We were upstairs, at a table overlooking the international departures atrium, sipping on frosted orange shakes I'd bought us from The Varsity.

Parker raised one eyebrow and said, "Okay. Good to know."

I took a sip of my shake and said, "When she moved to Hornby in first grade all the girls thought she was weird because her dad wouldn't let her play with Barbie dolls. He'd been to some Christian conference on the sexualization of American children and learned they modeled Barbie after a German adult novelty doll. Sadie said he came home and tossed her Barbies in the garbage. Called them seven-foot harlots with a shoe fetish living in a dream house of sin."

"Even Doctor Barbie?" Parker asked.

"Even Doctor Barbie."

"But she worked so hard to get through Barbie medical school."

"I know," I said. "But to make up for it he bought her a roomful of those Bible inspired dolls that looked like Barbies, except they all wore ankle-length tunics."

"You're making this up," Parker said.

"I swear. She had Mary, mother of Jesus. Ruth and Naomi. Rahab the prostitute …"

"Wait, hold up," Parker said, choking a little on her milkshake. "You're telling me her dad wouldn't let her play with Doctor Barbie, but Rahab the prostitute was okay?"

I laughed and said, "I'm not defending him."

"Did he buy her Adam and Eve with removable fig leaves too?"

"I don't recall."

"What about Job with removable boils?"

"Maybe."

Parker slid the salt shaker across the table and said, "Next time you see Sadie tell her I'm donating this to her collection."

I examined the shaker and gave her a puzzled look, and she said, "Lot's wife."

I shook my head and laughed.

"Because she looked back and turned to salt."

"Yeah, I get it."

"You can play with her for hours, then use her to preserve meat."

"I get it."

"She also adds flavor to bland vegetables."

"I get it."

"Okay," Parker said, "so her weirdo dad deprived her of Barbies as a small child. What does that have to do with anything?"

"I'm just saying Sadie was never very popular at school, because now it's easy to get the impression everyone always loved her.

"Fine, but it still doesn't make up for the fact she dumped you by text."

At some point in the last ten minutes I'd gone from telling Parker about Sadie to defending Sadie in a courtroom where Parker was the judge, jury, and executioner, and a guilty verdict was a forgone conclusion. I knew what I said next wouldn't help my case.

"Technically her dad dumped me for her by text."

Parker spit orange shake over the rail onto the atrium floor. A man below yelled at us.

"You're shitting me," she said loud enough that people started to look at us.

"Yeah … no."

"Edwin Green, please tell me you're shitting me. Even if you're not, tell me you are, because I can't live in a world where you're trying to win back the girl who had her Barbie-phobic dad dump you by text."

Against my better judgment, I pulled up the text on my phone and showed it to Parker. She read it and closed her eyes for a second, then screamed "Bitchwhore!" so loud everyone in the atrium stopped and looked our way. The people eating looked at us, the people ordering food looked at us, the people serving food looked at us, even people rushing to catch a flight stopped to look at us, and though I kept waiting for the normal buzz of a hundred conversations to resume, it never did. I suppose people in airports are always a little on edge, and it didn't help matters that Parker wore a T-shirt that said "Fight Terrorism" above a picture of the Olsen twins, so I grabbed her by the hand and pulled her toward the Delta lounge before security showed up and I had to discuss Sadie Evans with them too.

Chapter Twenty-Three

In which our hero's virginity is discussed,
and unlicensed psychiatry is practiced.

"Bitchwhore," I whispered after we'd shown our passports to the woman behind the desk and walked into the lounge where a sea of businessmen were drinking themselves sleepy before their flights. "I want to text that to Fitz. Is it one word or two?"

Parker didn't say anything. She was mad, or pretending to be, and either way I thought she'd become a little too overprotective of someone she'd only been friends with for forty-eight hours. We sat at a table with a view of the runway and after a while I said, "Look, if you'd rather not help me get back together with Sadie you don't have to. I didn't ask for your help."

She watched a plane take off and I wasn't sure she'd heard me, but a moment later she turned to me and said, "No, Edwin Green, this is my good deed and you and Sadie Evans will get back together—although the more I hear about her the less good my deed feels. But who am I to judge, maybe you've done something terrible and actually deserve her. You know when the gods want to punish us they answer our prayers."

It was strange to hear someone besides a film or music critic say bad things about Sadie. Everyone at school worshiped her, and because of that I'd missed out on a key element of the breaking up grieving process. Namely the part where friends badmouth your ex until you start to view the breakup as a good thing. I'm sure even back in the Paleolithic Era when a cavewoman dumped a caveman, all his cave buddies would come over and trash the offending party in hopes of cheering up their sad prehistoric friend:

"You invent fire. You can do much better."

"There are plenty of Megalodons in sea."

"We should never go near sea again."

But I didn't have any buddies, cave or otherwise, except Fitz, and when I told him after Black Saturday that I didn't want to talk about it he obliged. And sure, after a year most guys would have moved on, but even that wasn't an option for me, because the only thing any girl at school ever wanted to talk to me about was, you guessed it, my ex-girlfriend. My heart was trapped in romantic purgatory, and Sadie Evans was my only salvation.

Another plane took off and Parker said, "Or maybe my good deed should be making sure the two of you never get back together."

"What?"

"Nothing," Parker said, and smiled at me. I never got used to her smiling at me.

"Okay," I said. "Whatever. I'm not going to try and convince you Sadie is a nice person. But just let me say she never seemed like the type of person who'd have her dad dump me by text … until she did it."

Parker mumbled something else I didn't catch.

"She really was a sweet girl," I said, now sounding way too defensive.

"You don't have to defend her to me, Edwin Green."

"Good," I said. "I won't."

"That said, I think I can help you."

"Okay, how?"

"I'm no psychiatrist, but I've spent enough time with them that I can legally practice in six states. Do you want to hear my expert opinion?"

"Sure."

"It'll cost you five cents."

"Fine."

"You need closure," Parker said. "Sadie took your virginity and ran off with it and that's why you're still obsessed with her even though she treated you worse than shit."

"She didn't take my virginity," I said loud enough that half the people in the lounge looked up from their laptops. "We never got farther than—"

"I don't want the details, Edwin Green. Details are always vulgar."

"Fine," I said. "But we didn't have sex. She was a preacher's daughter."

"So? In my experience preacher's kids are the worst people on Earth."

"Yeah, well, you two have a lot in common."

Parker raised an eyebrow and said, "Like?"

"Like … okay, you know how on the last day of sixth grade girls were still gross and you should avoid them at all costs, but on the first day of seventh grade they were hot and pretty much all you thought about all day?"

"Uh … no."

"Right. Anyway, by seventh grade Sadie was unanimously regarded as the sixth hottest girl in our class, and—"

"Hold up. You ranked every girl in your class in seventh grade?"

"Not me personally, and not the entire class. Just the top ten."

"Is this list published somewhere? Can I see it?"

"It was more of an oral tradition."

"So you're telling me a girl on every magazine's Most Beautiful list was only the sixth hottest girl in her class of fifty girls at J. P. Hornby?"

I shrugged and Parker said, "Whatever, get on with the story, you pig."

"Like I was saying," I said, "In seventh grade Sadie found herself the focus of our collective hormone-riddled attention. But no one can go on real dates in seventh grade. You're totally dependent on your parents' willingness to drive you to the movies or the mall or wherever. But Sadie couldn't even do that. Even if your parents drove and sat between you at the movies she couldn't go. But everyone still tried. Buzz Booker asked her first, and she told him no, and though he later told everyone she was a lesbian, sixteen guys still lined up to try their luck and were all promptly rejected."

Parker laughed and said, "Okay, that sounds vaguely familiar."

"Exactly. You two have a lot in common."

"Like hell. We have exactly one thing in common. We both attract mouth-breathing football guys."

"Okay, you have one thing in common. Besides, Sadie was nice to all the guys she turned down."

Parker flipped me off and said, "So did you ask her out in seventh grade too?"

"I never asked her out."

"She asked you out?"

"Not exactly," I said. "She just invited me to church one Sunday, then the next, then the next. A month later she was telling people I was her boyfriend and we were making out in the pastor's study."

"Vulgar details," Parker said covering her ears.

I shrugged and said, "You're the one who wanted to hear all this. Anyway, I doubt I would've ever asked her out, on account of my undiagnosed case of Caligynephobia."

"You're afraid of calligraphy?"

"What? No."

"How do you invite people to your formal gatherings, Edwin Green?"

I laughed and said, "No, Caligynephobia, the fear of beautiful women."

Parker crossed her arms and said, "I think I'm offended. Why aren't you shaking in fear right now."

"Trust me," I said, "you scare the shit out of me."

Parker smiled and I looked at my feet and things were awkward for a moment before Garland hobbled up to our table and said, "Where the hell have you two been? Come on, we've got some international laws to break."

Chapter Twenty-Four

In which our hero commits criminal impersonation, a violation of Section 13A-9-18, Ala. Code 1975, and a class B misdemeanor.

"Wait, your lawyer is Lucian Figg? That guy on every billboard in Hornby?"

"Yeah," Garland said. "So?"

"Garland, your lawyer is a sleazeball."

"He's a lawyer, son, no need for redundancy. Now make the call."

Phase two of our plan involved me placing a handkerchief over the receiver of a prepaid phone Parker purchased at Walmart the night before, calling Morningview Arbor, and committing all manner of fraud.

"This will never work," I said, after we'd eaten either a late lunch or early dinner at El Taco, then spent the better part of an hour practicing the call in a quiet corner of the lounge.

"Son, back in 1982 I snuck into North Korea by holding up a ping pong paddle and telling the border guard I was on my way to the World Championship in Pyongyang. Trust me, this will work. But hey, if you've got a better idea, we're all ears."

I shrugged and called Morningview Arbor.

"Hello," I said in my deepest voice, "this is Lucian Figg, attorney at law."

Garland winced and Parker whispered, "Stop talking so formal. And don't change your voice, that's what the handkerchief is for."

Shaken, I tried to continue, "As you are aware, my client, Mr. Garland Lenox, is in Chattanooga today on a school field trip. I'm calling to inform you Mr. Lenox decided to stay in Chattanooga tonight with extended family. He will return to Morningview Arbor on Sunday morning."

I recognized the voice on the phone as the same nurse from that morning. She said something about this all being unorthodox, and against nursing home policy, and something else about the legal department and a release form and the potential for big headaches, so I went off script. "My apologies for any inconvenience. If you will email the release form I can fax it back to you in the morning from my office."

Parker's eyes widened and Garland began mouthing "no" over and over, but I didn't grasp the reason for their panic until the nurse from Morningview Arbor said something about the email address on file. "No!" I said, with more force than I'd meant to. "I've actually changed my email address. The new one is l-a-d-i-e-z-z-z-l-u-v-c-o-o-l-E at gmail dot com. Yes, three z's. Yes. Sorry again for the trouble. Thank you."

I hung up the phone and gasped for breath, and when I looked up, Parker and Garland were staring at me.

"What?"

"Nothing son," Garland said, shaking his head. "That was smooth."

"Cool E been smooth since he wore Underoos," Parker added.

"Shut up. I created that account when I was twelve."

"I'm just wondering why you stopped at three z's," Garland said.

"Shut up."

"Was Ol' Dirty Edwin already taken?" Parker asked.

"Shut up."

They both laughed and Garland patted me on the back and said, "You did okay, son. But I'm not gonna feel good about this until we're in the air."

We made the short walk to gate F9 where they'd just invited first-class passengers to board. I took out my passport and said to Garland, "Since we're in a hurry, maybe you can talk the pilot into taking off a few minutes early," but he didn't laugh.

"Not a bad idea," he said. "In 1975 I was on a BOAC flight to Stockholm with that disco group ABBA. We were in first class, and they'd just begun seating coach when the brunette one, I think her name was Anni-Frid, shouted at the pilot it was time to leave. Sure enough they shut the doors and took off with a half empty plane. I helped them write 'Fernando' on that flight."

"There must have been something in the air that night," Parker said, and when I looked over they both wiped the smiles off their faces and Garland said, "Son, you can't make this shit up."

Chapter Twenty-Five

*In which our hero reluctantly partakes in the miracle of flight,
and later enjoys some cashews.*

"Welcome aboard, Mr. Green," a flight attendant said while examining my boarding pass. "Seat 72K, you'll be in our upper deck. Please take the staircase ahead on your right." Walking up the steps I heard Garland growl behind me, "No I don't need any help getting to my damn seat."

Confession time: Before this I'd only flown once in my life, a two-hour flight from Birmingham to Orlando's Magic Kingdom when I was seven—I only had a passport because we drove to Canada to visit Carl's weird sister three summers ago. The one plane I'd been on was small, no more than eighty people on board, all going to see a giant rodent. But now I was on a Boeing 747. A plane so big it (1) had an upper deck, and (2) had more than enough seats to accommodate everyone at J. P. Hornby, and (3) would surely never get off the ground. I realized 747s had, at some point in the past, flown, but I was struggling to picture this particular behemoth soaring into the sky, and I may have freaked out a bit.

By the time we made it to our seats I was sweating somewhat heavily for a cool day in April, and after I stood up and sat down for the sixth time in less than a minute, Parker asked, "Are you okay?" I was in the single seat on the front row, Parker and Garland had the two seats behind me. Well, the word seat doesn't do them justice. These were private thrones in the sky that at the push of a button transformed into private beds in the sky. They even gave us those nice noise canceling headphones and a little kit with a toothbrush, socks, an eye mask, and some body lotion. This was a nice touch, but what I really needed was a tranquilizer.

"I think so," I said. "I just haven't flown much."

Garland reached over my seat, squeezed my shoulder, and said, "Son, these things hardly ever crash, but if it does, odds are it'll be right here at takeoff."

I turned around and gave Garland my best "what-the-hell" look and Parker asked, "Is that supposed to make him feel better?"

Garland shrugged and said, "I just wanted him to know the suspense wouldn't kill him."

"Sir, can I offer you a predeparture beverage and snack?"

The flight attendant was standing in front of me with a tray full of drinks and nuts and I wanted to ask her who could eat at a time like this, but instead I took a Coke and some cashews and heard Garland say, "Excuse me, miss, I'm in a bit of a hurry."

The flight attendant flashed a Pan Am smile. "And what can I offer you, sir?"

"I'm not in a hurry to get my damn cashews. I'm in a hurry to get to Paris."

She laughed and rolled her eyes and said, "I'll go talk to the pilot and see what I can do."

Garland gave Parker and me a triumphant look, but our flight still backed away from the gate ten minutes late.

We were on a Delta flight operated by an Air France crew, so flight attendants made announcements in French first, then English. This was when I noticed another glaring hole in Garland and Parker's plan—they were counting on me to translate. I caught *Bonjour* in the welcome announcement, then the flight attendant began speaking so fast I only understood every eighth or ninth word.

"What's she saying," Garland barked from the seat behind me.

"It's the welcome message," I said, though I couldn't be certain. I looked back and tried reading the facial expressions of our fellow first-class passengers, because if the flight attendant was saying something like, "We've just received word from the tower that an elderly gentleman on this flight has escaped from his nursing home with the help of two young people who skipped school today. We ask that everyone remain seated while the air marshal Tasers them unconscious," it would have been obvious on their faces. But everyone looked bored, so I figured it was safe to assume they were listening to instructions on how to use a seatbelt.

"Son, aren't you going to translate any of this?" Garland asked again, but Parker said, "If you can wait ten seconds they repeat everything in English." I could hear them arguing like an old married couple behind me, but now I was less concerned about translating and more concerned about losing my lunch. The plane bumped across the tarmac, and the flight attendant said something about an emergency water landing, and I experienced all the symptoms of a full-blown panic attack. Mom and Carl didn't even know where I was, and when this plane crashed into the sea, how would they ever know I was on it? Would the airline call them? Would they be compensated for their loss? This whole thing made so much sense last night, and now it was suffocatingly obvious I'd made the biggest mistake of my short life. I gasped for air and unbuckled my seatbelt. The pilot told the flight crew to prepare for takeoff, and I noticed an emergency exit behind us. The door looked complicated but if I could get back there and open it I could jump out before the plane took off. Yeah, that would work. I stood up and a flight attendant shouted, "Sir, return to your seat immediately!" She didn't have to say anything though because just then the thrust from four Pratt & Whitney 4062 engines shoved me back against my seat. We were now hurtling down the runway at speeds I had not anticipated, though speed I suppose is a crucial element in lifting 364,000 pounds of aluminum alloy off the ground. Either way the emergency exit was no longer an option, so I put my seat belt back on, and shut my eyes tight, and when the rattling stopped I opened one eye and peeped out the window and watched Atlanta shrink into miniature. My ears popped, and as Georgia disappeared below the clouds I felt my heartbeat slow, and my muscles unclench, and at some point I realized oxygen was entering my lungs at regular intervals again. Playing it cool, I propped my feet up and enjoyed a few cashews and tried to forget I'd just strongly considered leaping from the upper deck of a rolling 747. Twenty minutes later, when the pilot turned off the seat belt sign, I stood up, stretched, and looked back at Garland and Parker. They both smiled.

We were going to Paris. Our terrible plan had worked. It had actually worked.

Chapter Twenty-Six

In which Garland Lenox takes advantage of the beveled Christofle flatware used in Air France's first-class cabin.

Actually our terrible plan hadn't worked, but we had no way of knowing it at the time. We ate dinner with real knives and forks—I even tried caviar for the first and last time—then the three of us indulged in hot fudge sundaes before the cabin lights dimmed. I suspected Garland and Parker would try to sleep, but the old man shouted for me to come sit on his ottoman.

I obliged and he said, "I thought you should know how I met Madeleine."

"Who?"

"Madeleine," Garland shouted and a woman behind us turned on her reading lamp to see what was the matter. "The woman you're taking me to France to find. Holy hell, son, try and keep up."

"How was I supposed to know her name was Madeleine? You said she was French, I figured she had a French name like Jacques or something."

"Jacques is a boy's name."

"Or whatever a French girl name is."

"Madeleine is a French girl name. Son, do you want to hear this story or not?"

I raised my hands in surrender and said, "Yes. Tell it already. Wait, do you mind if I record you again?"

"What the hell for?"

"A lot of people liked your last story," I said, "and it really pissed off the Omaha Prophetic Presbyterians."

Garland laughed. "Then by all means, son, record away."

"Wait, do you think she'd want to hear?"

Garland looked at Parker and said, "Don't wake her. She's heard all my stories a dozen times," then he launched into his tale. "Now I told you about that man in Chattanooga signing me up for the Air Force 'cause I walked into the recruitment center with that mechanic's boy. Well, I figured they'd try and make a mechanic out of me too, but somehow my paperwork got screwed up and they put me on a bus to something called the Aviation Cadet Classification Center in Nashville. The cigar-chomping officer I presented my papers to looked them over and said, 'Hell son, they've lowered the requirements but you still need a high-school diploma to be here.' Of course I didn't have a high-school diploma because I'd spent most of my childhood in the damn woods waiting for Doomsday, but I didn't mention that to him. I've always been able to read people. The day I met Elvis I knew he'd sell a billion records and die on the toilet, and I knew that fat bastard in Nashville wanted to do as little work as possible. Sure enough, he started moaning about all the paperwork it would take to get me where I needed to be, so I said, 'Sir, there must be a mistake, I do have a high-school diploma.' He glanced up and gave me a strange little smile, then scribbled something on my papers before handing them back to me and saying, 'You sure do. Right through that door, son, they'll show you where to go.'"

A flight attendant walked by and Garland stopped her to ask for an extra pillow before continuing his story. "In Nashville they shaved our heads and stuck us with half a dozen needles and tested us for a week to see if we'd be pilots, navigators, or bombardiers. Turns out I had 20/10 vision. Now that didn't mean much to me, I just knew back home I could shoot a squirrel from two-hundred yards, but the Air Force seemed to think I'd make a good pilot. Hell, I'd never even driven a car and they were about to let me fly an airplane. But first we had six weeks of boot camp. We ran, and did push-ups, and ran, and scrubbed toilets, and ran, and peeled potatoes, and then we ran some more for good measure. The only thing I remember more than the running was the shouting. They'd shout at you if you messed up, and they'd shout at you if you did something right. I wanted to remind them I'd volunteered for this shit, and a little gratitude wouldn't hurt, but something told me that would only make them shout louder. After basic we had four weeks of book learning on how planes work, the physics and math of it all. Then they tested us."

"Hold up," I said, "if you never went to school how did you manage to pass a physics test?"

Garland laughed and said, "I cheated like the devil. I was just lucky the fella next to me knew what he was doing. Anyway, when they were through with us in Nashville they loaded us on a train with blacked-out windows. None of us knew where the hell we were going, and one dumb ass kept saying they were shipping us straight to Europe on a train. I don't think that poor boy realized there was an ocean in the way. Rest of us guys called him Choo Choo after that—at least until the Germans shot him down over Antwerp. We wound up in Texas, learning to fly rickety old Stearman 75s at a civilian-run flight school, then to Louisiana for basic flight, and finally to Selma for advanced flying school.

When that was all over they handed me my wings, told me I was a flight officer, and assigned me to the 375th Fighter Squadron in Richmond. I spent a few months in Virginia training in a P-47 Thunderbolt, then in November they stuffed a bunch of us on a big boat called the Queen Elizabeth and shipped us to England. Did you know some Hong Kong tycoon bought that boat in the seventies and tried to turn it into a floating university, but some Chinese Nationalists set it on fire one night and it sank to the bottom of Hong Kong harbor?"

"I ... no ... I didn't know that," I said, and tried to steer the conversation back to the war. "So you were a fighter pilot? With the Aviator glasses and those cool leather jackets with the fur collars?"

"I suppose I was," Garland said, "though Bottisham was usually a little too cloudy for the shades."

"And you spent the war what, dogfighting the Luftwaffe?"

"Hell no. I told you, son, I didn't do shit in the war. I flew escort for B-17s, and that was it. We had permission to engage enemy fighters, but I never saw the first one."

"Did you fly on D-Day?" I asked.

"No, son, my war didn't last that long," the old man said. He stared out his window for a long moment, then turned back to me and said, "It was a few minutes after midnight on April 24th, and a fella named Joe Baggio and I were flying P-47 escorts for a Flying Fortress called the Savannah Smile dropping leaflets over Normandy."

"Leaflets?"

"Propaganda leaflets. Let everyone on the ground know the Germans were losing the war and we'd be there to liberate them soon. Anyway, we were on our way back to Bottisham when a German Focke-Wulf 190 came in from above and just lit us up. I was flying tail-end Charlie, and he came at me first with those twenty-millimeter cannons. Blew half my damn wing off, and I screamed into my radio, 'Bogie at four o'clock!' but I don't know who heard me. The Wulf went after Joe next, and it didn't take him long, then he should've gone for the Fortress—those bombers were so bulky a single fighter with a machine gun could take one down by itself—but for some reason he came back for me. My plane was chewed up, and the cockpit was filling up with smoke when I saw that German coming back to get a medal for blowing me out of the sky. I needed to get out of that Thunderbolt fast, but I was taking on too much fire. If I'd tried to crawl over the side and jump out, bullets the size of your fist would've ripped me in two. So I got my seat belt off, pulled the canopy back, and rolled that Thunderbolt hard as I could. When it was upside down I just fell out toward France and the Wulf never saw me."

"Bullshit," the eavesdropping man sitting behind Garland half-said, half-coughed, but thankfully the old man didn't hear him.

"That's insane," I said, and Garland waved me off and said, "Don't be surprised at the lengths a man will go to save his own ass."

The old man took a sip of water and continued, "Now I've been in some dicey situations before—The Shah of Iran once walked in on me playing chess with his favorite mistress—but I don't think I've ever been as scared as I was on that fall."

"Wait, can women not play chess in Iran?" I asked.

"Strip chess," Garland said with a wink. "But the thing was, you couldn't just jump out and pull your chute because the Germans would strafe you into Swiss cheese if they saw you drifting to Earth. So I fell, and prayed, and fell some more. You know that skydiving school out at the Riverton Airport?"

"Yeah," I said.

"The craziest fellas out there will sometimes deploy around two thousand feet, but that's about as low as they'll go. But even two thousand feet was too high for my comfort, so I waited and watched the ground get bigger and bigger. I've got no way of knowing how low I got, but I do recall the distinct smell of cow shit just before I grabbed the rip cord ring and pulled."

"Bullshit," the man behind Garland coughed again, but this time the old man jumped from his seat, grabbed the eavesdropper by his hair, and held a dinner fork to his neck.

"Not bullshit. Cow shit," Garland said. "Had it been a bull I wouldn't have made it out of the field alive. Now I appreciate your interest in my story, but if you want to hear the rest you'll have to watch it on the YouTube like everyone else. Because if I even suspect you're listening to us again I'm gonna pop that emergency door and toss your ass in the ocean—oh, thank you, dollface." The flight attendant was back with Garland's pillow, and her eyes drifted from us to the terrified man checking his neck for blood.

"Is … everything okay?" she asked.

"I think the three of us could all use another hot fudge sundae," Garland said.

"Of course," the flight attendant said, "but I need to ask that you return to your seat. Turbulence can occur unexpectedly, and for your safety, and …" She glanced back at the bullshit man who was still rubbing his neck. "… for the safety of your fellow passengers, we ask that you remain seated with your seat belt securely fastened whenever possible."

"Sure thing," Garland said, and handed her his fork. Then he gave the bullshit man a little slap on the cheek and said, "Now you enjoy your sundae," before turning to me and saying with a wink, "To be continued."

Chapter Twenty-Seven

In which our hero gets a croissant, the hard way.

I ate half my second sundae then tried to sleep, but I was still buzzing from (1) sneaking out of the country, and (2) hearing Garland's story about jumping from his burning fighter plane, and (3) witnessing an angry geriatric threaten to toss a drunken businessman out of a Boeing 747 from 37,000 feet, so I watched the second Avengers movie, then I watched an hour of the third hobbit film, then I stared out the window at the dark Atlantic Ocean below before finally dozing off. I dreamed we found Madeleine and brought her back to the States where we were all wildly famous. The four of us were in the back of an old convertible driving through a ticker-tape parade in Manhattan, and our driver was telling us we'd made the most famous Atlantic crossing since Charles Lindbergh, which was great and all, but I kept searching for Sadie in the massive crowd and never found her.

"Edwin Green." Someone was shaking my shoulder. "Wake up."

My ears popped and Parker said something about our descent into Paris and I felt like I'd woken up from one dream into another. I rubbed the sleep from my eyes and looked out the window half expecting to see the Eiffel Tower but only saw rectangular farm fields of varying shades of brown and green. Parker said something else.

"What?"

"Landing card."

"My what?"

"Your landing card." She handed me a slip of paper and said, "Fill this out and get your shit together. Once we land we need to get out of the airport, fast."

I mumbled something and she went back to her seat, and half an hour later our wheels touched down a few minutes past seven a.m. local time. "*Bienvenue à Paris*," the flight attendant announced, then repeated her welcome speech in English as we taxied toward our gate. But as everyone began to unbuckle and retrieve their luggage, the pilot announced something in French that drew groans from around the cabin. People returned to their seats and Garland said, "What the hell did he say son?" just as the pilot began to repeat his announcement in English. "Ladies and gentlemen, we sincerely apologize for the inconvenience, but for security purposes there will be a short delay. We must ask everyone to please remain seated until the tower clears us to disembark. Thank you for your cooperation."

One of the flight attendants stared at me while the pilot made his announcement, but quickly looked away when I took notice. I leaned my head into the aisle so I could see Garland and Parker and said, "I don't like this."

Parker looked scared, which scared me more because Parker wasn't scared of anything, but Garland said, "They probably don't have the jet bridge ready. You want everyone falling out the front door son?"

"I don't like it," I said again, and Garland growled, "Well worry about it then, see how much good it does you."

I turned back around and cursed under my breath. He was right, worrying wouldn't help anything, but he was wrong too, because there was plenty to worry about. I suppose had we been in coach we'd have seen the two soldiers in red berets board the plane—though there still wouldn't have been anywhere to run— but from where we sat they came from behind, and we didn't see them until one of the flight attendants pointed us out. "Mademoiselle Haddaway, Messieurs Lenox and Green, we will be escorting you off the plane," one of the soldiers said. "You will follow us please."

The bullshit man applauded as they ushered us down the aisle, and I wanted to tell Garland I'd told him so, but I was afraid if I opened my mouth I'd vomit. The soldiers, for their part, weren't intimidating. I mean they carried assault rifles, but they were also smiling and wearing funny hats and even offered to help Garland down the steps—"I can manage the damn steps just fine, Jacques." As we followed them up the jet bridge toward the terminal I recall not being half as scared of them as I was the trouble I'd be in once we got home.

A balding middle-aged man in a dark suit flanked by two more beret-wearing soldiers waited for us at the end of the tunnel, and when we reached him he smiled and said, "Welcome to France, I'm Martin Blair with the United States embassy in Paris." For just a moment I let myself hope that an embassy welcome with marine escort was part of Air France's first-class service, but Martin Blair continued and dashed any hope. "Three hours ago we received word the three of you were on this flight, and we were instructed to place you on the next plane back to Atlanta which leaves at 10:35 this morning."

Then the embassy man glanced at his watch and said, "Follow me please. I'd hate for you to come all this way and not at least have a croissant."

Chapter Twenty-Eight

In which blame is squarely placed.

It wasn't my fault they caught us, and it wasn't Parker's fault either, and though I'm not trying to blame anyone here, that only leaves one of us, so maybe I am trying to blame someone after all. Lucian Figg, Attorney at Law, kept a close eye on Garland's finances, because that's what Garland paid him to do—although twice on our trip I heard the old man refer to his lawyer as a thieving litigious troll. But the old man had money Lucian Figg, Attorney at Law, did not know about. A lot of money Lucian Figg, Attorney at Law, did not know about. A lot of money Lucian Figg, Attorney at Law, would never have known about had our plan not unraveled in such spectacular fashion. Here's what happened. At the Atlanta airport Garland paid $28,637 for three first-class tickets to Paris using a debit card tied to his numbered Swiss bank account. No problem there, because Lucian Figg, Attorney at Law, had less than no idea his angry old client kept a small fortune in a foreign bank. However, when the ticket agent scanned Garland's passport, ElderScan, a subscription service that monitors identity theft for $9.95 a month, alerted Lucian Figg, Attorney at Law, that someone had used his client's passport by sending him an email to the address on file, which unfortunately wasn't LadiezzzLuvCoolE@gmail.com. Lucian Figg, Attorney at Law, received this alert about the same time the three of us were testing massage chairs in Brookstone, but he was on the golf course and did not check his email until after dinner, at which point his client was thirty-seven thousand feet over Greenland.

Lucian Figg later claimed he kept his client's passport, along with sundry legal documents and financial statements, in a file cabinet in his home office. But after digging through Garland's file for twenty minutes, he recalled his client asking to see the passport a month earlier, because, he said his client claimed, "Looking at all those damn stamps might bring back some good memories."

ElderScan, on occasion, will send alerts by mistake, but since he could not lay eyes on the passport, Lucian Figg called his client's room around 7 p.m., but no one answered, because Herschel Thomas was watching *Meerkat Manor*, and Garland Lenox was jabbing the neck of a smartass business traveler with a fork. Lucian Figg hung up and called the front desk at Morningview Arbor, and this began a chain reaction of phone calls between Lucian Figg, Morningview Arbor, Delta Airlines, Air France, the State Department, the embassy of the United States in Paris, Aunt Marcy, and my mom and Carl. Morningview Arbor records phone calls for quality assurance, and the State Department records phone calls because they're the freaking State Department, and attorneys used transcripts from many of the calls made that evening as evidence in the various criminal and civil suits stemming from our little adventure. Here are some of the highlights.

Chapter Twenty-Nine

In which your call may be recorded for quality assurance.

WEDNESDAY, APRIL 15, 7:13 P.M. CST

LUCIAN FIGG — This is Lucian Figg. I'm trying to reach my client, Garland Lenox, but he's not answering the phone in his room.

BETTY DUNCAN, RN — Good evening, Mr. Figg. Your client isn't in his room.

LUCIAN FIGG — Well obviously, but do you know where he is? I need to speak to him.

BETTY DUNCAN, RN — He's staying with family in Chattanooga.

LUCIAN FIGG — Excuse me?

BETTY DUNCAN, RN — We spoke this afternoon. You said your client would be staying with family in Chattanooga for a few nights.

LUCIAN FIGG — I most certainly did not.

BETTY DUNCAN, RN — Yes, Mr. Figg, you did. Garland accompanied some students from J. P. Hornby to the National Medal of Honor museum in Chattanooga this morning, and you called a few hours ago and said he'd be staying with family through the weekend.

LUCIAN FIGG — Garland Lenox doesn't have family in Chattanooga. He doesn't have family anywhere.

BETTY DUNCAN, RN — That's not what you told me a few hours ago. You said they'd drive him back here on Sunday. I sent the release form to your new email address. You said you'd fax it back in the morning.

LUCIAN FIGG — I think you've confused me with someone else. My client is Garland Lenox. He's ninety years old, suffers from dementia, and cannot leave your facility without my express written permission.

BETTY DUNCAN, RN — No, we're talking about the same Garland Lenox, and you said he'd be staying with family in Chattanooga tonight.

LUCIAN FIGG — I did not.

BETTY DUNCAN, RN — Mr. Figg, are you calling me a liar?

LUCIAN FIGG — Yes, I'm calling you a liar because you are lying! Is there someone else there I can talk to?

BETTY DUNCAN, RN — Mr. Figg, there is no need to shout, if you'll …

LUCIAN FIGG — You're not seriously telling me you let my ninety-year-old demented client leave your facility with a group of high school students?

BETTY DUNCAN, RN — Mr. Figg, please calm down. Yesterday you spoke to Marcy Owens and gave your client permission to leave our facility …

LUCIAN FIGG — No, I did not …

BETTY DUNCAN, RN — Then we spoke this afternoon and you asked me to send a leave form to your new email address

LUCIAN FIGG — What the hell are you talking about? I don't have a new email address.

BETTY DUNCAN, RN — That's not what you told me five hours ago.

LUCIAN FIGG — Am I having a stroke? Is that why nothing you say makes sense? I think I smell burning toast.

BETTY DUNCAN, RN — Hold on, here's the note. You told me your new email address was L-a-d-i-e-z-z-z … oh, that can't be right. Dammit. Dammit, Parker.

LUCIAN FIGG — Hello?

BETTY DUNCAN, RN — Shit.

LUCIAN FIGG — Nurse, please tell me what's happening.

BETTY DUNCAN, RN — Shit, shit, shit.

LUCIAN FIGG — Nurse?

BETTY DUNCAN, RN — [Inaudible mumbling]

LUCIAN FIGG — [Inaudible shouting]

WEDNESDAY, APRIL 15, 7:39 P.M. CST

HORNBY 911 DISPATCH— 911, what is your emergency?

LUCIAN FIGG — This is Lucian Figg. I think some high school kids abducted my client and took him overseas.

HORNBY 911 DISPATCH— Please sir, calm down. You said your name is—

LUCIAN FIGG — Lucian Figg.

HORNBY 911 DISPATCH — The guy on all the billboards?

LUCIAN FIGG — What? Yes. I have a few billboards around—

HORNBY 911 DISPATCH —And all those commercials too.

LUCIAN FIGG — Yes, I advertise on television as well, but my client—

HORNBY 911 DISPATCH — That jingle gets stuck in your head, don't it? *Lucian Figg, he'll get you more, call 205-8994.*

LUCIAN FIGG — Right. Look, my client—

HORNBY 911 DISPATCH — Sorry. You said something about an abduction?

LUCIAN FIGG — Yes. My client's name is Garland Lenox. He's ninety years old and he lives in the dementia unit at Morningview Arbor. Two high school students snuck him out of the nursing home this morning and now they've left the country. I fear they're planning to ransom him.

HORNBY 911 DISPATCH — Whoa, hold on. If they're planning to ransom him this would technically be a kidnapping, not an abduction. I know it's confusing, because it's kids kidnapping an adult, and usually when you think of kidnapping you think of adults taking kids, because kidnapping has the word kid right there in the word, you know?

LUCIAN FIGG — Okay, kidnapping, whatever. Just help me, dammit!

HORNBY 911 DISPATCH — There's no need to yell, Mr. Figg. I'm just trying to get things straight, because if I transfer you to abductions you'll be talking to the wrong people. And no one over there can figure out how to transfer a call without accidentally hanging up on you, and then you'd have to call this number again and we'd be going through the same song and dance.

LUCIAN FIGG — I wish someone had abducted your [INAUDIBLE]

HORNBY 911 DISPATCH — What was that, Mr. Figg?

LUCIAN FIGG — Nothing. Let me start over. This is Lucian Figg, two high school students kidnapped my client.

HORNBY 911 DISPATCH — Please hold while I redirect your call.

WEDNESDAY, APRIL 15, 8:37 P.M. CST

ALICE MORRISON — Hello.

DANIEL HEALEY (STATE DEPARTMENT) — Hello. May I speak with the parent or guardian of Edwin Green?

ALICE MORRISON — This is Alice Morrison, Edwin's mother. Is something wrong? Is Edwin okay?

DANIEL HEALEY — Mrs. Morrison this is Daniel Healey with the State Department. Earlier today your son, a young woman named Parker Haddaway, and an elderly man named Garland Lenox boarded a plane in Atlanta bound for Paris, France.

ALICE MORRISON — [Laughter] I don't think so. Edwin had track practice today. And he's sleeping over with that boy who thinks he's a Hobbit. What's his name ... Tyler Godfrey. Edwin said they're working on a science project that measures the effects of sleep deprivation on Xbox performance.

DANIEL HEALEY — I'm afraid not, Mrs. Morrison. Delta Airlines and Homeland Security both scanned your son's passport, and surveillance video confirms he boarded the flight.

ALICE MORRISON — You're telling me a girl and an old man kidnapped my son?

DANIEL HEALEY — No, Mrs. Morrison. We believe all three of them willingly boarded the plane, although Mr. Lenox's attorney fears your son and Ms. Haddaway kidnapped his client.

ALICE MORRISON — My son is not a kidnapper.

DANIEL HEALEY — We don't believe—

ALICE MORRISON — Hold on, my husband wants to—

CARL MORRISON — This is Carl Morrison, Edwin's stepfather. Is Edwin okay? My wife said something about a kidnapping.

DANIEL HEALEY — No, Mr. Morrison. Your stepson voluntarily boarded a plane this afternoon with a fellow student and a ninety-year-old dementia patient.

CARL MORRISON — This must have something to do with Sadie Evans.

DANIEL HEALEY — The actress?

CARL MORRISON — Would you call her an actress? She plays herself in every movie.

DANIEL HEALEY — She was pretty good in *Back to the Future IV*.

CARL MORRISON — She was terrible. Wait, why the hell are we talking about Sadie Evans?

DANIEL HEALEY — You brought her up, Mr. Morrison.

CARL MORRISON— Okay, forget it. What are we supposed to do? About Edwin?

DANIEL HEALEY — Mr. Lenox's attorney is also his legal guardian, and he requested we intercept his client at the airport and place him on the next flight to Atlanta. We will want to question your son at the airport, but as long as everything checks out, he's free to stay in France, unless you would like us to put him on the next flight back to Atlanta as well.

CARL MORRISON — Of course we want him on the next flight back to—hold on, my wife wants to—

ALICE MORRISON — Did you say this had something to do with Sadie Evans?

DANIEL HEALEY — No, Mrs. Morrison. Your husband suggested that.

ALICE MORRISON — Oh. Well do you think Sadie might hear about this?

DANIEL HEALEY — We've no plans to alert the media if that's what you're asking.

ALICE MORRISON — Well, would you mind if we did?

DANIEL HEALEY — We'd rather you not contact—

CARL MORRISON — Sorry, Mr. Healey. We will not contact the media. Please make sure Edwin is on the next flight home, and have him call us as soon as he can.

DANIEL HEALEY — Yes, Mr. Morrison.

ALICE MORRISON — And tell him he's not in trouble. We know he's had a rough year and he's just trying to—

CARL MORRISON — No, you tell him he's in more trouble than he can possibly imagine and he's grounded for the rest of his natural life, and if he dies young and reincarnates we will track him down and make sure his new parents ground him as well.

DANIEL HEALEY — Uh … okay. Will do.

WEDNESDAY, APRIL 15, 9:07 P.M. CST

MARTIN BLAIR (ASSISTANT TO UNITED STATES AMBASSADOR TO FRANCE) — It's four in the damn morning.

DANIEL HEALEY (STATE DEPARTMENT) — Sorry, Martin. But we need you at Charles de Gaulle when Delta flight 8517 from Atlanta arrives this morning. Two high school students and an elderly man are on board, and we need you to intercept them and put them on the next flight back to Atlanta.

MARTIN BLAIR — Okay … why?

DANIEL HEALEY — Well the elderly man has dementia and isn't supposed to leave his nursing home, much less country.

MARTIN BLAIR — And the students?

DANIEL HEALEY — We're treating them as runaways.

MARTIN BLAIR — So two high school students and a dementia patient decided to run away to Paris? That's weird, right?

DANIEL HEALEY — The old man's attorney believes the students kidnapped his client and plan on ransoming him once they make it to Europe.

MARTIN BLAIR — But you don't believe that is their intention?

DANIEL HEALEY — No, but this attorney is a loudmouth so we'd like to do this quietly. Last thing we need is this guy going on CNN spewing nonsense. We've already spoken to the French ambassador. A small marine detachment is at Charles de Gaulle, waiting at your disposal.

MARTIN BLAIR — A marine detachment? For two kids and an old man?

DANIEL HEALEY — We're not expecting any trouble Martin, but you're old, and if the kids try to run now you'll have some marines there to catch them.

MARTIN BLAIR — I'm not that old.

DANIEL HEALEY — If you say so, Martin. Look, all you have to do is hold them in one of the questioning rooms at border control, treat them nice, and put them on the next plane back to Atlanta.

MARTIN BLAIR — Okay. Who am I looking for again?

DANIEL HEALEY — We're faxing this to your office right now. The old man is Garland Lenox. Ninety years old, five foot seven, white hair, and reportedly ornery as hell. He's traveling with Edwin Green, male, seventeen, five foot nine, brown hair, hazel eyes, glasses. And Parker Haddaway, aka Emily Bloom, female, seventeen, five foot ten, red hair, brown eyes, and may be traveling under an alias.

MARTIN BLAIR — A seventeen-year-old with an alias?

DANIEL HEALEY — Yeah, do you remember that incident in Florida a few years ago, with that crazy church from Iowa or somewhere?

MARTIN BLAIR — I've lived in Paris for thirty-five years Daniel. We don't get a lot of local church news from the States.

DANIEL HEALEY — Whatever, it's all in the fax, you can read about it on the way to the airport. Oh, and Martin?

MARTIN BLAIR — Yeah?

DANIEL HEALEY — The old man, Garland Lenox, he worked for [REDACTED] for thirty-five years after the war.

MARTIN BLAIR — No shit. I thought they were all dead.

DANIEL HEALEY — Apparently not, so like I said, let's try and keep this quiet, okay?

MARTIN BLAIR — Yeah, okay.

Chapter Thirty

In which Garland Lenox suggests a physically impossible place for the Assistant to the United States Ambassador to France to stick his own head.

"Instructed," Garland shouted. "You tell me just who the hell instructed you to place us on the next flight to Atlanta."

I suppose it's difficult for four machine gun-toting soldiers to escort three people off a plane without drawing a few stares, but no one in the terminal had paid us much attention, at least not until Garland began shouting like a crazy man.

"Mr. Lenox, try and stay calm—" Martin Blair whispered in what I suspect is the same voice he'd use to soothe a screaming baby, but Garland wasn't interested in staying calm.

"Is this about the fork?" Garland said, his voice a bit lower but no less angry. "Tell me you're not arresting me for poking that asshole with a fork. I didn't even draw blood."

"No, Mr. Lenox, your—wait, you attacked a man on your flight with a fork?"

Garland played dumb, and when Martin Blair turned to me I shrugged and nodded in the affirmative.

A hint of a smile flashed across the embassy man's face and he said, "Mr. Lenox, your attorney instructed us to place you on the next flight to Atlanta."

"My attorney instructed you," Garland repeated. "And if my attorney instructed you to stick your fat head up your ass I guess you'd do that too?"

One of the soldiers laughed but stopped when Garland said, "Laugh it up you cheese-eating bastard. If it weren't for me you'd be speaking German. Ta mère la pute."

While I wasn't exactly fluent in French, I did have an extensive vocabulary of French swear words and insults, like the one Garland just used to insinuate a French marine's mother worked in the world's oldest profession. The soldier, to his credit, remained calm, though his smile dissolved into a violent glare.

"Enough of this shit," Garland said to Parker and me. "Come on, let's get out of here." He tried to walk away but Martin Blair grabbed him by the shoulder, which was a mistake. Garland shoved him and began shouting even louder, "I'm a citizen of the United States of America and a veteran of a world damn war. I got a Purple Heart liberating this country and I'm free to do whatever the hell I want whenever the hell I want to do it, and I swear if you touch me again, I'll pull the arms off one of these snail eaters in the pretty hats and beat you to death with them."

"Ornery might have been an understatement," Martin Blair said to no one in particular before taking a deep breath and trying his luck with me. "Edwin, we've informed your parents of your whereabouts and they're worried sick about you. They've insisted we place you on the next flight to Atlanta as well."

"What about Parker?" I asked, but she said, "Edwin, don't."

Martin Blair hesitated, then said, "Ms. Haddaway's aunt has relinquished custody. She is now a ward of the state, and Alabama Youth Services instructed us to place her on the next flight to Atlanta as well."

"The hell she is," Garland shouted, as the ever growing crowd watched on. "If the boy's parents want him back home, so be it. But the girl is staying right here, and so am I, and there's not a damn thing you or these beret-wearing shitbirds can do about it."

Chapter Thirty-One

In which our hero learns global data costs up to $20.48 per megabyte.

Turned out there was something they could do about it. They could handcuff Garland and drag him shouting into a window-less room used by passport control to question suspicious passengers. The soldiers escorted Parker and me in behind him, and we sat in silence while Garland spent the next five minutes inventively cursing at no one in particular before slumping in a chair across from us in defeat.

"Hey," I said to Parker, who hadn't looked at me since we left the airplane, "you okay?"

She didn't look up, and when Garland caught my eye he shook his head to discourage me from asking her again. A minute later Martin Blair and one of the soldiers walked in with our bags and the tray of promised croissants.

"Look, Mr. Clean," Garland growled while Martin Blair removed his handcuffs, "that ambulance-chasing weasel has no right to tell me what I can and can't do."

"Mr. Lenox, I'm afraid he does," Martin Blair said, taking a seat near the door in case Garland charged him and he needed to get out in a hurry. "Lucian Figg is your legal guardian."

"Like hell he is," Garland shouted. "I came down with pneumonia just before Christmas, and when they discharged me from the hospital Lucian sent me to that damn nursing home. I told every nurse there who'd listen that I'd escaped from Bang Kwang Prison in Bangkok twice, so getting out of that dump wouldn't be a problem."

A quick smile flashed across Martin Blair's face, and I realized with Garland's fondness of aggrandized details that it wasn't a stretch for someone to believe he belonged on the crazy hall of a nursing home.

"Hell, I wouldn't have stayed as long as I did had those nurses not been so nice to me. And the Salisbury steak is really good. But listen, if Lucian's got some paper claiming he's my guardian, it's because he forged my signature or had me sign something when I was drugged up in the hospital. So I'd like to press charges against him, for being a lying asshole."

"Mr. Lenox, I've no doubt you're telling the truth, but you have to understand my hands are tied here. When the State Department wakes me up and tells me to put three Americans on the next flight to Atlanta, that's what I have to do, no questions asked. If there's been a mistake, if your attorney forged documents, they will straighten it out once you're back home. But my job, my only job, is to get the three of you back to your families, and that is what I'm going to do."

"You're not sending the girl back to her family," Garland said, and the three of us glanced at Parker, but she didn't look up.

Martin Blair frowned, shook his head, and mouthed the words, "I know," then said, "Again, Mr. Lenox, I'm terribly sorry, but I'm just doing my job here."

After a few painful moments of Garland trying to kill Martin Blair with his eyes, the embassy man turned to me and said, "Edwin, I almost forgot, your parents are expecting a phone call. Here, use my phone."

"I've got my own," I said, pulling my phone from my pocket. "But can I call them outside? I'd rather not have this conversation in front of everyone."

"Sure," Martin Blair said with an understanding smile, and motioned toward the door.

I stepped outside the interrogation room into a sterile hallway of flickering fluorescent lights, turned on my phone for the first time in ten hours, and watched as a logjam of text messages popped up. The first one was from Fitz.

FITZ: So this opportunity of questionable legality must have involved skipping a day of school. I hope you, sorry, I hope this hypothetical someone, isn't doing anything too stupid.

The next ten were from my mom and stepdad, eight from Mom and two from Carl, and they all expressed unprecedented levels of parental anger and worry, though the last two from Mom hinted that if I was somehow trying to get Sadie Evans's attention she'd be willing to help however she could. The last one from Carl warned that Coach Knox would likely kick me off the track team, which I took as good news.

The last text to come through was from my phone company.

VERIZON: Welcome to France. Dial +1 & 10 digit# to call US. Calls made and received $1.29/min. TXT send $.5, Receive $.05. Your global data costs up to $20.48 per 1MB.

I read all the texts and started to call home but couldn't do it. Mom would be all worried and overly nice and asking about Sadie, and Carl would be apoplectic and threatening all manner of cruel and unusual punishment, and I couldn't handle either right then. I texted Mom instead.

ME: Hey Mom. Can't call right now but I'm safe and they're sending us back to Atlanta in a couple of hours. Will call soon and try to explain. I'm sorry. I love you. Tell Carl I'm sorry and love him too.

Then I texted Fitz.

ME: So I'm in France with Parker Haddaway and that old man from the nursing home. I'm also in a shit ton of trouble. Will explain it all when I get home if Mom and Carl ever let me contact the outside world again.

He replied immediately.

FITZ: It's two in the morning jackass.

He didn't believe me, which was understandable, I wasn't sure I believed it either—the lack of sleep had given our detainment a nightmarish quality, and a part of me hoped at any moment my mom would wake me up for school. I sat against the wall and wasn't sure if I wanted to laugh or cry or sleep or vomit or try all four at once. My phone buzzed. It was Mom.

MOM: Thank God. Edwin we're worried sick. Call us when you can okay? It won't be too late. We'll be awake. We love you. Promise me you're okay?

I texted her back.

ME: I'm okay. I promise. Love you too.

I wasn't okay though, because (1) Garland was screwed. He'd missed his only chance to find this Madeleine woman, because as soon as we got back to Hornby they'd chain his old ass to his nursing home bed and throw away the key; and (2) Parker's dreams of a new life, whatever that meant, probably didn't involve living in a child services facility. I hoped her aunt was overreacting, but Parker did say something about going to seven schools in the last four years. Maybe she'd lived with as many aunts and there were no more aunts to live with. Either way, Parker was in a lot of trouble, and I began to regret enabling her on this hopeless journey because; (3) it wasn't even going to make me famous. I wasn't going on *The Today Show*, unless they did a segment on teens whose parents had grounded them well into middle age. Our little adventure might make the local news, but that would be it. Sadie would never know. News from Hornby didn't reach her anymore.

I wasn't ready to join the others in the most depressing room in France, so I took advantage of the airport Wi-Fi to post the video of Garland telling me about getting shot down over France to my YouTube channel. It wasn't going to make me famous either, but I figured it would blow Fitz's mind when he saw it in the morning.

Chapter Thirty-Two

In which Garland Lenox regrets calling Martin Blair
"Ambassador Assburger," among other things.

"Mr. Lenox, you mentioned liberating France. Were you part of the Normandy landings?"

Martin Blair, bless his heart, was trying to make conversation with Garland when I walked back in, but the old man just stared back, trying to will the embassy official to die of a heart attack no doubt.

I grabbed a croissant from the table and answered for Garland, "No. The Germans shot him down six weeks before D-Day."

"Oh," Martin Blair said, and we listened to the air conditioning hum for a while until Garland growled, "Caen," and we all looked his way. "They shot me down over Caen."

"Were you … did the Germans capture you?" Martin Blair asked.

"Cue Ball do you think I'd let the Germans capture me?"

Martin Blair dared to smile and held his hands up to show he meant no harm. Garland continued, "I jumped from my burning plane and landed in a cow pasture south of Caen. Landed right on top of a cow in fact, which was lucky for me, and a little less lucky for Bessie. Still shattered my left ankle. Got this too," Garland said, pointing to a long scar on his right forearm. "And do you see this," Garland asked, holding up a middle finger toward Martin Blair.

Martin Blair squinted at Garland's middle finger for a moment before realizing the old man was just shooting him a bird.

Garland laughed for the first time since getting off the plane while Martin Blair shook his head and forced a smile, then Garland kept going, "I didn't pull my cord till late, but the Germans still saw me fall. I could hear jeeps and soldiers shouting through the hedgerows, so I cut my chute and crawled toward a little clump of trees about two hundred yards away. A part of me thought it was pointless though. I had a busted leg and a .45 with one round left and I was leaving a trail of blood even a blind German could follow. But I wasn't going to no POW camp. That just wasn't happening. I figured at worst I could hide in the brush and ambush a couple of 'em before they took me out. I got lucky though. There was a river just past the trees. I checked the silk map I kept in my boot and was pretty sure it was the Orne, and if so, the lights I'd seen on my way down were Caen. Now if I'd had two good legs I could have spent a year in those hedgerows dodging the Germans, but in my condition the only chance I had was to make it to a town and find a member of the French Resistance. So I ate the chocolate bar from my survival kit and crawled into that freezing-ass river and floated toward Caen. Did you know army chocolate is heat resistant to one hundred and twenty degrees? Like eating a brown rock."

"I ... no, I've never had military chocolate," Martin Blair said, then waited for Garland to continue his story but the old man had lost interest, so after a moment Martin added, "That's an amazing story Mr. Lenox, and I do hope you know your country is eternally grateful for your service and sacrifice."

Garland growled and said, "I didn't sacrifice shit."

Martin Blair looked at me and I said, "I was taking Mr. Lenox back to Caen," then glanced over at Parker who still hadn't raised her head. "We. We were taking him back to Caen."

The embassy man frowned and closed his eyes for a moment. "You know," he said, "we hold remembrance ceremonies at the Normandy American Cemetery every year. Mr. Lenox, perhaps your family can bring you back for—"

"Remembrance ceremony? Mr. Clean, I remember the war just fine."

"Okay," Martin Blair said, "then why exactly were you trying to get back to Caen?"

"I'll tell you why," Garland said, and crossed the room and stood right in front of Martin Blair. "Because on April 24th, 1944, delirious from pain and freezing half to death, I crawled out of a muddy French river and hobbled down a cobblestone street of a Nazi occupied town and knocked on the first door I came to. And who answered the door but the most beautiful girl in the world. The girl who saved my life. The girl I loved and lost and promised I'd come back for one day. That's why I'm going to Caen, Mr. Blair."

Garland sat back down and Martin Blair stared at his shoes and the room grew uncomfortably quiet until the old man threw a Hail Mary. "Martin," he said, "have you ever been in love?"

I wanted to laugh out loud but bit my tongue.

Martin Blair looked up and a sad smile flashed across his face. He sighed and said, "I have. I still am. With someone I met here in France no less. We met while I was studying abroad during college, and that fall I changed my major so I could find a job in Paris and be near her. I moved here right after graduation and we've been together since." He looked back at his shoes and without looking up said, "I want to help you, Mr. Lenox, but they've tied my hands here. I hope you can understand."

Garland didn't say anything, and when Martin Blair finally looked up, a single tear rolled down his cheek. "How rude of me," he said with quick rub of his eyes. "Croissants with no coffee. Excuse me, I'll be back in, let's say, fifteen minutes."

Martin Blair left the room and Garland smiled at me.

"What?" I asked.

"I never thought we'd have an ally in Mr. Blair. Not after I called him a bureaucratic asshat. But I suppose he's not so bad after all." The old man stood up and said, "Grab our bags. Parker honey, snap out of it, let's go."

Parker lifted her head for the first time since we'd been in the room and wiped the tears from her face.

"Go where?" I asked. "What are you talking about?"

"It doesn't take fifteen minutes to pour three cups of coffee," Garland said, then he smiled and pointed toward the door and added, "and Mr. Blair conveniently forgot to lock the door on his way out."

"Wait," I said, "I don't think he ..." but Garland and Parker were already in the hall, so what else could I do but follow.

Chapter Thirty-Three

In which a former Beatle is implicated in the 1997 Asian financial crisis.

We finally caught a break. The room they detained us in was on the French side of passport control. Had it not been, we'd have stood in line over an hour waiting to have our passports stamped, only to have the border police arrest us again once they realized who we were. Instead, all we had to do was grab our bags and leave the airport, which we did, in various degrees of nonchalantness.

I never thought walking casually was hard until I actually tried to walk casually. Suddenly I was hyperaware of my extremities. My arms swung too much, then not enough. My gait stretched abnormally long, then I overcompensated and began shuffling my feet. I had no idea what to do with my hands, so I stuck them in my back pockets for some reason. And to keep my head from swiveling like a Disneyland teacup I stiffened my neck in a most unnatural way. In an effort to make sure no one noticed me I became the only thing they noticed. Garland was better at it. He was cool even. He said, "Son, when running isn't an option, you gotta pick a topic and try to have a normal conversation," so I tried.

"Your aunt's just mad at you, right?" I asked Parker. "She's not really turning you over to the state?"

"Son, how 'bout another topic," Garland said, and when I glanced over at Parker she looked equal parts furious and terrified, so I mumbled an apology to no one in particular.

Garland took over and said, "Okay son, pick a story. Would you rather hear about how I should have won the 1976 Ugandan Open, how Paul McCartney and I caused the Malaysian stock market to crash in 1997, or how I survived Elena Ceaușescu's real life version of the Hunger Games in Communist Romania?"

"I don't know. Whichever one really happened."

"They all really happened, son. You think I could make this shit up?"

"Okay, the first one then."

"They had me stationed in Kampala, living in a little one-bedroom house across the street from the country club. I played six or seven times a week back then, and was leading the tournament after three rounds. But Amin's people picked me up that night and took me to one of his palaces, and over dinner he told me it would be detrimental to national morale if a mzungu won their national championship."

"A mzungu?" I asked, as my arms slowed down and my legs sped up and my head began to bob naturally enough to blend in with the river of Parisians and tourists and businesspeople flowing through Charles de Gaulle.

"That's the Swahili word for white person," Garland said. "Anyway, I dumped a couple of balls in the lake on the back nine and finished a distant third."

"Didn't Idi Amin eat people?" I asked.

"Never in front of me," Garland said.

We walked into the arrivals hall and Garland said, "Help me think of a way to get out of here. If we can get into Paris we can disappear, but we've got to get there, and we don't have much time."

Getting out of an unlocked room was easy, but making it out of the airport apparently wouldn't be, even if Martin Blair had left the door unlocked and given us a fifteen-minute head start, which I still doubted was his intention.

"What about the rental car?" I asked. "Haven't you already reserved it?"

"Yeah. I reserved it in my own damn name," Garland said. "Besides, those rent-a-car places are slow as hell. Think of something else."

"Could we walk there?"

"It's fifteen miles from here, son, and I can walk about a hundred yards before I have to sit and catch my damn breath."

"Sorry," I said, looking around the arrivals hall and racking my brain for a way out. "What about the train?" There were signs everywhere pointing toward the RER B train to central Paris.

"They've got guards and cameras on those," Garland said. "If they didn't arrest us on the train they'd get us the moment we stepped off."

"A taxi? Uber?"

"No, they'll radio our descriptions to every driver in the city. We'd be sitting ducks."

"I don't know," I said. "I think we're stuck."

"No," Parker said, speaking for the first time since we'd stepped off the plane. "I'm not going back in that room, and I'm not getting back on a plane, and I'm not going back to Alabama, so you'd better—"

"There," I said, pointing toward a group of men wearing black suits and black ties holding signs with last names on them.

Garland laughed. "Son, you're a genius."

"Do you think it will work?" I asked.

"No," the old man said, "but it's our only chance. Come on."

The three of us stood off to the side and tried to read the names on the drivers' signs without being obvious about it.

"Look for one on hotel letterhead," Garland whispered. "We don't want 'em dropping us off at a damn business meeting."

"There, third guy on the left," Parker said. "Mr. Dufresne. Four Seasons Hotel George V."

Garland chuckled and said, "The Four Seasons? Miss Parker, you do have expensive taste," and without hesitating he walked up to the man and said, "Let's go, Jeeves."

"Mr. Dufresne?" the driver asked.

"No, I'm Napoleon Bonaparte. Of course I'm Mr. Dufresne and these are my grandchildren and we're in a hurry, so let's go, son."

The driver gave us a quick glance before picking up Garland's suitcase and saying, "Follow me, monsieur." Five minutes later we were on the motorway driving through the morning rain toward Paris.

Chapter Thirty-Four

In which hissssssssss

Before this trip I assumed pepper spray got its name because it's a chemical concoction that mimics the sensation of someone spraying pepper juice in your eyes. But it turns out the active ingredient in pepper spray is capsaicin, a naturally occurring compound found in, what else, peppers. So pepper spray doesn't mimic the sensation of someone spraying pepper juice in your eyes so much as it *is* someone squirting pepper juice in your eyes. Fitz told me later, because he's into weird stuff like this, that people who measure pepper heat measure it in something called Scoville heat units, and typical law-enforcement-grade spray measures between 500,000 and 5,000,000 Scoville units, depending on dilution. I can't say for certain how many Scoville units the pepper spray our driver kept under his seat contained, but I can say with all manner of certainty it burned with the intensity of a million suns when he sprayed it in my eyes.

Our escape was going well. Too well. Our driver, make that Mr. Dufresne's driver, had merged onto the A1 motorway, and the rhythmic bumping of the road combined with the light tapping rain on the roof combined with the fact I'd slept maybe one of the last thirty-six hours all but forced me to lean my head against the window and rest my eyes for a moment. I woke with a jolt fifteen minutes later when our driver blared his horn at a Vespa that cut us off on Boulevard Périphérique, the bypass highway that loops around Paris. It's disorienting enough to doze off in class and wake up not knowing where you are, but waking up on a foreign motorway in the back seat of a strange car with Parker and Garland was a whole other level of where-the-hell-am-I.

I rubbed my eyes and asked, "Where are we?" to no one in particular.

"We're in Paris," Garland said. "We left the airport twenty minutes ago. Are you okay, son?"

"Just sleepy," I said, and leaned my head back against the window, this time fighting to keep my eyes open.

I suppose even beautiful cities have ugly highways, and Paris is no exception. On first impression the French capital didn't look much different from Atlanta. I saw a few faceless glass office buildings, but it was mostly concrete walls and tunnels. Only the street signs and car brands looked foreign.

"So this is Paris?" I asked.

"Two million people live here son. It ain't all Eiffel Towers and bistros."

Parker sat between us, gripping the straps of her backpack so tight that her knuckles were white, and I tapped her on the leg and said, "Hey, you okay?"

She looked at me for the first time since the soldiers escorted us off the plane and asked, "Am I what?"

"Are you okay?" I asked again, and in a whisper she repeated each word of the question before blowing the cobwebs away with a quick shake of her head and saying, "Of course I'm okay," then she started rapping about Paris and eating crazy cheese.

"What?"

"Beastie Boys, Edwin Green. God, do you only listen to Sadie Evans albums?"

"Shut up," I said, and after a moment added, "but seriously, you're okay?"

"I'm okay," she said, this time with a smile. "I just lost myself for a minute there."

"I think we all did," I said, and wanted to squeeze her hand or hug her or something but I wasn't sure if I should, so I leaned over and asked Garland, "Is that your trick?"

"Son, I don't what you're talking about."

"I think you do. Telling people your sad story of lost love before asking them to recall a love of their own. It turns people into mindless zombies willing to do your bidding."

Garland winked. "That's just one of my tricks."

I smiled and leaned my head against the window and watched the concrete go by, but minutes later we looped off the motorway into a tunnel and popped out on the Avenue de la Grande Armée, a wide, tree-lined, stone-paved boulevard that looked like the Paris from postcards (and *Call of Duty: Modern Warfare 3*). The rain had begun to clear, and ahead in the distance, silhouetted by the morning sun, sat the Arc de Triomphe.

I let out a dumbfounded, "Wow," and as we crept through the snarl of morning commuters Parker leaned over me, her hand high enough on my thigh I had trouble breathing, and she craned her neck to get a better look at the beautiful apartment buildings lining the road while I tried and failed to be a gentleman and not look down her shirt.

"This is where good Americans go when they die," Parker said, and Garland said something about how this street didn't look much different fifty years ago when our driver's phone rang and he answered and launched into a heated conversation in French. Parker nodded her head toward the driver, but I shrugged. He spoke way too fast for me to translate, but after I heard the name "Dufresne" for the third time, I had a sneaking suspicion our free ride might be coming to an end. Less than a minute later we stopped at a traffic light and without looking back our driver said, "You are not Mr. Dufresne, no?"

"Well, no," Garland said, "not exactly. But I'm happy to pay you for your—"

It would be wrong to describe the next few moments as a blur because I didn't actually see anything. I just remember (1) the rage on our driver's face when he spun around to face us, (2) the hissing sound his pepper spray made when it left the canister, and (3) the pain when an undetermined number of Scoville Heat Units introduced themselves to my corneas. Pain like I've never felt before and hope never to feel again. I think Parker pulled me out of the car, but I can't say for sure. A symphony of honking horns filled the air, and our driver was shouting something, but his voice faded, and was soon replaced by other voices, then the sound of bells on an opening door.

"Son, how do I ask for water?" Garland yelled at me, but I was too busy rubbing my eyes and moaning to answer. He grabbed me by the shoulders and shouted again, "How do I ask them for water?" and I screamed back, "I don't know!" which wasn't entirely true because I'd mastered French bathroom vocabulary in a classroom setting, but now, with the pressure on, I couldn't even recall the simplest phrases.

I heard Garland say, "*Eau? Toilettes?*" and a woman somewhere said something in French I didn't catch. "*S'il vous plaît,*" the old man replied, and dragged me down a hallway to the bathroom.

"I'm going to die," I said.

"You're not going to die," Garland said, "it's just pepper spray," and he splashed the first handful of water on my face.

"Just pepper spray? It feels like someone deep-fried my eyeballs."

"Your glasses stopped most of it," he said, and grabbed my hands and pushed them into the running water. "Here, keep splashing water in your eyes and try to blink a lot. Parker and I will be waiting in the cafe."

"No, don't leave! I don't want to die alone." But he left me there anyway.

Chapter Thirty-Five

In which the Raven, never flitting, still is sitting, still is sitting

Spoiler alert: I didn't die. But I couldn't open my eyes for close to twenty minutes, and even then I could only hold them open for a few seconds before succumbing to an involuntary blinking fit. I gave my eyes one last splash, then six more, and wandered back down the dark hallway into the cafe where Parker waved at me from a corner table.

"See, you lived," Garland said as I walked over and stood next to him, then he pointed across the table and said, "Edwin, meet our friend Rémy."

A man with a five-day beard wearing a Paris Saint-Germain shirt sat across the table smoking an e-cigarette with his legs crossed in perhaps the Frenchest way possible.

I nodded and said, "Hi," and Rémy said, "Edwin. Like the Edwin Allan Poe? Quote the raven, yes?"

"Yes," Parker said, before I could say no. I turned to her and she shrugged and smiled.

"We should go," I said, but no one moved, so I added, "shouldn't we?"

Garland pointed toward the bar and said, "Parker, be a dear and buy Edwin a coffee," and before I could argue she grabbed my arm and pulled me away.

"What is going on?" I whispered as we stepped up to the bar.

Parker turned to me after ordering and said, "We're ordering espressos, Edgar Allan."

"I figured that much," I said, "but did you two forget we're sort of on the run from the law?"

"Shit," Parker said, "I knew there was something we forgot."

"Be serious. Did something happen while I was in the bathroom? Is getting out of Paris not important anymore?"

"Too important to talk seriously about," Parker said. I didn't laugh and she added, "Relax Edgar Allan."

"Stop calling me that."

"Okay, relax Edwin Green. We figured everything out while you were dropping the kids off at the pool."

"I wasn't—I had pepper spray in my eyes—wait, you did?"

"We did," she said. "Rémy is giving us his car."

"Rémy? That dude you met ten minutes ago? He looks like a bad guy from a Fast & Furious film."

"People aren't good or bad, Edwin Green, they're either charming or tedious, and Rémy is charming, plus he's giving us his car."

"Whatever," I said, "but even charming people don't just give strangers their cars."

"Of course they do," Parker said, and we took our espressos back to the table just as Rémy handed Garland his keys.

"Let me guess," I said to Rémy as we sat down. "While I was in the bathroom Garland regaled you with his tale of lost love, and now you feel compelled to help him however you can."

"No, this is not so," Rémy said. "What compelled me was, how do you say, the bling bling," and when he held up his phone I saw a wire transfer on his banking app and a number with a lot of zeros behind it.

"See," Garland said, "I've got more than one trick."

I shook my head and the four of us sipped coffee and made awkward conversation until Garland said it was time to leave. We followed Rémy from the cafe down a side street to a neon green Peugeot hatchback not much bigger than Morningview Arbor's security golf cart. "Is here," Rémy said, pointing toward the ugliest car in France. "Thank you again," Garland said. "And remember, whatever money you have left after you buy a new car is yours to keep."

"Yes," Rémy said, "this is too kind." Then he turned and walked back toward the cafe before stopping and saying. "I wish you all the good luck. Au revoir."

Garland popped the back hatch and tossed me the keys, and I asked, "Are you going to buy two more of these or do you expect us to all fit in this one?"

"What was that, son?"

"Nothing," I said, and Parker began rapping about people laughing at our hatchback.

I squinted at her in confusion and she asked, "Skee-Lo? I wish I was taller? A baller? Come on, Edwin Green, you have to know that one."

I shook my head and asked, "Do you have obscure rap lyrics for every possible occasion?"

"Outta my way, son," Garland growled, and pulled my seat forward so he could squeeze into the back seat. As he climbed inside I asked, "So how much did you pay that dude for his go-cart?"

"Enough for him to buy two more if he wants," Garland said, tumbling less than gracefully onto the back seat. Then the old man sat up and asked, "What do you have against Peugeot anyway? They make good cars."

"I'm sure they do," I said and tossed my bag into the open hatch before saying to him over the back seat. "I just wish you would've bought some stranger's SUV."

"Remind me tell you a story about beggars and choosers one day," Garland said as I slammed the hatch.

I laughed and looked across to the top of the car at Parker who was standing by the passenger door. "Shotgun," she shouted, even though there was no one left to call it. We climbed inside and before I could stop her she grabbed my phone and said, "I've promoted myself to navigator."

"Okay," I said, reaching for my phone and missing, "but why don't you use your phone?"

"Because international data is expensive, man."

"Whatever," I said, and cranked the car. "Just type Caen in to Google Maps."

"I know how to use a phone, Edwin Green."

"And we're not going to Caen," Garland said from the back seat.

"What?" I turned around. "Why not?"

"'Cause I didn't crash in Caen. I crashed in Saint-Lô. I told Baldy Caen in the unlikely event we ever made it out of that airport. Now when they start looking for us, they'll start looking in the wrong town."

"Brilliant," Parker said, then she hit me on the arm and said, "Straight ahead one hundred yards captain, then make a sharp left on Avenue de Malakoff."

It's hard to say what time my internal clock thought it was, but I was now wide awake. Seems espresso and pepper spray combined with an impromptu vehicle purchase and merging into rush-hour traffic in a huge foreign city was a potent cure for jet lag. Not a cure I'd recommend, but a potent cure nonetheless. I checked my mirror—Garland was already asleep in the back—then I glanced over at Parker and she winked. I tried to wink back, but my eyelids still weren't working properly, so instead I made the face people make right before they sneeze and she laughed. Then we both laughed because we'd actually pulled it off. We were about to disappear into a country of sixty-six million people.

We had no idea Rémy would soon call the Paris police to report his car stolen. The asshole.

Chapter Thirty-Six

In which our hero shrugs off an existential threat to his doll collection.

CARL: Edwin, if you don't call home right now I swear I will destroy every Star Wars doll in your room.

The preceding text message was from Carl. It was the seventh of eighty-four threatening texts he'd send over the next two days, though I missed most of them after Parker blocked his number in my phone. By then we'd been on the run for over an hour, and word had trickled back home that we would, in fact, not be on the next flight to Atlanta. We were still in Paris though, lost in the 8th arrondissement, because (1) Central Paris is a cluster of roundabouts, medieval one-way streets, bike lanes, and cross-walks, which would have been okay had we been the only ones driving, but (2) apparently every person in France was driving in central Paris that morning, and there was never even a chance to pull over and get our bearings, which still might have been okay with a competent navigator, but (3) Parker was perhaps the worst navigator in the history of navigation. Half the time she was reading my text messages and wasn't even looking at Google Maps, but we did see the Eiffel Tower eleven times, which was cool the first three.

"Your stepdad texted again," Parker said as I tried to successfully negotiate the Arc de Triomphe roundabout for the fifth time that morning, a new American record.

"Okay," I said, half paying attention.

"He says he'll destroy your Star Wars dolls if you don't call home."

"They're not dolls," I said, trying to ignore the shouting man in the car next to us who was upset I'd violated some unwritten rule of French traffic courtesy. "They're vintage action figures. And he's bluffing."

"I don't think so. He cut off Darth Vader's head," Parker said, shoving the phone in my face.

"The heads come off," I said, pushing her hand away.

"Uh oh. He melted Chewbacca in the microwave," Parker said, shoving the phone back in my face.

"That's a Snickers," I said, pushing the phone away again. "Just reply that I'm fine and I'll call home soon."

"Too late," Parker said, typing with her thumbs. "I told him we were on a train to Gibraltar and you'd call after our wedding."

"Dammit. No. Why'd you—"

"Because that's where John and Yoko got married."

I gave her a dirty look.

"Besides," she said, "you said you weren't going to call home until we found Madeleine so what does it matter? This way they might all think we're going south."

"Sure," I said, "but tell him the wedding part was a joke. Mom will flip out and she's stressed enough."

"I knew you'd get cold feet," Parker said, before losing focus again and saying, "Oooh, what's that?"

I risked taking my eyes off the road for a second and looked up at a massive white building on a distant hill overlooking Paris.

"I don't know," I said, "but it's beautiful. Maybe it's a castle. Does France still have a king?

"France beheads their kings," Parker said. "But Spain still has one."

"I doubt the King of Spain lives in France," I said, and we heard Garland growling from the back seat.

"It's a church," the old man said, slowly sitting up. He'd been asleep since we'd left the cafe. "It's called Sacré-Cœur, and it's on a hill called Montmartre. Best view in the world from that church's steps, and they've got these singing nuns … anytime they had me in France through the years I made a point to go up there to hear those nuns sing. Wait, why the hell are we still in Paris?"

"Because he/she can't drive/navigate," Parker and I said in unison.

Garland sighed and said, "Parker hon, see if Rémy was kind enough to leave a map in his car."

"There's a map on my phone," I said.

"And how far has that gotten us," Garland snapped. "Parker. Map."

Parker opened the glove compartment and began taking inventory aloud, "Owner's manual, gum, dental floss, mouthwash. Rémy is way into oral hygiene."

"We're looking for a map, dear," Garland reminded her.

"No map," she said, then began digging under her seat. A moment later she shouted, "Holy shit!"

I almost wrecked. "What?"

"Shit," she said again, and Garland leaned over the back seat to investigate. Using two fingers like she was holding a dead mouse by the tail, Parker pulled a small black pistol with a dark wooden grip from under the seat.

I didn't get a great look at the gun because taking your eyes off the road in Paris is inadvisable, but at first glance I thought it was a toy. In my defense it was the first time I'd ever seen a gun up close.

"What is it?" I asked.

Garland took the pistol and said, "It's a 9mm. SIG Sauer P938 if I'm not mistaken."

"Throw it out the window," Parker said, scooting up in her seat in an attempt to get as far away from the gun as possible.

"I'm not throwing it out the window," Garland said. "That'd be littering. Besides, we might need it later."

"In what scenario would we possibly need a gun?" I asked, but Garland ignored my question and began shouting driving directions. He was guessing, I think—we did pass the Eiffel Tower three more times—but half an hour later we found the motorway and headed west. Satisfied that we wouldn't get lost again, Garland lay back down. Parker reclined her seat, propped her feet on the dash, and started to put her earbuds in and I asked, "New Pornographers?" but failed to mention I'd downloaded the song she played me on Tuesday and listened to it seventy-six times already.

"What? No. Camera Obscura. I'm only listening to Scottish bands with female singers this month."

"It's still April," I said.

"Oh, you think I'm on the Gregorian calendar, Edwin Green? That's cute."

I wanted to reply, but sometimes she'd say things so bizarre the gears in my brain would grind to a halt, so I didn't say anything and she put her earbuds in and leaned her head against the window and fell asleep. I drove for maybe an hour and watched as the landscape became increasingly rural. Endless farm fields dotted by tiny French villages, each with a church tower standing tall on the horizon. I watched these forgotten towns pass in Parker's window, and then I watched Parker, the rise and fall of her breath, the part of her lips, the terror in her eyes when the wheels of Rémy's hatchback left the road and a tractor-trailer blared his horn as I swerved to get back on the motorway.

Garland moaned from the back seat but didn't wake up, and Parker looked at me like she knew I'd been watching her sleep, and I stared straight ahead like nothing happened. A few minutes later she shoved my phone back in my face and said, "Someone named Fitz said you should stop breaking international laws and call him right now."

"You know Fitz," I said. "He's in three of your classes at school."

"If you say so," Parker said, and handed me my phone. I called Fitz.

"Green, I dreamt you texted me last night and said you were in France with Parker Haddaway, which sucks because I'd rather not dream about you and Parker Haddaway. No offense."

"None taken," I said.

"But my mom woke me up thirty minutes earlier than normal and dragged me into the living room and unpaused the morning news and there was your ugly mug next to Parker's and some old geezer named Garland."

"We were on the news," I announced to the car, but Garland didn't stir and Parker had her earbuds back in. "What news?" I asked.

"I don't know," Fitz said, "whatever news my mom watches in the morning."

"Yeah, but was is it like local Birmingham news, or—"

"No, it was the NBC one. *The Today Show*. They played a clip of the old man's attorney, then Al Roker made a couple jokes about you guys, then they moved on to a cooking segment."

"Shit," I said.

"Yeah, shit," Fitz repeated. "You didn't mention this hypothetical plan of questionable legality involved kidnapping some old man. You know, if you wanted to be famous for doing something illegal you didn't have to go all the way to France. You could have just threatened the President on Twitter without leaving your bed."

"We didn't kidnap him. Wait, is that what Al Roker said? That we kidnapped him?"

"That's what the old man's lawyer said. He was on the court-house steps shouting about the old man being out of his mind and that you and Parker planned to ransom him or something."

I tapped Parker on the shoulder and when she took out her earbuds I said, "Garland's lawyer went on national television this morning and told the world we kidnapped him and we're hold-ing him for ransom."

"Bitchin'," Parker said.

"No, not bitchin'," I said to her, then to Fitz, "We didn't kid-nap him. He wanted us to take him to Europe to find a woman he met during World War II."

"So you thought, 'Hmm, if I help this crazy old man find some French chick he hooked up with seventy years ago my su-per famous ex-girlfriend might notice me again.'"

"Pretty much."

"Well, it looks like your dumb plan might work. Too bad you're going to prison. You should call Al Roker and tell him your side of the story."

"Yeah ... or better yet," I said, "I've posted a couple of videos of Garland telling his story, can you send those to every news outlet you can think of?"

"Sure," Fitz said.

"Actually wait, give me twenty minutes. I've got a better idea."

Chapter Thirty-Seven

In which Garland Lenox doesn't believe in miracles on ice.

"Wake up."

"No."

"Garland, wake up! Your stupid lawyer is on television telling the world we kidnapped you for ransom."

The old man sat up and rubbed his eyes, then leaned between the front seats and laughed. "That sounds about like Lucian."

"Look," Parker said, showing him an Associated Press article she'd found on my phone.

"I can't read print that small," Garland barked.

"Fine," Parker said, and began reading the article out loud. "Birmingham, Alabama — Garland Lenox, a ninety-year-old World War II veteran, is missing, and his attorney fears the dementia patient is the victim of a kidnap-for-ransom plot. Lucian Figg, attorney for the missing man, told reporters gathered outside the Jefferson County courthouse that two high school students from nearby Hornby, Alabama, recently befriended his client and coerced him aboard an Air France flight bound for Paris, France. 'The State Department and United States embassy in Paris are aware of the situation,' Figg said, 'but failed to intercept my client and his abductors at Charles de Gaulle Airport.' When asked if he had received a ransom demand Figg declined to comment, only saying that, 'Garland Lenox is a hero, and we pray for his safe return.' Anyone with information concerning—"

"Okay, dear, I get the gist," Garland said.

"Why'd you even hire that guy?" I asked. "Didn't the name Lucian Figg tip you off that he might be evil?"

Garland laughed and said, "I didn't hire him. I hired his daddy, Lucian Senior—though I guess his name was just as bad. Lucian Junior took over when his daddy died two years ago. He's a moron, but I liked him alright until he stuck me in that damn nursing home."

"Well we've got to get our side of the story out there," I said, glancing back at Garland in the rearview mirror.

"No son, we've got to find Madeleine," the old man said. "That's why we're here, remember?"

"Yeah, but everyone in the world thinks we kidnapped you."

"So what? Everyone in the world thinks we beat the Soviets in hockey at Lake Placid, but I know for a fact Ronald Reagan offered the Russian goalies ten million each to throw the game. Paid them in Liberian dollars so no one could trace it back to the US, then staged a coup in Liberia a month later so their currency would plummet and the goalies wouldn't get anything. Man, ol' Ronnie hated the Ruskies."

"Okay, but—wait, really?"

"You can't make this shit up, son."

"Whatever," I said. "I'd still rather the entire world not think of me as a kidnapper. Besides, if we can get our side of the story out there they might not be so aggressive in tracking us down."

"He's got a point," Parker said. "And it's a good chance to make your lawyer look like an idiot."

Garland chuckled. "Alright, alright. You had me at make my lawyer look like an idiot."

A few kilometers later we pulled off the motorway at a service area, which is like a rest area in the States, except these have gas stations and restaurants, both a welcome sight considering we were starving and had wasted most of Rémy's gas circling Paris. I parked at an open pump, and while Garland watched me fill up the tank Parker went inside in search of nourishment.

"Is the metric system screwing me up," I asked Garland looking at the prices on the screen, "or is gasoline here crazy expensive?"

"Nope, they call it petrol, and it's about $5.50 a gallon," Garland said, handing me his debit card.

"No wonder they all drive glorified golf carts," I said, and took the card. "Wait, should we be using this? Won't they be able to track our purchases like cops do on television?"

"Not that card," Garland said. "Swiss banks are sticklers for privacy."

I examined the card. It didn't even have his name on it, just a long series of numbers. "Why do you have a Swiss bank account?" I asked.

"To keep my Swiss money," Garland said, and left it there.

Parker came back and handed me a bright green can of something called Gini.

"Do they not sell Coke?" I asked

"It's time you drink something besides Coke, Edwin Green. Consistency is the last refuge of the unimaginative." Then she tossed me a weird little tin of candied fruit and said, "Here, you need to broaden your horizons."

"No, I need calories," I said, and tossed the fruit back to her before going inside to buy a Coke and a family-size bag of Cool Ranch Doritos. Then the three of us sat and snacked on a picnic table in the parking lot median while I began recording Garland on my phone. "Okay," I said, "just tell the world what's going on."

Garland frowned at the camera and said through a mouthful of potato chips, "What, now?"

"Yeah, whenever you're ready."

The old man washed his chips down with swig of whatever nasty French soda Parker bought him and said, "Hello America, this is Garland Lenox, coming to you live from somewhere in France. I just wanted to take a moment and assure everyone back home I'm fine, and I wasn't kidnapped, despite what that asshole of an attorney of mine is telling anyone who'll listen. Hell, knowing Lucian he'll go on television after this and say my captors forced me to make this statement, and that I'm blinking SOS signals." At this Garland began to blink in exaggerated fashion and a Boy Scout in Arkansas was the first to notice the old man actually blinked the word "asshole" in Morse code, "but I can assure you that is not the case. If anything I talked these two kids into taking me to France, and if that's a crime, well, I'll face the music when we get home. But until then we're on a mission to find Madeleine Moreau, the beautiful woman who saved my life seventy years ago during the war. It may take us a few days, but I know we'll find her, and then we'll surrender and the kids can go back to school and I'll go back to my damn nursing home and you'll never hear a peep out of ol' Garland Lenox again. So to anyone out there trying to find us, just back off and let us do what we came here to do." Then Garland pointed at Parker and said, "Parker hon, anything you'd like to say to the folks back home?"

I turned my phone toward Parker and she jabbed a finger at the camera and said, "If you want to see the old man again you'll leave ten million dollars at the base of the Eiffel Tower by midnight."

Garland laughed out loud and I flipped the camera around toward myself and said, "She's joking. Tell them you're joking."

I pointed the camera back at Parker and she said, "I'm joking." Then added with an evil villain's laugh, "It's twenty million dollars."

I sighed and put the camera back on Garland. "Tell them she's joking."

"She's joking," he said between laughs. "It's thirty million dollars," and then they both cracked up.

I flipped the camera back around on myself and said, "I promise they're joking. Don't leave thirty million dollars at the base of the Eiffel Tower. Oh, and hi Mom, hi Carl. Sorry I haven't called you back, but as you can see, I'm fine, and now you know why I had to help Mr. Lenox. I should be home in a few days and you can ground me until I'm thirty-seven, okay? Love you both."

I hesitated before pointing the camera back toward Parker and asking, "Anything else?"

"Don't you think French gas stations are lovely in the spring?" she asked.

"I do," I said.

"I can't think of a nicer place to hold an old man for ransom."

"Damn it, Parker," I said, and turned the camera toward Garland who was still laughing. "Anything you want to add?"

"Did I mention that my lawyer is an asshole?"

"Yes, a few times."

"And that I wasn't kidnapped, and no one is holding me for ransom, and that my attorney is truly an asshole?"

"Yes."

"Then I guess that's all the news from France," Garland said, and I stopped recording.

I posted the video to my YouTube channel and texted Fitz to say it was ready for worldwide distribution.

Twenty minutes later CNN was the first network to air it in its entirety.

Chapter Thirty-Eight

In which speculators get their speculation on,
and our hero confronts an oblivious bilingual.

In a rush to be first, CNN aired our video unedited, and the anchor, his talking head contained in a small box at the bottom of the screen, visibly flinched every time Garland referred to his attorney as an asshole. You can still watch the CNN video on YouTube. It has 8.9 million views and it's hilarious. The next sixty-three times CNN aired the video that day they bleeped out Garland's more colorful nouns and adjectives, however his disdain for Lucian Figg was still abundantly clear.

In less than half an hour CNN assembled a roundtable of experts to speculate on every aspect of our story. Their legal expert, a balding man in suspenders, weighed in on whether Garland, Parker, or I had broken the law. "Having not been with them for the last twenty-four hours I cannot say for certain," the legal expert said, and the host nodded. "That said, the old man's language perhaps violated YouTube's terms of service, and your network will certainly face FCC fines for airing it uncensored." Next the historian, a bespectacled little old lady in a cardigan, spoke at length on the more than 60,000 US servicemen who married foreign women during and immediately following World War II. "Soldiers falling in love with women in countries they've conquered or liberated is not a new phenomenon," she said, but the host had to cut her off, when for no apparent reason she began talking about Attila the Hun. Finally, the psychologist, a black man with a British accent, speculated on our individual motives. "The older man, Mr. Lenox, appears to be grappling with his own mortality. By returning to the love of his youth he's trying to reclaim his youth." The host began to ask a follow up question but a producer interrupted. Lucian Figg was on the line, calling to defend himself against allegations of assholery. But when the host grilled Lucian on his unsubstantiated claims of kidnapping and ransom, Garland's attorney released a profanity-laced tirade of his own that, if not cut short by an impromptu commercial break, would have resulted in CNN receiving the sort of fine networks receive when pop stars reveal their nipples during the Super Bowl. This did little to refute Garland's claims, and Lucian Figg, Asshole at Law memes flooded the internet minutes later.

Had a plane crashed, or a kid fallen in a gorilla cage at a zoo, or Sadie Evans walked out of a restaurant, the networks would have pushed our story to the back burner. But obviously April 16th was a slow news day, and similar roundtable conversations were happening simultaneously on Fox News and MSNBC. Half an hour later the three networks somewhat suspiciously arrived at the same narrative—this was the feel good story of the year, and perhaps the most romantic thing anyone could remember. And unless Parker and I actually did issue a ransom—and apart from Lucian Figg no one believed we would—everyone was rooting for us to find Madeleine. However, each network had a team of researchers frantically digging to find out anything and everything they could about Garland, Parker, and me, just in case ratings demanded a change in narrative.

Back in France, the three of us cruised down Autoroute 13, unaware of our ever-growing celebrity status back home. We remained unaware for the next few hours because Parker, apart from navigational duties, was also in charge of scanning news sites for any mention of our escapades. But instead she'd discovered Candy Crush, and though she neglected her two primary jobs, she did pass level 350 for me, so I can't be too upset.

A few kilometers past the service area Garland announced, "Now, if you two don't mind, I'm going to resume my nap. All this getting kidnapped has wore me slap out."

"Sweet dreams," Parker said, not looking up from her game.

"Wait," I said, catching his eye in the rearview mirror, "you speak French."

The old man leaned forward and said, "What are you jabbering on about, son?"

"You speak French," I repeated.

"The hell I do."

"But you do," I said, "and I was under the impression you needed me here to translate."

"And drive," Parker said, again her eyes never leaving my phone.

"We do need you to translate," Garland said, and tried to lie back down.

"Tell him he spoke French," I said to Parker, who cursed loudly as her game ended.

"You spoke French," she said, then started a new game.

"When?" Garland demanded, leaning back between our seats.

"In the airport you told one of the soldiers his mother was a whore," I said, and Garland laughed because at times he had all the maturity of a twelve-year-old. "Then in that cafe in Paris you asked where the bathroom was, and the thing is, your French sounds better than my French teacher's, so I'm starting to doubt you brought me here to translate."

"And drive," Parker added again.

I watched Garland in the mirror. He looked genuinely confused.

"Garland, *où avez-vous appris parler en Français?*" I asked.

"I don't know where I learned it," Garland said, looking even more confused that he'd understood my question. He sat back to think, and a moment later leaned between our seats again and said, "You know, I probably picked up the whore stuff in the Army. We all knew how to say things like, "Your mother has a penis," in French and German, you know, in case we ever found ourselves in a situation where such language was appropriate."

"When would it not be appropriate?" Parker said and we both ignored her.

"As for the other stuff," Garland said, "I hid with Madeleine for nearly three months, and she tried to teach me a little French. I bet some of it's just coming back to me."

"Wait," I said, "you lived with her for three months?"

"Son, I was in a German occupied town with a broken ankle. Making a run for it wasn't an option." He cleared his throat like he was about to dive into another story so I snatched my phone away from Parker.

"Dammit, Edwin Green, I was almost—"

I turned on the camera, pressed record, and handed the phone back to her. "Just film Garland," I said. "His adoring fans may demand another video soon." I was more right than I knew.

Chapter Thirty-Nine

*In which not knowing the New York Yankees won the
1943 World Series can get your ass shot.*

Of all the Garland videos we made that week, the story of how
he met Madeleine was my favorite. Throughout the video, the
sun cast a dark shadow over the back seat, and you only see the
details of the old man's face when he'd get excited and lean forward. Behind him, out the rear window, the sun shines bright,
and on both sides of the road are endless fields of yellow flowers.
If Best Cinematography in a YouTube Video were an Academy
Award category, Parker would have walked away with the Oscar
that year.

"I tapped on the first door I came to," Garland said, "but
no one answered, so I started to bang harder and harder until a light came on upstairs. There were French phrases written on the back of our maps, and I practiced saying, '*Je suis un
pilote Américain,*' while waiting for someone to answer the door.
I heard footsteps inside, and the turn of a lock, then the door
cracked open just enough for one eye to peek out. A girl inside
said, 'Monsieur?'

"I said, '*Je suis un pilote Américain*,' much louder than I'd meant to, and that one eye widened and the door flung open and the girl grabbed me by the collar and yanked me into the house. She was tall, or at least she looked tall from the floor, and she was thin, too thin, from the rationing. I watched her look up and down the street before gently closing the door and turning back to me, her white nightgown fluttering in the breeze I'd let in. And in that moment, as she pushed a strand of long brown hair from her eyes, I was quite certain I'd died in that plane crash and gone to heaven, because I was looking at an angel. Then she leaned down close and whispered, 'You shit-for-brains American fool. Are you trying to wake every German in town?'" The old man chuckled and said, "Right about then I began to doubt her angelic credentials.

"She scowled at me and demanded 'Why? Why are you in this town, hitting this door at four in the morning?'

"I asked her, 'Why do you speak English?'

"She jabbed a bony finger into my chest and said, 'No. I ask the questions now.' That's when I started to think I'd have been safer outside with the Nazis. I pointed at my leg and said, 'I'm injured.' Thought maybe then I'd get a little compassion, but she just mocked me. 'Oh, you hurt your leg,' she said. 'So what? So you must bring the entire Nazi army to my door?'

"I told her I didn't know it was her door, it was just the first door I came to, and if she wanted me to I'd leave, but she shushed me with a raised finger. I watched her pace the room, every few seconds peeking out the curtains, then glaring at me with disdain, but after a few minutes, when she'd decided the Nazis were still asleep and not on their way to her door, her face softened and she bent down to look at my ankle.

"She said, 'So mine was the first door you came to. I guess today is my lucky day.' Then she added, 'Your ankle, it is badly broken.'

"I looked down at my ankle, felt a sharp blow to the side of my head, and don't remember much after that. Later she confessed to hitting me upside the head with a bronze candlestick.

"I woke up the next morning when the sun came streaming through the window of the attic bedroom she'd put me in. To this day I still have no idea how she even got me up there. I doubt she weighed a hundred pounds. Thanks to her my head throbbed with every beat of my heart, which I suppose would have been okay had it somehow taken my mind off my shattered ankle, but instead I ended up with excruciating pain on both ends of my body. I sat up in bed best I could and rubbed my eyes and found her sitting in a chair at the end of my bed with her legs crossed and a Luger P08 pointed right at my heart. It might have been sexy had it not so damn terrifying.

"She said, 'Good morning, monsieur,' and leaned forward in her chair.

"I said, 'It'd be a helluva lot better if you weren't pointing that gun at me.'

"She looked at the gun like she'd forgotten it was in her hand, then looked at me and said, 'A girl cannot be too safe, no? What, with Nazis all over town and American aviators knocking on doors at all hours of the night.'

"I told her I supposed not, and she smiled and said, 'Now you will answer my questions, because I must leave soon, and if you are a German spy I will need to kill you before I go.'

"I tried to laugh but nothing much came out, so I told her, 'I'm not a damn spy. I told you I'm an American pilot. The Germans shot me down last night and I spent four hours floating in some freezing ass river before hobbling through town to your door. Are you suggesting I'd break my leg on purpose just to throw you off?'

"She shrugged and said, 'Germans can be weird.'

"This time a little laugh came out and I said, 'I'll give you that. Now get on with it. Ask me your questions so you can stop pointing that damn gun at me.'

"She said, 'Okay, tell me who won your World Series last year.'

"I told her I hadn't a clue and she cocked the Luger. 'Now hold on,' I said, 'I'd never even heard of baseball until I joined the army last year. Some crazy preacher back home said the world was ending and my parents believed him. I spent most of my childhood living in the woods waiting for Jesus to come back.'

"She considered this long enough for sweat beads to form on my forehead before finally lowering the gun. 'Alright,' she said, 'even a German would not make up a story that weird.'

"I exhaled and said, 'Now, aren't you glad you didn't shoot me. You'd have never gotten these sheets clean.'

"She smiled and said, 'I wanted to believe you, but it is my job to be cautious.'

"I sat up a little more and asked, 'Now will you tell me how you speak English so well?'

"She pointed at the radio in the corner of the room and said, 'We learn some in school, but mostly I learn from listening to the BBC. When the Germans came in 1940 they confiscated some radios, though not all. But this January someone shot and killed a German soldier and the Nazis arrested several men from town and confiscated all the radios they could find. They did not find mine though, because this is a hidden room. Now I have one of the few radios left in town. Every night I listen, and in the morning I give a report to the Resistance leaders.'

"I shook my head and said, 'You're a member of the French Resistance?'

"She stood up and said, 'Do not act so astonished, monsieur. Just because I am young and a woman does not mean I cannot do my part.'

"I held up my hands in surrender and said, 'You're right. I'm sorry. So can you get me back across the Channel to England?'

"She shook her head no. 'We have helped many pilots back across the Channel,' she said. 'And some we have sent south to Spain. But the invasion will be soon. Probably it is best now to hide, and the Allies will come to you.'

"I knew we were in a strategic Nazi controlled town, and I wanted to tell her when the Allies did come rolling through it wasn't going to be like some damned homecoming parade, but with my ankle I wasn't going anywhere anyway, so I didn't argue. I said, 'Well I sure am lucky I knocked on the door of a family of French resisters. Where are your parents?'

"The mischievous smile left her face for a moment and she said, 'My parents are dead, monsieur. My mother before the Germans came. My father after.'

"I told her I was sorry, and we were both quiet for a long time before she nodded toward some milk and bread on the table next to me. 'It is not much,' she said, 'but it is all I have for now. I will try and bring something more when I return this evening. When I tell the leaders I have an American pilot in my house they will provide.'

"I looked over at the food and said, 'Wait, you made me breakfast before you knew if you'd have to shoot me?'

"Her smile returned and she said, 'I would have let you eat breakfast either way. We are not animals.' Then she stood to leave and said, 'There is a bathroom down the hall. Stay upstairs today and do not look out the windows. The Germans know I live alone, and so does the Larue boy next door who watches my window hoping to see me changing clothes. If they inspected the house again and found the radio it would be bad, though not as bad as if they found an American pilot.'

"She turned to leave and I said, 'Wait, where are you going?'

"She held up a couple of books and said, 'To school, monsieur. It is Tuesday. Then I go to piano lessons.'"

"Wait, hold up," I said, interrupting Garland's story. "She was taking piano lessons in the middle of World War II?"

"Yep," Garland said. "Hell, kids in Saint-Lô went to school on the Monday before D-Day. That little town went about its business as usual. Folks went to work, and kids went to school—there were just Nazis everywhere. They even had movies and a theatre until January when someone shot that German soldier in the street, then the Nazis clamped down on 'em a little more."

"That's weird," I said. "Right?"

"Not too weird," Garland said. "They had me in Salisbury posing as an oboe instructor during the Rhodesian Bush War. I was there for two of the worst years and never had a student miss a lesson. 'Course I told 'em I was the oboe player for the Rolling Stones so all the kids thought I was the real shit."

"I thought you taught bassoon," Parker said.

"Bassoon, saxophone, oboe," Garland said, "I taught all the woodwinds, dear."

"Okay, so she left for school," I said, trying to get Garland back on track.

"Right," the old man said, "She turned to leave but I didn't want her to go, so I blurted out, 'How old are you?'

"She stopped and said, 'Seventeen monsieur.'

"I said, 'Well I'm only nineteen so how about you stop calling me monsieur.'

"She said, 'Will I call you G.I. Joe?'

"I said, 'You can call me Garland.'

"She smiled and said, 'Garland. Okay Garland, you can call me Madeleine.'

"Then she turned to leave again and I said, 'Madeleine, wait.' She looked back and I said, 'I think I love you.'

"Madeleine sighed and shook her head and said, 'Yes, you told me this twelve times last night after I knocked you out. Now get some rest.'"

The video abruptly cuts off here, but not before you hear Parker shout, "My God, Edwin Green, stop the car!"

Chapter Forty

In which our hero breaks for canola.

Not long after we'd made our service station video Garland had me exit the motorway. We were getting close to Caen, and since that's where Martin Blair thought we were heading, Garland thought it best to take back roads the rest of the way to Saint-Lô. And though Parker's navigational abilities hadn't improved much since leaving Paris, we'd made some progress, until that is, she grabbed my wrist and I stomped the brakes and Rémy's hatchback performed a terrifying, if not X-Games-worthy, 360 before sliding to a stop on a lonely country road ten miles northeast of Caen.

"What the hell!" I shouted and turned around to check on Garland who'd tumbled hard into the floorboard.

"Look," Parker said, "isn't that the most beautiful thing you've ever seen?"

On the left side of the road, as far as the eye could see, was a waist-deep field of yellow flowers. It was picturesque, but we'd passed fields like this one for the last hour, so I wasn't sure exactly why Parker had nearly killed us to stop and see this particular one.

"Those are canola flowers," Garland said, pulling himself up slowly, "and they smell like old socks dipped in mustard."

By now Parker had her window down and said, "I think they smell lovely," then she slapped me on the knee and said, "Come on." She was out the door before I could stop her.

I turned back to Garland and he gave me a shrug, so I climbed out of the car and followed Parker into the field of flowers. She was twenty yards ahead of me, skipping and running a hand across the tops of the flowers. It's a moment I still dream about, only in my dreams she never turns around, she just keeps skipping farther into the field. But that day she stopped and spun around and waited for me to catch up.

"What do you think about this, Edwin Green?"

"It's ...," I started to say, but never came up with anything.

"Such a wordsmith," she teased, and skipped away again.

"Shouldn't we be getting back on the road?" I asked, chasing after her.

"We're stopping to smell the flowers, Edwin Green. The literal flowers."

She stopped and I caught her again and said, "Roses. You're supposed to stop and smell the roses. Not mustard-sock flowers. No one stops to smell mustard-sock flowers."

"There's no accounting for taste," she said, then grabbed me by both hands and started spinning us. We spun faster and faster until her red hair and the yellow flowers and the blue sky blurred into a rainbow. A rainbow that made no guarantees God wouldn't flood the Earth again but bewitched me to the point I wouldn't mind if he did. I wanted to stand there and spin with her forever, but after a few moments I realized more spinning would soon lead to vomiting, and I said so. Parker laughed, and I laughed, then we fell, me on the ground, and her on top of me, and we laid there and laughed and tried to catch our breath.

"What would you do without me, Edwin Green?"

"I'd have us in Saint-Lô already," I said.

She pretended to look at a watch she wasn't wearing and said, "No. You'd be in algebra. And you've got to admit, this is way better than algebra."

"It's …," I started to say, but again never came up with anything, this time because my brain was allocating all its resources toward convincing me I should kiss Parker that very instant. Well, not all its resources. There was a tiny voice in my head trying to remind me why I'd actually traveled to France in the first place, but the kiss-Parker-now-you-fool part of my brain soon bludgeoned that tiny voice with a stale baguette, and I counted down from five in my head to get my courage up. But then a French policeman shouted "*Levez-vous!*" and sort of killed the mood.

Chapter Forty-One

In which objects in mirror are closer than they appear.

"What did he say?" Parker asked.

"He either wants us to stand up or undress," I said, "but considering the context …"

Parker stood up with her hands raised, then looked at me and whispered, "He's a little guy."

"Okay, so?"

"So I think we can take him. He doesn't even have a gun."

"That's a terrible idea," I said, and stood next to Parker with my hands in the air. The policeman was ten yards away. He had a neatly trimmed mustache and wore dark blue pants with a light blue shirt. He reminded me a little of Lando Calrissian, only he was white and spoke French.

"What did he say?" Parker asked after the policeman shouted something I didn't catch.

"I'm not sure, everyone here talks too fast."

"Tell me again how you won the top French award?"

"I did figure out he wanted us to stand up," I said.

The policeman yelled something else and we stopped arguing and looked back at him. Parker was right, he was small, and apart from the baton hanging from his belt, he didn't appear armed. But he'd parked his little blue patrol car behind Rémy's, so even if we knocked him down and ran for it, we'd still end up in a car chase, and as a general rule, I try to avoid car chases.

The policeman spoke again and this time I caught the words, "*voiture volée*" and cursed under my breath.

"What?" Parker said.

"He said something about a stolen car. I think he's accusing us of stealing Rémy's car."

"Shit," Parker said. "What's the French word for sorry?"

"Pardon. Wait, are you going to apologize for stealing a car? I don't think that will—"

"Pardon," Parker said, walking toward the policeman with both hands still held high over her head. "Pardon. Pardon. Say it, Edwin Green."

"Pardon," I said.

"Louder," Parker said.

"Pardon," I said again, this time with feeling.

We succeeded in confusing the policeman for a moment, but then he pulled his baton and began waving it at us and shouting in agitated French.

We stopped, then Parker proceeded to perform a brief medley of early Outkast songs for the confused policeman, and in one of the more terrible seconds of my life I understood she'd only been trying to distract him long enough for Garland to sneak up from behind. Sneak up from behind with that damn pistol.

"No," I said, looking at Parker. "Tell me we're not doing this?"

"Well we're not letting the French Barney Fife arrest us, Edwin Green, so if you've got a better idea you'll need to implement it in the next six seconds or so."

I looked back at Garland, and following the panic in my eyes the policeman turned around only to see a ninety-year-old man aiming a gun at his face.

"Garland, please don't shoot him," I begged, and Garland said, "Son I'm not going to shoot him. This thing isn't even loaded. But Pierre here doesn't know that, do you Pierre?" And he thrust the gun toward the policeman, who flinched and dropped his baton and likely wet his pants.

"Don't just stand there, get to the car," Garland growled at us, "and son, how do I tell this fella to stay put?"

"'*Restes*,' I think. Or maybe '*resteras.*' I always confuse my tenses."

"*Restes! Resteras!*" Garland shouted at the policeman who shrugged like that went without saying.

Parker and I waited on the road as Garland backed up, leaving the policeman twenty yards away in the field of canola flowers. "Here son," Garland said to me, "keep this pointed at him," and he tried to hand me the gun.

"No," I shouted. "I'm not pointing a gun at a policeman."

"Dammit son, I told you it's not loaded," Garland shouted back, but I walked away so he handed the gun to Parker, who wasn't nearly as bothered by the pistol now that she knew it wasn't loaded.

Parker rapped about having five in the clip and one in the hole and her intentions of making a body turn cold, then she laughed at herself, and the poor policeman looked equal parts baffled and terrified.

And this is where my memory of that moment's events begins to blur. Not because I'm trying to avoid prosecution—the French Barney Fife later corroborated my story—but because traumatic events involving large explosions can affect the memories of eyewitnesses. I was in the car, watching Garland in the mirror until he ducked behind the policeman's car, then I glanced back at Parker. She was still rapping, and had either just said, "… and Parker don't stop, cause it's one eight seven on a rural French cop," or "… and when Parker pulls out her jammy get ready cause she might go blaw!" when she squeezed the trigger on what was in fact a very loaded gun. A bullet exploded from the barrel and missed the policeman's head by maybe six inches. Parker screamed and dropped the gun, and the policeman screamed and took off running through the canola field, and I put my head in my hands and tried hard to wake up from what had to be a terrible dream. Seconds later Garland slammed the door and said, "Drive son."

I didn't respond because I thought maybe if I didn't, none of what just happened would be real.

"Dammit son, drive," Garland shouted, this time slapping me on the back of the head. "Drive fast."

So I stomped the accelerator, and we squealed down that sleepy French road, and though I didn't want to know, I was about to ask Garland what he'd been doing to the policeman's car when I saw the explosion in my rearview mirror.

That's when I realized I'd spend a large part of my life in a French prison.

Chapter Forty-Two

In which our hero learns simultaneously comforting and
terrifying information about capital punishment in France.

Smoke from the flaming police cruiser was still in my rearview
mirror when I screamed at Garland, "What the hell did you do?"
The old man didn't answer, but continued to look out the back
window and admire his handiwork while Parker held her face in
her hands and laughed.

"This isn't funny," I shouted at her. "They're going to kill us.
They're going to kill us all dead and bury us under a prison so
our ghosts will have to haunt a jail cell for eternity. Garland what
the hell did you do?"

"I soaked one of Rémy's old T-shirts with lighter fluid, stuck
it in that cop's gas tank, and lit it," Garland said, turning back
around and leaning between the front seats. "It was much louder than I expected. Gotta be the most exciting thing to happen
around here since the war."

"They're going to kill us," I repeated. "They're going to line
us up against a wall and shoot us all in the face."

"Will you calm the hell down, son, they're not going to kill
us."

"You don't know that," I said. "You didn't even know you spoke French."

"I do know that," Garland said. "France did away with the death penalty in 1977, so no, they're not going to kill us. But even if they did reinstate the death penalty just for us they still wouldn't shoot us. They'd use a guillotine."

"The guillotine is much more romantic," Parker said, and I glared at her.

"Why did you have to blow up his car?" I asked Garland.

"So he wouldn't follow us," Garland said.

"You could have taken his keys. Or shot out his tires. There didn't need to be a fireball." I glanced in my side mirror. We were a few miles away now but I could still see the black smoke rising into the air. "The fireball was completely unnecessary."

"He'd have used his radio," Garland said. "I wasn't being rash, son. Unless someone happens to drive by and pick that poor man up we've got at least an hour head start, and we'll need it to dump this car and disappear."

I started to reply but didn't know what else to say. Garland had a point, I suppose—the point being if we're willing to run from a policeman, blowing up his car made perfect sense. And none of us wanted this trip to end in a field only sixty miles from Saint-Lô. But if Garland could blow up a police car without hesitation, I worried about what he might do were our situation to become more dire. I just kept telling myself that (1) Garland blew up the car, and (2) Parker shot at the policeman, and (3) apart from frolicking through someone's canola field—and French trespass laws are pretty lax—I hadn't done anything wrong. Yet.

"Where are we anyhow?" Garland asked.

Parker looked at the map on my phone and said, "Belgium, no wait, this map is upside down."

I grabbed my phone from her and said, "Reviers. About ten miles north of Caen, ten miles east of Bayeux."

"You shouldn't look at your phone while you drive," she said, grabbing it back from me.

"You shouldn't shoot at policemen," I snapped back, and she mumbled under her breath, "Damn, it does indeed feel good to be a gangster."

"Martin Blair thinks we're going to Caen," Garland said, "so that's a no-go. I know Bayeux has a train station. Find the address."

Parker began pressing buttons on my phone and I grabbed it from her again and asked the little robot inside, "Where is the train station in Bayeux, France?"

The robot replied, "Gare de Bayeux is located at Station Square, 14400 Bayeux, France. Would you like directions?"

"That'll do," Garland said. "Now get us there fast, and while you're at it ask that robot where we can buy some new clothes in Bayeux. We look a little too much like ourselves."

Chapter Forty-Three

In which our hero gets something he'd almost forgotten he wanted.

"There," Garland said, "between those two."

It was a fifteen-minute white-knuckle drive later and we were in Bayeux, ditching Rémy's hatchback on a residential street a few blocks north of the city center. I parked between two other hatchbacks—I think eight out of every ten cars in France are hatchbacks—in front of an endless row of three-story beige apartment buildings, and while Parker and I grabbed our bag from the hatch, Garland began rather indiscreetly tampering with the license plate on the yellow car in front of ours.

"What the hell are you doing?" I asked, but he shushed me and proceeded to switch Rémy's plate with the one he'd just removed.

"Let's move," the old man said once he'd tightened the last screw, and we left the car with the keys in the ignition. "They'll be looking for a bright green hatchback with Rémy's tag number," Garland said once we'd rounded the corner, "but they're not going to find that car in Bayeux now are they?"

"I guess not," I said, though I didn't share his certainty that swapping two license plates had us out of the woods. In fact,

I was still quite certain a team of French special forces would sweep in at any moment to arrest us or shoot us or maybe both. I wasn't homesick, but I wanted to go home. I'd signed up for helping an old man find his girlfriend, not shooting at cops and blowing up cars and swapping license plates to stay one step ahead of the law.

"We need to split up," Garland said once we reached a bridge crossing the Aure, the narrow river that runs through Bayeux. "They may not be looking for us yet, but they will be soon, and when they do they'll be looking for two kids with an impossibly handsome older gentleman. You two meet me at the train station parking lot in one hour."

"You said we shouldn't take trains," I said.

"We're not taking the train, son, but if I told you my plan you'd get all upset like you do."

Just the mention of a plan that would upset me upset me, and I cursed and pulled my hair and began walking in small circles mumbling that I wanted to go home. Garland knew he was losing me, so he looked around and pulled Rémy's pistol from his coat pocket.

"What the—" I began to say, but he hushed me with a finger, wiped the fingerprints off the gun, and tossed it into the green water. "We won't be needing that anymore," Garland said, then turned to me and asked, "You feel better now, son?"

I watched the ripples on the Aure fade as Rémy's pistol sank to the bottom, then said to Garland, "I guess." I still didn't see how things would end well, but at least now we'd lowered our odds of dying in a shootout. "But if you'd got over your aversion to littering a little sooner we'd be in a lot less trouble."

"Maybe, but we'd also be under arrest," Garland said and tousled my hair. "Now you two go buy us some new clothes and I'll see you at the train station in one hour."

"What are you," Parker asked Garland, "size 6?"

"You flatter me dear. Train station. One hour. Don't be late."
Then he turned and hobbled off down the sidewalk.

"Let's go, Edwin Green," Parker said, grabbing me by the
hand and leading me alongside the Aure into town.

We walked in silence for a while, but as we passed through
the branches of a willow Parker inexplicably began singing "The
Humpty Dance."

"How are you not freaking out?" I said. "You almost shot a
policeman."

"If I had a dollar for every time I *almost* shot a policeman,"
she said.

"This isn't funny. We're in a shit-ton of trouble."

"No, Edwin Green, we're not. I may be in trouble, and Garland is definitely in trouble, but you've done nothing wrong. I
swear I would have brought Buzz Booker had I known you'd
worry so much."

"Sorry," I mumbled, and she squeezed my hand. I'd forgotten
she'd been holding it the entire time. Then she kissed me on the
cheek and said, "That's okay. Now will you try and relax and enjoy yourself a little. You're in France, you jackass." She pointed
ahead toward a small waterfall between a row of moss-covered
medieval buildings. The buildings were blanketed with pink and
white flowers, as was the waterwheel which no longer turned in
the current, and ahead in the distance were the towers of Notre
Dame Cathedral—not the one you're thinking of though—apparently every town in France has one. It was perhaps the loveli-
est place I'd ever set foot; however, I struggled to appreciate the
vista because Parker Haddaway had just kissed my cheek and
rendered the rest of the world irrelevant.

We kept walking and stumbled out onto the Rue Saint-Jean,
a narrow, bustling street full of shops and cafes and people, and
in a matter of maybe ten minutes I'd gone from wanting to go
home to wanting to stay with Parker in this French town forever.

"Come on," Parker said, "clothes," and I followed her through the crowd to a store called I.Code, but as we walked inside my phone buzzed. It was Fitz.

"I should take this," I said.

"Okay, Edwin Green, but I'm going to pick out your outfit." She spun me around and lifted my shirt to see the size of my jeans, then slapped me on the ass and walked into the store. An old French woman saw the whole thing and scowled at me like I'd said something bad about soft cheese, so I walked farther down the street to avoid her glare and answered my phone.

"It's happening," Fitz said.

"What's happening?"

"What do you think, Green? You're famous," he said. "All three of you are famous."

It took a full five seconds before I remembered why I'd actually come to France. I hadn't thought about Sadie Evans since we'd escaped from Charles de Gaulle, which, not counting sleeping hours, was by far the longest I'd gone without thinking about her since Black Saturday.

"I tweeted that video you sent me," Fitz continued, "and all the news networks picked it up, and they haven't stopped talking about you all morning. It's crazy. They're not even making us do work at school. We're just watching you guys on the news."

"That's good," I said.

"Good? Dude, this is all you've talked about for twelve months. Your YouTube videos, they all have millions of views now. Millions."

"Shit," I said.

"Yeah, shit."

I'd walked back toward the clothing store and saw Parker through the window. She held up a short red leather mini-skirt and I gave her a thumbs-up. She shot me the bird and I laughed and Fitz said, "What?"

"Nothing," I said. "So, have the networks made the Sadie Evans connection yet?"

"Not yet," he said, "but I'm sure they will soon. Want me to tweet them?"

I was still watching Parker through the window and said, "What?"

"Do you want me to tweet them, about Sadie?"

"No," I said. "Don't worry about it. I've got to—"

"Oh shit."

"What?"

"Dude?"

"What?!"

"Green, some guy on CNN just said you guys shot a cop."

Chapter Forty-Four

In which public opinion takes a nose dive.

An underling for the Ambassador of France to the United States was live on CNN when the news broke we'd shot at a French policeman and blown his car to tiny little bits. The underling, a dark-haired man in a trim-fitting suit with a knit tie, told the host that even though we'd entered the country illegally, the French government was not particularly concerned, and most, if not all of France, was rooting for us to find the woman we were looking for. Later the same underling, his name was Marcel, fought back laughter while conveying his country's universal bemusement that the embassy of the United States in Paris was somehow unable to detain two children and a ninety-year-old man. Then, while the host and the underling speculated where in France we might go next, the breaking news alarm sounded, and a reporter in Paris told CNN's viewers we'd bombed a regional police headquarters and shot and wounded at least one officer. Twenty minutes later he corrected his report, but I still meet people who insist Parker shot a French policeman. When the reporter threw it back to the host, the ambassador's underling was gone, and half an hour later the French embassy released a statement that contained words like "grave threat," "relentless pursuit," "swift apprehension," and "remorseless punishment."

Parker wasn't the least bit concerned about CNN's erroneous report. "Did we shoot a police officer?" she asked, carrying two shopping bags full of new clothes.

"No, but—"

"Then don't worry about it," she said, handing one of the bags to me. "They'll correct it, or they won't, either way it doesn't matter."

"Yeah, but I don't want people thinking we shot a cop."

"People are stupid, Edwin Green. They'll think what they want."

What worried Parker was that the news, however inaccurate, of our run-in with French authorities, had already reached the United States. We were probably now on France's most-wanted list, if they have such a thing, so we walked as fast as we could without running to the train station, and stood at the entrance to what we assumed was the parking lot for the Gare de Bayeux, but Garland was nowhere in sight. The station and the Hotel de la Gare were across the roundabout, and maybe I was being paranoid, but I said to Parker, "We look suspicious just standing here."

"Should we sit?"

"No, that would—"

"Should we dance, Edwin Green?"

Parker sang some song about never trusting a girl with a big butt and a smile while doing the Carlton and I had to beg her to stop.

"It's been an hour already, where is he?" I asked after she stopped dancing.

"For the sixth time I don't know," she said, then started singing again, "Par-ker is poison."

"Please, enough with the Boyz II Men."

"Bel Biv Devoe."

"Whatever," I said, and walked up the sidewalk to look farther down the road. When I came back Parker was still humming to herself and I said, "He's been arrested. I know it."

"He's probably eating dinner across the street," Parker said, "or maybe he found Madeleine and they're in that hotel having gross old-people sex."

"Ugh. Why would you even think about—" I began to say, when an engine revved from the back of the train station parking lot. Tires squealed, and seconds later a dark green minivan barreled toward us. We jumped out of the way and the van slid to a halt and Garland Lenox leaned out of the driver's side window grinning like an asylum escapee.

"No!" I shouted.

"What are you gonna do, son, walk to Saint-Lô? Get in, both of you, and Edwin take the wheel please. I hit three cars trying to back this thing out.

I dropped my bag in protest and said, "No. This is insane. I'm not getting inside that van."

Parker had already climbed into the passenger seat and Garland said, "Son, there's a time and a place to discuss this. The time is fifteen minutes from now, and the place is inside this damn van. Now get in ... please."

I mentioned earlier I was cautious by teenage standards, and though evidence points to the contrary, I stand by my statement. But I'm also willing to admit that perhaps I wasn't quite as cautious as I thought. Scientists believe the reason and judgment compartments of our brains aren't fully developed until we reach our midtwenties. Case in point, a few weeks before this trip I tried to throw a twelve-pound shot put over my car after track practice. It landed in the middle of the hood and left the mother of all dents. This to say teenagers, even cautious ones, make poor decisions, and mine to drive a stolen van wasn't my best.

But in my defense, being awake for something like forty hours straight had, cognitively speaking, left me with the thought process of a high-functioning Labrador. It doesn't make sense now, but I remember thinking as long as Garland didn't tell me he'd stolen the van, I wouldn't technically be driving a stolen van. Schrödinger's minivan, if you will. I cursed and climbed into the driver's seat.

"Step on it, son," Garland said. "The less time we can spend in a stolen van the better."

"Damn it," I said. "I'm not supposed to know it's stolen."

"Did you think I bought it in the parking lot?"

"It's a lovely van," Parker said while leafing through the glove compartment and fishing under the seats. "No gun in this one though."

"Good," I said. "The last thing we need is another gun. You know people visit France all the time without breaking any laws. Why'd you have to steal a car?"

"Because we needed another car," Garland said, "and people leave their cars at train stations for days at a time."

"But what if they come back tonight?"

"What if Jesus comes back tonight? Son, you worry too damn much. I watched a family park this van. They had half a dozen children and more luggage than you'd need to sail around the world. We've got time to find Maddie and get this car back to Bayeux before that family gets back from Euro Disney or wherever the hell they went. So we're just borrowing it, if you think about it."

"If I think about it I have trouble breathing. And why is there a screwdriver in the ignition. Oh God, did you hot wire it?"

"Well the owners forgot to leave us a key," the old man said.

"You've got to teach me how to do that," Parker said, pointing at the screwdriver.

"Oh it's easy," Garland said. "The night before the 1981 Daytona 500 I hot-wired Richard Petty's Buick and took it for a spin. Broke the track record for fastest lap, but it was unofficial of course." The old man must have saw me roll my eyes because he added, "I wouldn't make that shit up, son. Oh, and watch your knees. I didn't have time to tape that starter wire and it'll shock the hell out of you."

"We're going to die," I mumbled.

"We're not going to die," Garland said. "Now drive like the police are chasing us and try to relax a little."

Chapter Forty-Five

In which Parker Haddaway silences the lambs.

After twenty minutes of trying to follow Garland's instructions to drive "fast but casual," the old man made me pull over at a service station so he could piss.

"Just leave it running, son," he said, climbing out of the van.

"I wouldn't know how to turn it off if I wanted to," I replied.

It was twenty minutes after seven on what was by far the longest day of my life, and my body kept alternating between heart-pounding terror and can't-keep-my-eyes-open exhaustion, sometimes in the same minute, so I took the opportunity to re-caffeinate. When I climbed back into the van with an energy drink so potent it would be illegal back home, Parker was flipping through a French tabloid she'd found under her seat. "Hey look, Edwin Green," she said, holding the magazine for me to see, "it's your shitty ex-girlfriend."

"Yeah, she's big in France," I said.

"So is Burger King," Parker said and I laughed. "By the way, I have a new Sadie theory."

"And if I don't want to hear it?"

"I'm going to tell you anyway," she said, and then she told me. "At first I thought Sadie was, you know, a bitch."

"I believe 'bitchwhore' was your exact phrasing."

"Right, but now I don't think that is entirely accurate. Don't get me wrong, I still think she's a bitchwhore, but I'm starting to think she might also be evil, like serial-killer evil."

I sighed and Parker said, "Hear me out. You know how all these serial killers keep a collection of their victims' fingers in a shoebox in the back of their closet."

"If you say so," I said, holding up both hands to show Parker my digits were all accounted for.

"Well that's Sadie," Parker said. "Only she collects hearts. That's why she emails you once in a blue moon. She's checking her shoebox to make sure your heart is still inside. She'd let you go if she weren't afraid someone else might pick you up. Trust me, Edwin Green, if Sadie thought for one second you were interested in another girl she'd lose it. She'd probably eat someone's liver with some fava beans and a nice Chianti." Then she held up the tabloid article about Sadie and asked, "How do you say 'World's Worst Person,' in French, because I'm pretty sure that's what this caption says."

"Funny," I said.

"What's funny?" Garland asked, climbing into the back seat.

"Parker's jealous of my ex-girlfriend," I said.

"Only because she's seen Ryan Gosling naked," Parker said, and I scowled at her.

"Enough bickering," Garland growled. "Drive, son."

I pulled back onto the road and Parker leaned her head against the window while Garland laid down across the back seat, and I said, "No. No more naps. You've both slept plenty and I've had to drive all day. Someone has to talk to me if you expect me to stay awake until Saint-Lô."

"Son, fifteen years ago they had me in Delhi and I wound

up refereeing an eighty-seven-hour cricket match between India and Pakistan without even knowing the rules. I was so sleepy I dismissed Sachin Tendulkar by mistake and almost started World War III, but did I complain?"

"Okay, but—forget it," I said, and turned the radio to a French rap station. Garland lasted six seconds before he begged me to turn it off. "Fine," he said, "where was I with Madeleine?"

"In her hidden bedroom with a broken ankle," I said. "Parker, record."

"Aye, aye, captain," Parker said.

"Okay," Garland said. "So Maddie was seventeen, a member of La Résistance in Saint-Lô, and the prettiest girl I'd ever laid eyes on. On her way to school that first morning she stopped by the post office and told the leaders an unexpected visitor had dropped in the night before, and with my broken ankle they decided it was too risky to move me. She came home that night with a few extra rations and made dinner. We ate upstairs, me in bed, her at the little table with the radio, and we listened to Radio Londres, the BBC broadcast operated by the Free French across the channel in England."

"Dum dum dum dummm," Parker sang for no apparent reason.

"What?" I asked.

"That's how the show began each night," Garland said. "It sounded like Beethoven's 5th, but Maddie told me, 'It is the letter V in Morse Code. V for victory.' Then she pointed at the red V she'd painted on the wall behind my bed, right next to this ugly ass painting she said her uncle had saved from the Nazis. After the drums a man would say, *'Ici Londres! Les Français parlent aux Français!'*"

"London calling. The French talking to the French?" I asked, with about thirty-percent confidence in my translation.

"Something like that," Garland said. "The entire show was in

French, and I understood maybe two words of it. The man on the radio would deliver personal messages, and Maddie would write them down, but when I'd ask what he said she'd always shush me. Later she'd translate the messages for me but they never made much sense. Always stuff like, 'The parakeet is wearing a blue sweater.' It was all coded though, secret orders for the resistance, and the people she delivered them to in the post office knew exactly what they meant."

"We turn right here," Parker said.

"Right?"

"Yes, Edwin Green, right."

I turned right and Garland said, "The second day Maddie feigned illness and stayed home from school. A doctor friendly to the cause stopped by and put my leg in a cast, but he couldn't bring crutches 'cause it would have looked suspicious, so I had to hobble around on a broom best I could. The Resistance sent word back to England that I was alive, which came as some shock to the Army since they'd already listed me as killed in action. Word came back that I was to stay put. Plan was, when the army rolled into Saint-Lô, I'd just roll out with them. But that was a terrible plan."

"Why?" I asked.

"Because after a week I was crazy in love and sure as hell didn't want to fight anymore."

"You were in love after one week?"

Garland smiled. "Hell son, I don't expect you to understand, but Maddie, she was ..." The old man went quiet for a moment, then said, "The thing is, when you meet the one, the one you've dreamed about and hoped and prayed actually existed somewhere out there in the world, when you meet her, you know it. You know it in an instant. You don't even fall in love with her, because you were in love with her before time. Before either of you even existed. When you meet her you'll know it because you feel whole, for the first time, and it's the best damn feeling in the world."

"Hold up," Parker said, "you told me you fell in love with Madeleine because she had, and I quote, 'A great pair of gams.'"

Garland laughed until he started coughing, then said, "I don't recall saying that," then he turned to me and added, "but son you should have seen her legs."

I laughed and Parker stuck her tongue out at Garland and the old man sighed and said, "Those six weeks together, before the invasion, they were just about perfect. Maddie would come home in the afternoon and cook dinner and we'd sit upstairs on the bed, listening to the BBC, and when Radio Londres went off we'd just sit and talk. Maddie wanted to know everything about America, but all I knew was life in the Appalachian Mountains with a family of Doomsday preppers. So I told her about our training, and my train trip to New York, and our little boat ride across the Atlantic. Then I made up a bunch of shit, and I think she knew I was lying, but I kept it entertaining enough she didn't care. When we'd run out of things to say we'd just lie there, and she'd run her fingers through my hair and sing. Her voice, it was so beautiful, and she'd sing these French songs I'd never heard. So many nights I fell asleep to the sound of my angel singing. That's why I didn't want the army in Saint-Lô. Maddie and I, we were just two kids playing house, and I didn't want it to end."

"How old was Maddie when the Germans came?" I asked.

"Twelve or thirteen," Garland said. "She remembered life before them, but by then it had been so long she said she'd forgotten what it was like to walk down the street and not see Nazis. Maddie used to get so angry when she'd talk about the people in town who thought the Germans had been more than fair. She curled up next to me on the bed one night and said, 'People say we still have our movies and our fairs and our schools, so life isn't too bad. But we've lost all freedom. These people say mind your business and live your life and listen to the Germans and when the war is over things will be back to normal. But these people, they only say these things out of fear. They are scared, too scared to fight, so they cower and capitulate, and they do not even realize all they have lost."

"Keep straight here," Parker said, interrupting the story.

"Wait, are you sure?"

"Positive," she said, "now finish your story, Garland. I believe you were about to attempt to convince Edwin Green that Madeleine kissed you first."

"She did kiss me first," he said, laughing from the back seat.

"A likely story," Parker said.

"Son, I swear," Garland said. "It was that same night, up in my room. She began talking about how the Allies would be in Saint-Lô soon, and how she couldn't wait to see American bombers flying low over her city, and American tanks rolling through the streets. 'Soon,' she said, pointing toward the window. 'This will all be over soon.'

"And I said, 'You know what, I wish they'd take their time,' and after I'd said it she turned on me like a circus lion going after its trainer.

"She jumped up from the bed and said, 'How can you wish this? What gives you the right to wish this? Have you lived with these animals for four years? Have you watched them line up men and shoot them in the street? Have you gone to bed every night wondering if tomorrow is the day they will shoot you too, or send you to a labor camp? No, you have not. You have been here two weeks, and you are not entitled to wish for anything but liberation.'"

"Smooth," I said, and Garland told me to shut up.

"I told her I was sorry," he said, "and I tried to explain when the Americans rolled into town they'd toss me in the back of a Jeep and take me far away from her. Her face softened and she sat down next to me and put one hand on my cheek and said, 'When this is over, when the Germans are no longer in France, we can do whatever we want. You will come back to me, or I will come to you. This with you is nice, but it is only a half-life. When we are free our lives will be whole again. We will have to be apart, but when we are back together it will have been worth it. You will see.' Then she leaned in and kissed me. It was my first kiss."

"Wait, that was your first kiss?" Parker interrupted. "You were like twenty-five."

"I was nineteen and I'd been living in the woods since I was twelve," Garland growled. "Like I said, she kissed me and said, 'When the Nazis are gone Saint-Lô will still be here, and I will still be in Saint-Lô waiting for you.' Then I kissed her, and kissed her again, and, well, you can use your imagination from there."

"Gross," Parker said, "I'd rather not."

"Wait," I said, "this isn't right. That's the ocean. Parker, where the hell are we?"

"Brief detour," she said.

Chapter Forty-Six

In which Parker Haddaway performs a good deed.

Even by quaint French village standards, the seaside village we found ourselves in was ridiculously quaint and French, except for one strange detail—I was quite certain I'd just seen an American flag flying on someone's front porch. We drove through town until a few hundred yards before the sea a roundabout split the road making way for a long strip of grass that ran toward an imposing monument perched above the beach. More flags flew on either side of the monument—American, Canadian, British, and others. "Where are we?" I asked, parking the van alongside the road.

"Omaha Beach," Garland said, and he opened his door and stepped out of the van.

Parker and I followed him but kept our distance as he stood in front of the massive concrete monument. The script at the top was in French, and below the English translation read, "The allied forces landing on this shore which they call Omaha Beach liberate Europe - June 6th 1944." Behind, on the beach, the high tide had almost reached another monument, this one a sculpture resembling enormous shards of metal stuck in the sand.

Parker whispered for me to wait where I was and she walked over to Garland and grabbed his hand. She said something to him I didn't catch, and he put his arm around her, and the two of them stood there for another minute or two before turning around and walking past me to the van.

"One more stop," Parker said when I climbed in the van, which we'd left running because we didn't have a key. This time Parker gave perfect turn by turn directions, and minutes later we arrived at the very locked gates of the Normandy American Cemetery.

I parked the van next to a no parking sign and said, "It's closed."

"To the public," Parker replied.

"Yeah, that's us. We're the public."

"Speak for yourself, Edwin Green." And she and Garland got out of the van and had already crawled under the gate by the time I set the parking brake and followed them. We walked through an empty parking lot and across a brick road before passing through some trees into the cemetery. The graves, marked with simple white crosses or the occasional Star of David, stretched out in perfect lines as far as I could see. We followed behind Garland as he walked through the cemetery, and stopped when he knelt to examine one of the crosses.

"Did you know him?" I asked, after he got to his feet.

"I never met this man," he said, "but in a way I suppose we all knew each other." He pointed to the date on the marker and said, "He died on D-Day. A lot of them did." Then I realized where I'd seen this cemetery before, and I asked Garland, "Have you ever seen *Saving Private Ryan*?"

Garland looked at me and said, "Son, would you want to watch a movie about all your friends dying starring Forrest Gump?"

"I guess not," I said.

"Well me either," he replied with a wink, and continued his walk through the field of crosses.

We followed him until he stopped under a gnarled oak tree and the three of us looked out on the cemetery. The sun was setting behind us, and beyond the cliffs a man with a dog was walking along Omaha Beach. I began reading the dates on the surrounding crosses and a lump rose in my throat when I realized many of the soldiers buried there were only a year or two older than me.

"I've always felt so much guilt about the war," Garland said, looking straight ahead. "All these men, my brothers, here on this hellish beach getting blown to bits, and where was I? Holed up in bed with a beautiful French girl."

I began to protest but Parker put her hand on my shoulder and I stopped. Garland kept talking. "The night before the invasion we were lying in my bed listening to the BBC and the man read a poem with a line about 'monotonous languor.' Maddie jumped off the bed and turned the radio up louder than she'd ever dared before. She kept repeating phrases that made no sense to me. John has a long mustache. The Cotentin is a peninsula. The sirens have bleached hair. The dice are thrown. 'Tonight,' Maddie said when the broadcast was over. 'The Allies land tonight.' Soon we could hear the big guns down on the coast. Huge, Earth-shaking roars that rattled the windows to our room even though the beaches were twenty-five miles away. There was lots of noise in the streets too, not just Germans, but French people too, ignoring the curfew. Planes would buzz the town, and if the German antiaircraft guns lit up the sky with orange tracers, we knew it was the Allies. We sat up all night and dreamed about our lives after the Germans were gone and the war was over. Where we'd live. What we'd do. I wanted to stay in Saint-Lô. She wanted to come back with me to the States."

A bird landed on one of the crosses in front of us and we watched it until it flew away. "The next morning it felt like the whole town was out in the streets," Garland said, "and like a couple of idiots we joined them."

"Wait," I said, "You went outside? Where all the Germans were?"

"Maddie gave me some of her father's clothes and his old hat," Garland said. "It was stupid, but we were young and in love and, no offense, teenagers do stupid things sometimes."

"Like breaking old geezers out of their nursing homes and taking them to France," Parker said.

"Exactly," Garland said and smiled. "Anyway, people were everywhere. Not celebrating, but smiling, and exchanging knowing looks. 'So it is true?' Maddie asked a woman she knew. 'Yes, the Allies landed last night,' the woman whispered. 'They will be here by nightfall.' Maddie squeezed my hand with excitement just as a truck full of Nazi soldiers drove past and ordered everyone to stay indoors until further notice. I fought the urge to give them the finger and stared down at my borrowed shoes instead."

"That's incredible," I said.

"But I should have been flying that day, son," Garland said. "I should have been doing my part. If I had been some of these boys might still be alive, not in this damn cemetery."

"Dear Miss Haddaway," Parker said, and Garland and I both turned toward her. She held a handwritten letter, and continued to read, "I cannot begin to thank you enough for taking the time to write. My father didn't talk about the war much, and us kids knew not to pry, but we all knew the name Garland Lenox. The story of Mr. Lenox's heroic actions during the early hours of April 24th, 1944 was the only war story my father ever told, and he told it because he believed, if not for Mr. Lenox, he would have died that night. But he also told us the story of Garland Lenox to help us understand how the actions of one person can ripple through generations. I won't bore you with the details of mine or my siblings' life stories, but I speak for us all when I say because of Garland Lenox we've lived our lives mindful of the exponential effect our good and brave deeds have on others. After the war my father returned to Kansas, married my mother, and ran a sporting goods store in Salina for forty-five years. He had six children, twenty-two grandchildren, and I've enclosed a photograph of us all at Papa's 84th birthday party in 2010. He died six months later. Miss Haddaway, thank you again for reaching out, and promise me you will give Mr. Lenox the biggest hug from me. Sincerely, Martha Alsobrook Moore, Oldest daughter of Captain Pete Alsobrook, United States Army Air Force, 1941–1946.'"

Parker handed Garland the photograph and while he looked at it she said, "You weren't flying on D-Day because on April 24th, 1944, your plane was heavily damaged by a German Focke-Wulf 190. Still, you could have flown back across the English Channel to safety, but you didn't. You knew the B-17 you were escorting wouldn't stand a chance against the quicker German plane, so you doubled back and engaged him, and soon he was on your tail. But just before that Wulf blew you out of the sky, you rolled your heavily damaged plane, dropped from the open canopy, and took out the pilot by sending seven rounds from your .45 through his windshield."

Garland started to speak but Parker kept going, "I don't know everything about you Lieutenant Lenox, but I know you were awarded the Distinguished Flying Cross, and the Silver Star, and the Purple Heart. I know you won enough aerial victories during Big Week alone to qualify as a flying ace twice over. And I know if not for you there would be ten more crosses in this cemetery. But you saved every man in that B-17, and they went on to fly on D-Day, and then they all went home and lived long, happy lives." Parker handed Garland a stack of photographs and letters and said, "I tracked them down. Every crew member from the Savannah Smile. Three are still alive, the rest of the letters are from their children. Children who grew up knowing that if not for the actions of a man named Garland Lenox, their fathers would not have lived through the war."

Parker and I watched Garland read the notes and softly weep, and when he'd finished Parker said, "Garland Lenox, you are the bravest man I know." The old man hugged her, and though I couldn't hear what he said in her ear, he must have thanked her because after a moment Parker said, "Alright you're welcome, that's enough hugging and crying. Let's get back to that stolen van before we get into trouble."

Parker walked between us through the darkening cemetery, holding both our hands, and once we were back in the van I said to Garland, "I can't believe you shot down a plane with a freaking pistol. That's some real Chuck Norris shit."

"I guess," the old man said in a sudden burst of modesty.

"Seriously, how are you not famous?"

"Son, it wasn't a big deal," Garland said. "Joe Baggio had already cracked the Wulf's windshield for me, and besides, a fella named Baggett did the same thing in the Pacific."

"Oh, well if it's happened twice I guess it isn't that impressive after all," Parker teased.

"You hush," the old man said to Parker, then to me, "and you drive."

I'd recorded the entire cemetery scene on my phone but didn't share the video until much later because it wouldn't have taken folks long to figure out where we were. But as of this morning the video has 842,516,985 views, making it the 50th most-viewed video in YouTube history, placing First Lieutenant Garland Lenox between Rihanna and a finger-biting British baby, right where he belongs.

Chapter Forty-Seven

In which there's plenty of room at the Hotel Vue de la Rivière.

We arrived in Saint-Lô at a quarter past ten on a day that felt like it began six weeks ago, entering the town from roughly the same direction as the 29th Infantry Division did in 1944, though encountering considerably less German artillery. After listening to Garland's stories a part of me expected Saint-Lô to exist in a time warp—that we'd find the city unchanged from the night the old man crawled out of the river seven decades earlier—but that was not the case. Saint-Lô stood apart from everything we'd seen in France, and not necessarily in a good way. On our drive toward the city center we passed a number of concrete buildings that somehow looked both futuristic and dated, like props from a 1950s sci-fi film, and I wondered aloud why every other French town looked ancient, and this one looked like it just sprung up after the war.

"Most of it did," Garland said.

"Well what was here before the war?" I asked.

"The same beautiful little town that had been here for a thousand years," Garland said.

"I don't understand," I said. "What happened to Saint-Lô?"

"The Allies liberated it, son. They liberated it by bombing it right off the damn map."

"Wait, while you and Maddie were still here?"

"Yep."

"Shit."

"Yep."

No one said much after that. Garland and Parker peered out their windows while I drove somewhat aimlessly through town. It was late, but a few people still sat outside a café on Rue Torteron. We passed the remains of the old city walls and drove over the Vire, the bridge adorned with flags of countries that helped liberate France. Circling back across the river into town and stopping on a side street I said, "Okay, any idea where Madeleine might live?"

Garland laughed and said, "Son, as much as Maddie would appreciate the irony of me banging on her door in the middle of the night again, I think it best our reunion wait until morning." Then he pointed across the street at the sign for the Hotel Vue de la Rivière and said, "I'll be staying there tonight."

"Wait, do we have reservations?" I asked

"I have several," Garland said and Parker laughed.

"No, I meant—"

"Son, I know what you meant," Garland said, slapping me on the back. "And no, I don't have a reservation to stay at the Hotel Vue de la Rivière, but I'm guessing I won't need one. If a hotel has "river view" in its name but doesn't actually offer a view of the river, you can usually count on a vacancy. You two won't need reservations either, because you're staying somewhere else."

"Where?" I asked.

"Hell if I know," Garland growled, "but it can't be here. They're looking for us now. Really looking for us. So the three of us can't just waltz into some hotel together and ask for a room. The receptionist would say, '*Bonjour*, I just saw the three of you on the six o'clock news, please have a seat while I phone the police.'"

Parker had pulled up the Hotel Vue de la Rivière on my phone and said, "Good news Garland, you picked the sixth ranked hotel in Saint-Lô."

"Out of how many?" Garland asked.

"Eight."

Garland laughed and said, "Doesn't matter. There's a restaurant right there under the hotel. I'm going to have dinner and go the hell to bed. You two have your choice of the five nicest hotels in town, or the two worst I suppose. Tell 'em it's your honeymoon. They might even give you a bottle of champagne." He got out of the van and leaned back in Parker's open window and said, "Just make sure you're back here at eight tomorrow morning. We've got a busy day ahead. Au revoir kiddos."

Chapter Forty-Eight

In which a Saint-Lô Creperie receives free advertising

I've been too hungry to sleep, and I've been too sleepy to eat, but until that night in Saint-Lô I'd never been both at the same time. Parker, who'd slept on the plane and somehow napped on and off throughout the day, said she was starving, so now we were sitting at a table outside Le Caryopse, a creperie near the banks of the same river Garland floated down more than half a century ago. Our waiter brought our drinks and took our order and I sipped my Coke hoping it would wake me up long enough to eat but not a minute longer.

"Where are we going to stay tonight?" I asked and Parker grabbed my phone off the table and said she'd find a place. While she searched, a city bus crossed the bridge and let out its solitary passenger. As it drove away I said to Parker, "So do you really believe Garland shot down a German plane with his pistol?"

"I can believe anything," Parker said without looking up, "so long as it's incredible."

"No wonder he likes you so much," I said, but she pretended not to hear me. A minute later she asked, "Did you consider shooting down a German plane in your quest for fame?"

"I think we're allies with Germany now," I said. "Besides, fighting in wars doesn't make people famous anymore."

"God, I wish," Parker said.

I watched a stray cat scamper past us before darting down the alley toward the promise of food scraps, then I looked back at Parker. She was biting her bottom lip while scrolling through hotels on my phone and I think I would have stared at her for hours had she not glanced up and noticed me.

"What?" she asked.

"I don't know," I said. "It's weird. I still don't really know anything about you."

Parker put down my phone and said, "You know plenty about me. You know I drink my coffee black. You know of my long running beef with the Olsen Twins. You know I'm not a slave to Pope Gregory XIII's shitty-ass calendar."

I laughed and said, "Okay, I know more about you than I did on Monday. But just like surface stuff."

"Those who go beneath the surface do so at their own peril, Edwin Green."

I was trying to think of a response to that when my phone buzzed and Parker handed it to me. "Someone named Fitz," she said, joking, I think.

"Green," Fitz began, "the FBI or CIA or somebody just left school and they asked everyone about you and Parker, like were you friends or dating or whatever, and everyone was like, 'No, Parker doesn't even talk to people.' But when they checked the school's security cameras, they saw the two of you kissing in the hall."

"I'm sorry, what?"

"You. Parker Haddaway. Security Camera. Green, why the hell didn't you tell me you and Parker Haddaway made out in the hall?"

"I wasn't entirely sure it happened," I said.

"Whatever, I'm still kicking your ass when you get home."

"Fair enough."

"So anyway, the CIA or whoever must have leaked the video, because CNN played it an hour ago, and now that old man's lawyer is back on television saying you two had a secret relationship, and you're some sort of modern-day Bonnie and Clyde."

"No we're not."

"Well, you did shoot at a cop."

"Accidentally."

"And you blew up his car."

"Okay, it's not a terrible comparison."

"Anyway," Fitz said, "you'll probably want to pull up CNN. They're about to interview Sadie Evans."

"I don't really care to listen to her talk about her new album again," I said.

"No Green," Fitz said, "they're interviewing her about you."

Chapter Forty-Nine

In which our hero eats a crepe and recounts his blackest Saturday.

Parker was staring across the roundabout at the tall tower atop Saint-Lô's ancient city walls when I said, "So, do you happen to remember kissing me in the hall at school on Monday?"

"I kiss so many boys in the hall," she said, "but now that you mention it, yes, I do seem to recall that particular kiss."

"Right, well, the school's security camera caught us, and CNN somehow has the footage, and now the networks think we're some sort of modern-day Bonnie and Clyde."

"Oh fun, I wonder who they'll get to play us in the movie? Faye Dunaway is probably a little old for me," Parker said, not particularly concerned the media now appeared to be rooting for us to die in a rather violent shootout.

"Oh, and CNN is about to interview Sadie … about me."

"And you want to watch it?"

"Sort of."

"Well turn it on," Parker said, so I launched the CNN app and propped my phone against the salt shaker so we could both see it. When the fifteen-second advertisement for an allergy medicine ended, Sadie Evans's photograph appeared on screen above the words, "ALERT: Mega-star childhood friend of French fugitive."

"Childhood friend? Bullshit. She was my girlfriend, CNN."

"They once reported a boy was flying over the desert trapped inside a balloon," Parker said. "Don't take it personally."

Sadie appeared via telephone from her Hollywood home, and there was an awkward lag between the host's questions and her answers. "Thank you for taking the time to be with us, Sadie," the host said. "A lot of people don't know this, but you and Edwin Green were childhood friends."

"We were," Sadie said. "Edwin was my first boyfriend back in Alabama."

My stomach clinched when Sadie said my name, and Parker said, "That's not a flattering photograph. She's got to be more careful with the Russian Botox."

"That's right," the host said. "Edwin Green was there the night America discovered you, right here in Atlanta, on the Braves' Kiss Cam."

"I wasn't with her, I was kissing her," I yelled at my phone.

"The what?" Parker asked.

"This Kiss Cam," I said pausing Sadie's interview, "at the Braves game. You seriously don't know any of this?"

Parker rolled her eyes and said, "No, Edwin Green, I do not. I've never had much interest in Sadie Evans's origin story."

Scholars differ on when exactly the Kiss Cam came to be, but most agree it happened in Los Angeles, at a Dodgers game. Looking for something to entertain fans between innings, the Dodgers began showing couples on their video screen. Two unsuspecting baseball fans would find their heads superimposed inside a large heart, and they would either kiss to loud cheers, or not kiss to loud boos—I always thought it was weird fans booed couples who didn't kiss. What if they were brother and sister, or mother and son? All this to say the Kiss Cam is everywhere now, and teams even hire actors to stage elaborate break up fights on camera. It's stupid, but people are stupid, so I guess it works.

I finished explaining the Kiss Cam just as the waiter arrived with our crepes, ham and cheese for me, strawberry, banana, and all the powdered sugar the chef could find for Parker. She took a bite of her crepe and said, "So people go to baseball games hoping to see brothers and sisters kiss? That explains a lot."

"Sort of," I said, unpausing the video. The allergy medicine advertisement played again. "That's how Sadie was discovered," I said, "at a Braves game. They were playing the Nationals, and it was Faith and Family Night, so Sadie's dad loaded up the Hornby Christian Fellowship youth group into the church van and drove us to Atlanta. There were twenty of us sitting together in the half empty upper deck. Sadie and I were a couple rows in front of everyone else, and—wait, they're showing it now, just watch."

Parker picked up my phone and I didn't protest, I'd seen the video so many times I could replay it in my mind whenever I wanted. It was the middle of the fifth inning, and fans were cheering and booing the couples kissing and not kissing, when Sadie and I found ourselves staring at ourselves on the centerfield Jumbotron. I mouthed the words, "Oh shit," and the stadium erupted in laughter because everyone could read my lips. Sadie grabbed my arm, and we exchanged panicked looks before both turning to look at her father, who gave the impression he could turn green and burst out of his clothes Incredible Hulk-style at any moment. I covered my mouth and whispered something to Sadie. It's impossible to tell on the video, but I was telling her if we just waited a moment they'd move on to the next couple and it would all be over. I never finish telling her this though, because she grabbed my face and kissed me to thunderous applause.

Parker leaned my phone back against the salt shaker and said, "So you're telling me Sadie Evans is famous because a bunch of baseball fans thought she kissed her brother?"

I laughed and said, "No, she's famous because she won America's Next Celebrity."

"I still can't believe that's a television show," Parker said, "and people actually watch it."

"Well, they do," I said, and stopped to watch the CNN host ask Sadie about the rumor she'd been cast to play Scarlett O'Hara in Quentin Tarantino's remake of *Gone with the Wind*. Sadie wouldn't confirm or deny the rumor, but said she'd always admired the director's work, which was a lie because I knew for a fact the sight of blood, real or fake, made her sick.

"Okay," Parker said, "I'm still missing something here. So if you kiss someone on the Kiss Cam you get to be on America's Next Celebrity?"

"No. It was our particular kiss that … okay … so I closed my eyes when we kissed, because that's how you kiss, right?"

"Unless you don't have eyelids," Parker said. "Like a shark. Or a snake."

"Right, well you'll love this part then. Sadie didn't close her eyes. She watched herself kissing me on the Jumbotron, and Sadie has these eyes that, well, let's just say Buzzfeed ranked our video 87th on their 100 Sexiest Videos of All Time."

"Buzzfeed must have a crazy strict internet filter if they think that's the 87th sexiest video on the internet," Parker said.

"Yeah, well after watching that kiss, men all around Turner Field had very inappropriate conversations about a sixteen-year-old girl, and one of those men, Paul Dupree, was an agent with Universal Talent Conglomerate. He was in a luxury box with his sleazy Hollywood friends, and after he saw Sadie on the Jumbotron he borrowed a pair of binoculars and found us in the upper deck. Ten minutes later he was sitting next to Sadie, whispering promises of fame in her ear."

"Merci," Parker said to the waiter as he refilled her coffee. She took a sip and said, "So her fame is a total fluke? I always assumed it was because she could sing or something."

I unpaused the video and the allergy medicine commercial played once again before the CNN host asked Sadie about her new album set to drop next month, and while Sadie launched into a rehearsed soliloquy full of music industry buzzwords, including the phrase, "It's grungy soul, think Adele meets Nirvana," I rolled my eyes and said to Parker, "No. Her dad used to make her sing solos in church, but they were awful. Auto-Tune is her friend."

Parker laughed and said, "That's the first bad thing I've ever heard you say about Sadie Evans." I shrugged and she asked, "So this Paul guy swooped in and took her away to Hollywood?"

"Sort of," I said. "I didn't hear much of what he said. Just caught a few words like "beautiful young lady," "rich," "famous." Sadie's dad came down to find out why a grown man was talking to his daughter, and after a handshake the three of them went back to Paul's luxury box. They didn't return until the 9th inning, and when they did Sadie's dad made us leave. We didn't even stay for the Christian concert and firework show."

"Christian fireworks are the worst anyway," Parker said, and waved for our waiter and asked for the bill. After he left she pulled a wad of euro notes from her pocket and I said, "On the drive back to Hornby she told me Paul was a talent scout, and that she was going to Hollywood."

"Have you tried to contact Edwin Green?" the CNN host asked Sadie, and Parker and I both stopped to look at my phone. There was a longer than normal pause on the other end of the line, then Sadie said, "No. Edwin and I haven't spoken in a long time."

"The minute she told me she was going to Hollywood I knew we were through," I said. "She didn't say we were breaking up, but I knew. On the drive home she sat up front with her dad, and the two of them dreamed and conspired, while I sat in the back seat and—"

I was going to say cried, but stopped when the CNN host said, "Alright Sadie, now before you leave, we have to get your reaction to that bombshell video we aired earlier this hour."

Parker and I watched the video of our kiss in the hallway, and just as Sadie was about to respond the battery in my phone died.

"Shit," Parker said. "That was the first time I was ever actually interested in something she had to say. So you haven't seen her since she left Hornby?"

"Nope," I said. "She called once her first week in Hollywood, and again after the first episode of *America's Next Celebrity*, then a few days later I got the text from her dad. Two days later, on the second episode, that Seacrest look-alike who hosts the show said, 'So Sadie, I hear you're single again,' and Sadie was like, 'Yes I am,' all flirty and shit, and the studio audience actually cheered, and I may have thrown my television across the room."

Parker laughed and I said, "Are you a psychopath? When someone tells you their most painful story, you don't laugh."

"I'm not laughing at your pain, Edwin Green," Parker said, and she pointed at the television screen inside the restaurant which was currently showing security camera footage of the two of us kissing in the J. P. Hornby hallway. "I just think it's funny every time someone kisses you they become famous," then she leaned over and kissed me again.

"Now come on," she said, dropping a couple pink ten euro notes on her powdered sugar-covered plate, "let's go find a hotel room."

Chapter Fifty

In which Parker Haddaway questions our hero's personal hygiene.

"This can't be the right way."

Even with Google Maps we'd spent half the day lost, but now Parker was spouting out directions based on instinct I guess, and I feared we were more likely to end up in Italy than find our hotel. She had, using lessons Garland taught her on the drive from the cemetery to Saint-Lô, managed to crank the van, but she also had us on a dark and winding road that, had this been a horror film, would have led straight to a chainsaw wielding maniac. Under normal circumstances I suppose I would have turned around; however, when a girl kisses you and says, "Let's go find a hotel room," the circumstances are anything but normal.

"Yes, Edwin Green, it is. Turn left here."

"If you say so, Magellan, but I seem to recall spending most of the day—"

Before I could say "lost" I realized the road we were now on was in fact a long ribbon driveway leading through two ancient lion-topped stone columns to a moonlit sixteenth-century French manor.

"Oh. Wow," I said.

"You're welcome," Parker said.

"Wait, we can't stay here. That's a castle. You can't just spend the night in a castle."

"We can do whatever we want," Parker said, and I parked the van and together we walked into the Manoir de Litteau. The dark lobby smelled of pipe smoke and coffee, and we stood in the entrance, not knowing where to go, until a woman behind a desk in the corner of the room greeted us in French. We walked over, both of us wearing backpacks and at least one of us feeling out of place. "*Bonjour*," I said, and Parker began whispering, "Tell her we'd like the suite."

"I don't know the French word for suite," I whispered back, then tried to ask the woman about a room for the evening.

"Tell her it's our honeymoon and we intend to have all manner of sex in their nicest room," Parker whispered, and this time I shushed her.

The woman clicked on her keyboard and said in perfect English, "I believe Mademoiselle would like the honeymoon suite for the evening, yes?"

"Yes," I said, and turned to see Parker Haddaway blush for perhaps the first time ever.

The woman introduced herself as Valerie, the manor's owner, and she told us the top floor suite was available for the night. "I will need to see a passport please," Valerie said, and I reached for my passport but froze because if I showed this woman my passport our wakeup call would almost certainly involve machine-gun toting French Commandos. My mind raced through our options and running back out the door appeared to be the best one, but as I turned to Parker I saw her hand Valerie a red passport I'd never seen before. When Valerie walked into the next room to make copies I turned and whispered, "What the hell was that?"

"One of my other passports," she said.

"Why do you have other passports?"

"For such a time as this, Edwin Green."

By now my eyes had adjusted to the dark lobby and I could see a man and woman sitting in the far corner of the room near an unlit fireplace, the woman sipping a glass of something, the man holding the pipe I smelled upon entering.

"Okay," I said, turning my attention back to Parker, "but how do you have other passports?"

"Wouldn't you rather not know?"

I conceded I wouldn't with a shrug, and a moment later Valerie returned with Parker's other passport.

"My husband will assist you with your bags shortly," Valerie said, after Parker paid her in cash. I pointed toward my back and said, "We can carry them."

"Of course monsieur," she said, and showed us to the staircase that led to our suite on the manor's top floor.

The door to our room looked older than the United States, and it opened with the turn of the medieval key Valerie had entrusted us with. I stepped inside and gawked. The suite was all ceiling beams and ancient hardwoods and antique furniture. The canopy bed itself belonged in the Louvre, and it was larger than my entire bedroom back home.

Parker followed me in, set her bag on the breakfast table, pointed at the bed and said, "What's up with the rose petals?"

Pink and white rose petals were strewn across the duvet and I said, "You told her it was our honeymoon, and we intended to have all manner of sex in their nicest room."

She laughed and said, "Oh right," then walked over to open the large window looking out on the manor grounds. I could hear frogs croaking in the distance, and after a moment Parker turned to me and said, "You can have the first shower."

"I shower in the morning," I said, and she made a face.

"What?"

"Nothing," she said, and shook her head in mock disappointment.

"What? Don't you like to start your day with a shower?" I asked.

"I start my day with coffee," Parker said, "and I end my day by washing off hours' worth of dirt and grime so to not wallow in my own filth all night."

"Whatever, I'll sleep on the couch," I said, immediately regretting it.

"You will not sleep on the couch," Parker said. "That's the largest bed in Europe. It was probably Andre the Giant's. If you stay on your side your filth won't rub off on me."

"I wasn't worried about my filth rubbing off on you."

"Oh, were you worried I wouldn't stay on my side," she said with a wink. She was joking, but my knees buckled nonetheless.

"That's not what I—"

"Go to bed, Edwin Green," she said, and picked up her bag and went into the bathroom. I changed into some track shorts and a J.P. Hornby T-shirt and put on some deodorant out of guilt, then I laid down and would have passed out except for the fact that (1) a girl was showering less than twenty feet from me, and she'd left the door cracked enough that I couldn't see anything inside, but couldn't look away either and (2) that same girl, who was obviously messing with me by leaving the door cracked open, would soon crawl into bed with me, at which point (3) nothing would probably happen, but *anything* could happen. Twenty minutes later Parker came out wearing a T-shirt so long I wasn't sure if she was wearing anything underneath. And though there was enough room for the entire Dallas Cowboy offensive line to sleep on my left side, she crawled in on my right, curled right up next to me, kissed me on the cheek, and promptly fell asleep. I, on the other hand, was wide awake for the next two hours because, well, because I was in a French castle, curled up next to Parker Haddaway in bed, and every sixty seconds or so I had to remind myself to breathe.

Much later, after I finally passed out asleep, Parker snapped a selfie of us in bed and posted it to my Instagram with the caption, "Catch us if you can. #Bonnie&Clyde."

Chapter Fifty-One

In which our hero suffers for fashion.

"*Bonjour monsieur,* this is your wake up call."

I don't recall exactly what I said to Valerie when she called to wake us up at seven the next morning, but it was likely (1) an incoherent slur of mumbling, cursing, and apologizing, preceded by (2) the crashing of the lamp I knocked off the nightstand when her call jolted me from a most pleasant dream about spending the night in a French castle with Parker Haddaway, which was followed immediately by (3) a moment of confused and silent awe when I looked down and realized—oh shit, that wasn't a dream.

Parker was still asleep next to me, her face aglow in the golden sunshine streaming through the open window. I thought about kissing her good morning—I should have kissed her good morning—but instead I said, "Wakey, wakey," then cringed because I said, "Wakey, wakey." She pulled a pillow over her head and extended a middle finger in my direction. "We've got to leave in thirty minutes," I said. "I'm taking a shower."

"Don't. Care." Parker said.

I smiled and said, "Aww. That's the first thing you ever said to me," but she didn't stir, so I grabbed my bag and stumbled to the bathroom. My phone was charging by the sink because after years of tourists complaining, the Manoir de Litteau had installed American power sockets in their bathrooms, while the rest of the sockets remained European and useless. I unplugged it and saw a confusing text message.

FITZ: Dude! I need details!

I replied.

ME: What?

He didn't reply—it was midnight back home—so I climbed in the shower and stood there half asleep until the hot water ran out. There was still no reply from Fitz when I got out, so I started to dress in the clothes Parker bought for me in Bayeux, but after pulling up my pants yelled, "Parker, what the hell?" I stumbled out of the bathroom, found her sitting at the breakfast table sipping a cappuccino, and forgot what I was going to say. She wore a soft and swaying green dress she must have bought the day before, and she'd braided her auburn hair in a crown with a few strands falling on her cheeks, and when she smiled at me I thought I might as well go blind because nothing I'd see for the rest of my life would ever compare.

"Valerie cooked a breakfast with no hog," she said, pointing at some croissants on the table. "I even ordered you a Coke since you're a weirdo who won't drink coffee."

"I think …," I began to say, but found it was impossible to look at her and form a coherent thought.

"You think what, Edwin Green?" she asked, and I snapped out of it.

"I think I will never, under any circumstances, let you buy my clothes again," I said, and motioned toward my pants. Well, my half pants. She'd bought me a pair of houndstooth capris and a denim button down shirt so tight I couldn't legally wear it in Alabama.

"You look great," Parker said, fighting back laughter.

"It would help if you could say that with a straight face."

"The woman in the store yesterday told me that's the newest look from Milan. Besides, you heard Garland, we looked too American. No one will suspect you're from Hornby now."

I turned to look at myself in the bathroom mirror again and said, "Maybe not, but why do I have to look like I lost a bet, and you get to look ..." I wanted to say amazing. I should have said amazing. Why the hell did I not say amazing?

"I look what?" Parker asked.

"Normal," I said, and she stood up and smoothed her dress with her hands. "Edwin Green, please tell me I look better than just normal." Then she twirled and her dress rose high enough to take a year off my life.

"I ... that's not ... yes, sorry, you look very nice," I conceded rather ineloquently, and Parker said, "A girl shouldn't have to beg for compliments, Edwin Green."

"No, seriously, you look—"

"Nope. Too late," she said, and tossed me my backpack. "Let's go."

The streets of Saint-Lô were quiet as we parked outside Garland's hotel. The old man sat waiting by a window in the lobby and walked outside to meet us.

"Good morning men," Garland said as we stepped out of the van.

"It's freezing," I said, through chattering teeth.

Garland looked me over and said, "Hell, son, no wonder. Are those long shorts or short pants?"

"Everyone in Milan dresses like this," I said.

"Oh, I've no doubt," Garland said.

"Ask her," I said, "she bought them."

Garland turned to Parker and said, "My dear you look lovely this morning."

Parker curtsied and returned the compliment. Garland wore a dark tweed suit with a tam cap, and I was more than a little annoyed I had to be the only one dressed like the lead singer of a Slovakian electronica band, but I let it go.

"Alright kids," Garland said, "let's find my Maddie."

Chapter Fifty-Two

In which strangers are accosted in the Capital of Ruins.

"*Excusez-moi, savez-vous Madeleine Moreau?*"

A man in a dark suit slowed down long enough to shake his head and say, "*Non,*" before hurrying along to the bank or wherever he worked. This was disappointing, but a marked improvement over the first four people I'd asked that morning, three of whom avoided eye contact and kept walking, while the fourth, a woman opening her shop on Rue Havin, flashed a canister of pepper spray and stared us down while we slowly backed away.

Asking random strangers on the streets of Saint-Lô was my idea, and perhaps it was not the most efficient way to find Madeleine, but it was better than Garland and Parker's plan, which was nonexistent. No one moved at Garland's call to action outside his hotel because no one had given any thought to how we'd actually find this woman once we got here.

"Wait, we're sure she lives in Saint-Lô, right?" I asked, but no one replied. "Tell me someone bothered to look her up before we flew across the ocean and blew up a police car and stole a van and—"

"Edwin Green, shut up," Parker said.

"Oh shit. You didn't did you? Did you even check Facebook? I think they have Facebook in France. I mean, what if she's married? How awkward will it be when we show up and her husband answers the door and—ow, dammit!"

Parker hit me harder than Fitz ever had, and her glare led me to believe if I said another word she would kill me on the spot and toss my corpse in the Vire. I shut up.

"She's not married," Garland said. "I told her I'd be back, and she told me she'd wait. I'm back, and she will still be waiting."

I wanted to say that expecting a woman to wait for a man she hasn't heard from in seventy years was asking a lot, but Garland wasn't paying me for my opinions, so I kept them to myself and apologized instead.

"That's alright, son," the old man said, "she might not even be in Saint-Lô. Hell, I almost don't expect her to be after what happened. Lord knows I couldn't live here again. But it's a small town, someone will remember her. Someone will know where she is. We'll find her, I know it."

"Okay," I said, trying to focus on what now felt like a helpless mission, "do you remember where she lived? We could try there first. Maybe the people who live there now will ..."

My voice trailed off as a frown crossed the old man's face and he shook his head no. "Her house was right there," he said, pointing across the street at four-story stone building with Préfecture de la Manche written on the front facade. "There were row houses all the way down to the old city wall, but they're all gone. I don't know this place. I don't even know where—"

Garland lost his train of thought and walked away. We followed him for a block until the fresh pavement gave way to ancient cobblestone, and turning the corner we saw yet another church named Notre Dame, except this one was different than any church I'd ever seen. One of the two towers was just gone, like a giant child had reached down and broken it off while pitching a fit, leaving a sad, solitary tower waiting for its soul mate who'd never return. Parts of the exterior were intricately carved, but large sections were blank, constructed from newer greenish bricks. I wondered if the town ran out of money while building the church and just never got around to finishing it. "What's wrong with that church?" I asked Garland, who'd been standing still, staring at the strange cathedral since we'd rounded the corner.

"Not a damn thing," the old man said, and we followed him up the steps of the church, but the carved bronze doors were locked. "This says there's a weekday mass at noon," I said, reading a sign near the entrance, "and the church office opens at nine-thirty."

"We can come back," Garland said, and that's when I suggested asking strangers if they knew Madeleine. We walked past the church down Rue Carnot, each of us asking a stranger in turn, each of us eliciting some form of no in response. Most of the stores were not open yet, but I did step inside a pharmacy and asked the man behind the counter if he knew Madeleine. "Non," he said, before I'd even finished asking my question, so I tried to ask again and he literally chased me from his store with a broom. We kept walking through town, and in succession a young mother walking her young daughter to school had never heard of Madeleine, then an old man reading a newspaper on a park bench had never heard of Madeleine, and finally a thirtysomething man wearing the same half pants as me and randomly enough walking a cat on a leash had never heard of Madeleine either.

We passed a Subway, and Parker wondered aloud who the hell would eat at Subway in France, and then we stumbled across Saint-Lô's outdoor market, where neither farmer, nor butcher, nor fishmonger, nor cheesemonger, nor anyone else selling almost anything you could possibly want had ever heard of Madeleine Moreau. Defeated, we sulked past the ruins of Saint-Lô's prison, where American flags flapped in the morning breeze, and stopped at a café to regroup.

After ordering coffee for Garland and Parker, I tried my luck with the barista, "*Savez-vous Madeleine Moreau?*" The woman smiled, repeated the name, and brought her hand to her chin while she thought. "She was," I began to say, "how do I say this, she ... *elle a vécue avec vous à Saint-Lô en 1944.*"

The woman's smile faded, and when I repeated my question she glared at me and turned away with a huff.

"That woman is probably going to spit in your coffees," I said when I sat down.

"What the hell'd you say to her?" Garland asked.

"I'm not sure," I said, "but she didn't like it."

A few minutes later the woman brought three coffees and some pastries we didn't order and sat down at our table. Then, in English, she said, "I do appreciate your attempts at the French language, however, I do not appreciate your insinuation that I was alive in 1944." Garland and Parker laughed and the woman smiled as I apologized in English and French until she forgave me. Then she said, "This woman you look for, perhaps you will try La Matin vue Tonnelle? It is, how do you say, a retirement house. My grandmother lives there now. It is possible someone there will remember your Madeleine."

We thanked her again, and thirty minutes later parked our stolen and hot-wired van in the visitor's lot at La Matin vue Tonnelle.

Chapter Fifty-Three

*In which Garland Lenox tries to singlehandedly undo
decades of Franco-American relations.*

"What'd she say, son?"

"She said they have no one here by that name," I said to
Garland, after asking the nurse behind the reception desk at La
Matin vue Tonnelle about Madeleine. The old man looked disappointed, and I tried not to show my relief, because walking
into that depressing French nursing home my mind couldn't
help but drift back to Morningview Arbor and all those men
and women staring at the test pattern on the television in the big
room. In that moment I didn't want to find Madeleine, not if she
was strapped to a bed babbling on about escargot and Gérard
Depardieu, and I doubted Garland wanted to find her that way
either.

"Well, ask if someone here might remember her," the old man
said, and I tried to explain to the nurse that Garland was a soldier
during the war, and the Germans shot him down over Saint-Lô,
and he'd hid in Madeleine's house. The nurse nodded while I spoke,
but apparently I'd only managed to ask my first question again, be-

cause she told me that no one named Madeleine lived there.

"Okay, let me try again," I said. "*Les residents … vivant vivants … pendant la guerre?* World War Two?"

The nurse asked me to repeat myself twice more before picking up her phone, and with a finger she motioned for us to wait on a couch in the corner. Five minutes later an orderly pushed an ancient French man into the lobby and parked him in front of us. "*Je vous présente, Thibaut Larue,*" the nurse said, and the old man in the wheelchair scowled at us before saying something about how we'd interrupted his television viewing, and that we'd better have something important to ask him. I stood up and tried to thank him for his time, but he waved off my pleasantries mid-sentence and unleashed a barrage of French swear words that made the orderly laugh and the nurse blush and slap his wrist. In that moment I realized we'd just met the French version of Garland, so I got to the point and asked if he knew a girl named Madeleine Moreau during the war.

Thibaut Larue thought for a moment, or maybe he fell asleep. I repeated Madeleine's name again and finally the old Frenchman's eyebrows rose in recognition and he began to speak.

"What's he saying, son?" Garland asked.

"He knew her," I said, trying to listen and translate and stop Garland from interrupting all at the same time. "He said she was a little older than him. A very pretty girl. She was his girlfriend, or maybe he wanted her to be his girlfriend, I'm not sure—"

"She wasn't his damn girlfriend," Garland snapped, and he was off the couch jabbing a finger into Thibaut's chest before Parker or I could stop him. "She wasn't your girlfriend," he growled, and while Parker and I pulled Garland back onto the couch, the old Frenchman spat and swore.

"*Il est désolé,*" I whispered to Thibaut, hoping the nurse and orderly hadn't noticed Garland's outburst. "*Pardon. Il est désolé.* Garland, tell him you're sorry."

"No."

"Garland, apologize now," Parker said.

"*Pardon,*" Garland mumbled, and Thibaut grunted and waved off our apologies and continued talking about Madeleine.

"He says he remembers the day her father shot a German. No, the day the Germans shot her father. There were rumors she helped the Resistance."

"We know all of this," Garland growled. "Ask him what happened to her. Where is she?"

I asked Thibaut, "*Savez-vous où elle … uh … habite maintenant?*"

The old Frenchman shrugged and began to speak. "He says after the bombings there was only confusion," I said. "She did not die though, he would know if she died. He says he lived in Saint-Lô after the war, but many left and did not return. She is one who did not return."

"Does he remember anything else?" Parker asked, and I urged the old man to recall anything else he'd heard about Madeleine. He shrugged, and I tried to explain why we were looking for her, hoping Garland's story of lost love would compel him to think a little harder, but when I got to the part about Garland and Madeleine being in love and living together for months, I saw an unmistakable flash of jealous rage in the old Frenchman's eyes. He began to speak again, but his tone had changed, and now he looked only at Garland.

"He says she probably went to Paris," I said. "Many young people went there looking for work." Then he kept talking but I stopped translating.

"Son, what's he saying?" Garland barked.

"I'm not sure," I lied.

"Son," Garland shouted, pointing at the smirking old Frenchman, "what the hell is he saying?"

I sighed and said, "He said she probably became a prostitute, a lot of them did."

Garland slumped back on the couch and Thibaut appeared to take great pleasure from the pain he'd caused, but he took significantly less pleasure from what happened next.

"You son of a bitch," Garland shouted, and before Parker or I could stop him he'd wrapped both hands around the old Frenchman's neck and the two of them tumbled to the floor. The nurse screamed, and the orderly came running and tried to separate them, but Garland had somehow managed to apply a crossface chickenwing on Thibaut who was in turn attempting to claw Garland's eyes out. I've no doubt they would have fought to the death—which honestly wouldn't have taken long considering their age—had the nurse not shouted something about calling the police as she ran behind the reception desk. At that, Garland let go of Thibaut with one final slap to the cheek and said, "Alright kids, I think visiting hours are over."

"*Merci beaucoup!*" Parker shouted as the three of us ran for the door.

Chapter Fifty-Four

In which a lovely French town is bombed out of existence.

"Who is it?"

"Edwin. Open the damn door."

Parker opened the door to the hotel room and I barged past her and shouted at Garland, "You beat up a ninety-year-old man."

"Mama said knock him out," Parker sang and I turned to her and yelled, "This isn't funny. None of this is funny."

"Shhh," Parker said, and I said, "What? Am I causing a scene? You know I'm not the one who assaulted an old French dude in a wheelchair." I turned back to Garland and repeated, "You beat up a ninety-year-old man."

"Son, you keep saying that like it's a bad thing."

"It is a bad thing," I shouted before slumping into a chair in the corner of the room and pulling my hair. "It's a really bad thing."

I like the sirens in Europe. They make even the mildest fender bender sound like a Jason Bourne movie. However, when you know you're the reason for the sirens they lose some of their appeal. We'd squealed out of the La Matin vue Tonnelle parking lot on two wheels and raced back toward town at speeds our van was not designed to handle, then I parked our borrowed vehicle outside the Museum of Fine Arts, leaving it there for good. From the museum we split up, each of us making our separate way back to Garland's room, and by the time I got there the sirens had stopped, but I knew it wasn't going to take the police long to figure out the old man and two teenagers who caused a scene at the nursing home were in fact the three most wanted people in France.

"It's only a bad thing if you do it," Garland said, "but when another ninety-year-old does it it's just a fight. A fight I won by the way. Parker dear will you bring me a glass of water, I'm feeling a little—" Garland stumbled back on the bed and Parker rushed over to check on him while I ran to get a glass of water.

"Is he okay?" I asked, handing Parker the water.

"I'm fine," Garland barked, but he didn't look fine, and Parker stopped. him from getting up. "Drink," she said, putting the glass to his lips, "and rest a minute."

No one could tell Garland what to do, but he listened to Parker and leaned back against his pillow. Once I was sure he wasn't about to die I walked over to the window and peeked behind the curtain, half expecting to see a swarm of police cars, but only seeing an old man hobbling past with a baguette. It's hard to open your eyes in France and not see an old person hobbling past with a baguette.

"What are we going to do?" I whispered when Parker joined me at the window.

"I don't know," she said. "But he needs to rest. He's too old for this much running around."

"I'm not too old to hear every damn word y'all are saying," Garland said from the bed, and we sheepishly turned to face him.

"Hell, just last month I won the decathlon at the geriatric Olympics in Singapore. I can handle a ten-block walk."

Parker laughed and said, "Now I know you made that shit up. I saw you every day last month."

"Maybe it was two months ago," the old man said with a wink. Then the smile faded from his face and he said, "Look, she's not in Saint-Lô. I think I always knew she wouldn't be. Who the hell could blame her?"

"Why wouldn't she have come back here?" I asked. "What happened?"

"Now might not be the—" Parker started to say but Garland waved her off.

"It's fine, dear," he said, and turned to me. "The Devil came here, son, and he brought hell with him, and when it was over there was nothing standing and no one left to say what had even happened." The old man sat up a little more in bed and took another sip of water. "Just after noon on D-Day an American bomber hit the main transformer in town and we lost power. We couldn't see the plane or the bombs from our window, but we felt the blast and we saw the smoke. Later we heard a man in the street shouting that he'd watched it happen. Said the Americans hit the transformer with two precision bombs. A lot of folks in town, and Maddie was one of them, believed the American bombers were impossibly accurate. Like we could drop a bomb in a crowd and only kill the Germans. Four or five hours later a dozen bombers came back and destroyed the train station. This time we watched from our window, or tried to watch. You know sound can kill you if it's loud enough, and the concussion of those blasts knocked us both on the floor and neither of us dared to look out the window again until it was over. After that I begged Maddie to go to the country, like the leaflets told us to do, but she wanted to be there when the Americans marched into town and raised the French flag, so we stayed."

I pulled back the curtain again and looked out toward the train station across the river, but the big government building across the street blocked our view.

"You see anything?" Garland asked. I shook my head no and he continued his story. "About eight that evening the bombing began for real. The first one hit so close it knocked us both off the bed. I shouted at Maddie to run and I hobbled behind her and we hid in a closet under the stairs. There was no hiding from the sound though. Those bombs screamed like demons as they fell, and when one hit close it sucked the air from your lungs before hammering you with an unholy roar. Every bomb sounded like it hit the house, and I wanted to be strong, for Maddie, but I was terrified. Best I could do was hold her so she couldn't see the fear on my face. When I caught my breath I tried to tell her we'd be okay, but she just kept saying, 'I don't want the liberation. Not like this. I don't want it.'"

Garland shook his empty glass at Parker and she got him a refill. He took another sip and set the glass down and rubbed his eyes. "I'm not sure how long the first bombing run lasted," he said. "It felt like days but they say it only lasted a matter of minutes. When it was over I pulled Maddie from the closet and we stepped outside into Armageddon. Her street was a smoldering ruin, and dust-covered men and women were running and shouting, except I couldn't hear them at first. The sound only came in short waves, like invisible hands were covering and uncovering my ears. We sat on Maddie's stoop because we didn't know what else to do, and a little later a man grabbed me by the arm and pulled me around the corner where others were digging through rubble. I helped them dig, but I never knew who or what we were digging for. We never found them either way. And after a while, maybe thirty minutes, maybe two hours, I went back and found Maddie still sitting on the stoop. She had to be in shock, because when I asked her questions she wouldn't even look at me. She'd just stare straight ahead at nothing."

The old man sighed and paused for a moment, and I wanted this story to go off the rails like his stories usually did. I wanted him to talk about his twenty-four-hour engagement to Audrey Hepburn, or recount the time he played doubles tennis with Kim Jong-il, or even reassert his claim that he invented the internet by accident, because the story he was telling was hard to listen to. But instead Garland wiped his eyes and said, "Night fell, but the burning city still glowed, and after a long while I asked Maddie one more time if she wanted to go to the countryside, and this time she shook her head yes. We walked a few blocks but had to turn around because a stretch of row houses had collapsed in the street, and that's when the bombers returned. We watched a rocket scream across the sky and destroy an apartment building not two blocks from us, and we turned to run, but I couldn't move fast enough because of my leg, and the storm caught us out. Soon the bombs exploded so fast you couldn't tell them apart, they were just one long ghastly roar. If there's music in hell, son, that's what it'll sound like. We moved through sparks and fire and the blinding flash of sixty thousand pounds of explosives until we saw through the smoke the silhouette of one of the few buildings left standing: Notre Dame.

"The church from this morning?" I asked.

"The church from this morning," Garland said. "There were others packed inside, huddled in the nave, and we squeezed in with them. I held Maddie tight, but a bomb hit close, and parts of the church collapsed. Shock waves tossed people on top of each other and against walls, and at some point I realized my folks were right all along—this was the end of the world, it had to be. When the bombs stopped falling, the church was so black and quiet I thought I'd died, but the sound of people coughing and spitting up dust brought me back to life. No one spoke, but after a while we left the church and stepped into the most terrible scene you could imagine. There were no German occupiers, no American liberators, there was no Saint-Lô. It was gone, wiped off the map in one night. All that remained was some of the church and a few dust covered people, wandering the streets like ghosts. At some point I took Maddie's arm and we followed a small crowd from town into the country where we stopped at the farm of a man named Herpin, and there we cried and prayed and tried to wake up from our nightmare."

Garland finished his water and stood up and walked over to the window where I'd been standing. He peeked behind the curtain and shook his head and said something I didn't catch, then he sat back down and said to me, "Son, that's why Maddie would never come back here."

"I'm sorry, Garland," I said, before asking, "So are … are we giving up?"

"No. Maybe. I don't know, son."

"Garland, we're going to find her," Parker said and I agreed without conviction.

"Sweetheart, that's awfully kind of you to say, but we're not going to find Maddie. I'm calling Jonas."

"Who?" I asked, but they both ignored me and Garland added, "And you need to go. Now. Before it's too late."

"Wait, go where?" I asked, but they both ignored me again and Parker said, "I'm not leaving yet. We want to try the church one more time."

"Okay," Garland said. "But you need to be moving soon. If you're here when the police arrive—"

"I know. If I didn't know better I'd think you're trying to get rid of me," Parker said and leaned down and kissed Garland on the forehead. "We'll be right back, and then I'll go. I promise."

Chapter Fifty-Five

In which Parker Haddaway tells all … almost.

"The church is that way," I said to Parker as we walked out of Garland's hotel and she turned the wrong direction.

"We're not going to the church," she said, so I shrugged and followed her in the opposite direction, toward the medieval town wall.

"Okay," I said, jogging a little to catch up, "but you've got to tell me what's going on. Who is Jonas? Where are you going?"

Parker didn't look at me, but said, "Jonas is Garland's banker. He's moving some money into an account for me."

"Okay," I said, hoping she'd elaborate, but she didn't, so I asked again, "Where are you going?"

"I'm not going anywhere, Edwin Green."

We passed a couple of girls younger than us sharing a cigarette, and when we reached the wall we walked along the ramparts, stopping at a turret to look out over the town. Cars below navigated roundabouts to cross the two flag-draped bridges over the Vire, and on the far side of the river a train pulled into Gare de Saint-Lô. "So you're staying here?" I asked, "in Saint-Lô?"

Parker waited on the train's whistle to stop blowing and said, "No, but I'm staying in Europe. At least for a while. I told you Garland promised me a new life. Well, this is it. I'm not going back to America. I'm never going back."

There had always been a mysterious quality to my relationship with Sadie Evans. I didn't pursue her, I didn't ask her on a date, but one Sunday night after church I found myself making out with her behind the counter of Hornby Christian Fellowship's coffee bar. It used to freak me out that something like Sadie and me could materialize out of nothing because I knew it could disappear just as easily. "Edwin, don't ruin the best times of your life trying to figure out when they're going to end," Sadie used to tell me when I'd lament that there were no guarantees we'd always be together and as happy as we were then. "If you're happy now, then be happy," she'd say, and after she left I told myself if I were ever happy again, I'd stop trying to predict the future and just let myself be happy. Even so, after the last few days with Parker I couldn't help but make a handful of assumptions about our future together. And though I hadn't had time to discuss these assumptions with her yet, I can tell you they did not involve her staying in Europe and me going back to Hornby.

"What?" I said, my heart jumping into my throat. "No … we … you've got to …"

"Edwin Green, I owe you an explanation," she said, and motioned for me to sit next to her on a stone bench. I hesitated, then sat, and she said, "Remember when I told you I'd lived with seven different relatives in the last four years?"

"Yeah."

"Well I never told you why," Parker said and stared up a fluttering blue and yellow municipal flag before turning to me and saying, "It's because I killed my parents."

"You killed—wait, what?"

"I killed my parents," Parker said, then noticing the look on my face said, "God, Edwin Green, I didn't murder them, but I'm the reason they're dead."

"I … I don't understand," I said, and after a long silence Parker spoke again, but she wouldn't look at me, which wasn't like her at all. She just stared out over Saint-Lô and said, "My parents weren't married when Mom got pregnant. She was in college, majoring in Irish literature, and Dad played bass in a band. This awful rap-rock-ska band called Flaccid Confederacy that was somewhat famous in central Florida, but only because their three-hundred-pound drummer played in a gigantic cloth diaper."

I laughed but Parker still wouldn't look at me. "When I was born Dad quit the band to take care of Mom and me," she said. "He worked at Disney World for a while—he was one of the Seven Dwarves—but they fired him after he kicked a kid who wouldn't stop pulling on his beard. After that he bounced around construction jobs for a year before joining the army for the insurance and a steady paycheck. That was 2002, and they sent him to Iraq the next year." Parker laughed to herself and said, "I was too young to remember his first deployment, but when he went to Iraq the second time I was seven, and I gave myself stomach ulcers worrying about him. I was in the hospital for a week and had to see a counselor until he came home. The army deployed him again in 2011, this time to Afghanistan, and before he left Dad sat me down and explained that he had a desk job. 'I sit at a computer all day and order food and toilet paper for all the other soldiers,' he told me. 'You don't have to worry about me because I have the safest job in the army.' So I didn't worry about him, and one morning after breakfast he walked out of the mess tent and a sniper shot him in the stomach. He died en route to a hospital in Germany."

I slid over and put my arm around her and said, "I'm so sorry

Parker."

She looked at me and said, "If I'd never been born he would've never joined the damn army. He'd be alive and he'd still be in that terrible band doing what he loved."

Had this been a movie, an angel would have appeared to show Parker how much worse life would have been without her, but no angel appeared, perhaps because she was at least partially right. Had she not been born her dad would have never joined the army, although I sort of doubted he'd still be the bassist for Flaccid Confederacy. I tried to console her and said, "Parker, that's not—" but she wasn't finished.

"We lived in a little town outside of Orlando," she said, again looking off into the distance, "and it was big news when they flew Dad's body home for the funeral. I guess anytime a soldier from a small town dies it's big news, at least in that small town. Mom didn't want to tell me about the protesters, but I saw it on the news, so she just said that there might be some bad people at Dad's funeral, and I decided I'd be ready for them."

"Protesters?"

"The Omaha Prophetic Presbyterian Church."

"Oh God, not them."

"The world is a stage, Edwin Green, but the play is badly cast."

"Parker, I'm so sorry."

She waved off my condolences and said, "They weren't at the church service, but on the drive to the graveside our motorcade went right past them. Mom told me not to look but I did. They screamed at every car that passed, and one little girl about my age spit on the hearse. The city wouldn't let them get closer than a thousand feet, but when the preacher got up to say a prayer you could hear them chanting. Then the bugler played taps, and they chanted even louder, and that's when I lost it. I jumped from my chair and took off toward the protesters with at least twenty people from the funeral chasing me. It's funny, there were only about ten Prophetic Presbyterians at the protest. I'd expected there to be hundreds of them, but I guess it's hard to find that many homophobic lunatics free on a Tuesday morning. I recognized the tallest one with the long beard and funny hat. It was Jeff Pirkle, Raymond Pirkle's son, who'd transitioned his dad's church from fearmongers to hatemongers. When I got close he smiled, and he reached out like he was going to pick me up. Like I was his daughter and I was running into his arms. He didn't see my mom's steak knife until it was three inches into his thigh.

"Wait, that was you? I remember that, it was huge news."

"That was me."

"But that girl's name wasn't—"

"Parker Haddaway? No. It was Emily Bloom. You know what Andy Warhol said about the future?"

"Yeah, that everyone would be famous for fifteen minutes."

"Right. Well that soup-can-loving bastard failed to mention that in the future everyone would be famous for fifteen minutes whether they want to be or not. I didn't want the fame that came from stabbing that piece of shit in the leg, and Mom didn't want it, we just wanted Dad back, and for everyone to leave us alone. But because some sniper shot my dad in the stomach we were in the news, and because we were in the news the worst church in America put us on their radar, and because I did what everyone in America wanted to do to Jeff Pirkle, his church set up shop in our town and followed us and harassed us and filed three dozen lawsuits against our family. I found Mom in the bathtub a month later. She'd slit both wrists."

I cursed softly and began to say something, but Parker wasn't finished.

"After that you'd have thought the bastards would have quietly gone back to Omaha, but instead they announced plans to protest my mother's funeral as well, so Mom's family had her cremated, and we held a small memorial service out of town. A local judge threw out all the OPP's suits against me on account of their being assholes, but they still didn't leave town. They showed up at my school, and at my grandparents' house where I was living, and a couple months later I went to live with my dad's aunt in Louisiana. Since then I've changed my name twice and lived with half a dozen increasingly distant relatives who all inevitably get tired of my drama and show me the door. Aunt Marcy—she's really like a first cousin twice removed—she was my last chance. There are no long lost cousins willing to put up with my shit, so she turned me over to Youth Services like she'd threatened to do a dozen times. Thankfully the OPP's lost track of me, but they'll never stop looking. Anytime they protest you can usually spot a sign that says, "God hates Emily Bloom."

"Does anyone at school know about this?"

"Aunt Marcy talked to Principal Denham before I moved to Hornby, so she knows, but that's it. She passed word down to the teachers that I've had a troubled past and they should give me some space, but no one knows exactly what my troubled past entails. Edwin Green, you can't imagine how shitty the last four years have been, but then a few months ago I met Garland, and one day he told me about his parents making him live in the woods because of some crazy preacher, so I told him my story about stabbing a crazy preacher in the leg. That day he offered me enough money to get away and start a new life. Just like that, with nothing in return. But I couldn't take it, you know? You can start over in life, but not if you leave things unfinished."

"Wait, so you are Hindu?"

Parker smiled and said, "I'm not particularly religious, unless there's a religion that believes God overestimated his ability somewhat when he created man."

"Okay," I said, "So before you took Garland's money you wanted to do something good to make up for stabbing that preacher?"

"Hell no, I'd do that again right now. To make up for killing my parents."

"Parker, you didn't kill your—"

"I'm not arguing with you, Edwin Green. I had to do something good. Something for my mom and something for my dad."

"So you're helping Garland find Madeleine," I said, and Parker said, "No, I reminded Garland he was a hero. We're never going to find Madeleine, she—"

Parker stopped talking as a helicopter appeared on the horizon, followed by another, and then another.

"Uh, do you think those are for us?" I asked.

"Could just be a coincidence," Parker said, just as the Jason Bourne sirens roared to life all over town. "Or maybe not," she said, and we took off toward Garland's hotel.

Chapter Fifty-Six

In which Anderson Cooper doesn't know what he's talking about.

"Jonas had a man deliver your chariot," Garland said to Parker as we burst into his hotel room. He tossed her a key and added, "Candy-apple red and a little more reliable than your old one. It's waiting across the street. Dear, you might want to get moving."

"What, the helicopters?" she asked. "They're probably after some other fugitives in town."

The old man frowned and Parker said, "I'm joking, but I wasn't leaving without a goodbye kiss." Garland couldn't help but smile.

I walked past them to the window and peered out behind the curtain. The street was empty, but sirens still roared in the distance, and I could see one of the four helicopters hovering near the train station. "Where's the remote?" I asked, but no one answered so I turned on the television at the box and began flipping through the channels until I saw an aerial view of Saint-Lô.

"Les fugitifs à Saint-Lô," Parker said, reading the words on the screen. "See, it doesn't say which fugitives. I think we're good."

I tried to laugh and my phone rang. It was Fitz.

"Green, I really want to talk about you and Parker Haddaway sexing it up, but there are more important things—"

"Hold up, who said we—"

"Not now, man. Parker, her real name is Emily Bloom, and she's the same girl that stabbed that crazy gay-hating preacher in the leg in Florida when we were in like seventh grade and—"

"Dude, calm down, I know."

Fitz caught his breath and said, "Okay, but did you know Anderson Cooper just said French marines have the three of you holed up in a hotel in some town called Saint …"

"Saint-Lô?"

"Yeah, Saint-Lô."

"He's wrong," I said, then glanced out the window to make sure the marines hadn't arrived in the last sixty seconds. "At least for now," I added.

"That's good, I guess. Did you guys find the woman?"

"No."

"Damn," Fitz said.

"I know."

"So what are you going to do?"

"I don't know."

"Well don't do anything stupid, okay?"

"Everything we've done so far has been stupid, why would we change strategies now?"

Fitz laughed and said, "You know what I mean. Just be safe man."

"We will."

I hung up the phone as Garland and Parker finished their goodbyes. "What are we going to do?" I asked.

"Parker is going to leave," Garland said, then pointed at the door and added, "now."

"Okay, I'm leaving," she said, and picked up her backpack.

"And I'm going to turn myself in and go home," Garland said. "You're welcome to join me, or you can hide under the bed and play hide-and-seek with the French army."

"No," I said. "We can't give up now. Not in Saint-Lô. We can still find Madeleine if we—"

"Son, it's not going to happen. Believe me, I'm thankful for everything you've done. Everything you've both done," he added, turning to Parker. "But we're not going to find her. Now go, dear. You've got everything you need, so please, get the hell out of France."

Parker walked over to Garland and they embraced one last time. *"Au revoir mademoiselle,"* Garland said as they pulled away, and the old man put one hand on her cheek and whispered something I didn't hear, then he kissed her on the forehead and said goodbye again.

Parker turned to me with open arms and said, "Edwin Green." I didn't want to hug her because I thought maybe if I never said goodbye she'd never leave, but I walked across the room to her anyway. We hugged, and she put her hands on my shoulders and held me at arm's length and smiled and said my name again. I wanted her to stay. I wanted her to go back to Hornby and be my girlfriend and for us to live happily ever after. But now that I knew the rest of her story I accepted that none of that would ever happen, so in lieu of a bumbling attempt at a romantic farewell speech, I just smiled back at her and tried not to cry.

That's when Sadie Evans called.

Chapter Fifty-Seven

In which our hero pisses out an old flame.

"Shit. It's Sadie," I said, and Parker said, "Well answer it, Edwin Green."

"Okay … wait, are you leaving? Will you wait?"

"If you are not too long I will wait for you here all my life," Parker said, much to Garland's annoyance.

"Uh, hello," I said, walking into the bathroom for some privacy. I caught a glimpse of Parker as I closed the door and she winked.

"Edwin, my God, are you okay? What are you doing?"

"Hey Sadie. I'm about to surrender to French authorities. What are you doing?"

She laughed. I could always make her laugh. "It's good to hear your voice," she said.

"You too," I said, even though she'd spent the last year losing her southern accent and didn't sound like the Sadie I used to know.

"So you're okay?" she asked. "I mean, you're safe? You're not going to do something stupid, right?"

"Yeah, I'm okay. I don't think they're going to shoot us or anything."

"Edwin, the men on the news have guns. They look like marines or something."

"Oh, I'm sure," I said. "Garland did blow up a car, and Parker almost shot a policeman in the face. That was an accident though. The shooting part. Garland blew up the car on purpose. But still, as long as we hold our hands over our heads I can't imagine they'll shoot us, you know?"

"So that girl, Parker, are you two a thing?"

I glanced at my phone. Thirty-seven seconds. It took her thirty-seven seconds to ask about Parker.

"Maybe," I said, and the conversation marinated in awkward silence.

"I saw the video of you two kissing at school," Sadie said after a moment.

"Okay," I said.

"And there was that picture of you two in bed."

"Okay," I said, not knowing exactly what she was talking about.

"So, did you two like fuck or whatever?"

I hesitated here because (1) I'd never heard Sadie curse, at least not in person. She'd obviously cursed a lot since moving to Hollywood, half her movies were R-rated and one of her albums had explicit lyrics, but it still sounded so weird to me that I had to pause, which (2) gave me a moment to relish the fact that Sadie was totally jealous of Parker Haddaway, and she'd probably spent the better part of the last twenty-four hours wondering if we'd slept together, but she'd have to just keep wondering because (3) pardon my French, it was none of her fucking business.

"Sadie," I finally said, "why do you care?"

"Are you mad at me Edwin?"

"No," I lied. "Just tell me again why you called?"

"Edwin, this isn't like you. Why ..."

"Why what?"

"Why ... why did you do all of this?"

I took a deep breath and came clean. "I did it to get your attention, Sadie. I thought if I became famous you'd want to get back together."

"Dammit Edwin, you don't want to get back together with me."

"You're right," I said, "I don't. Not anymore."

This time Sadie hesitated, and when she spoke again she sounded different somehow, like an actor breaking character. "You know I'm not really dating Trevor. Our entire relationship is fake. Everything here is fake. He's had the same girlfriend since eighth grade. She goes to college in Liverpool. Our publicists arranged our relationship for the, what'd they call it, the mutual benefit of our brands. Our dates are fake, our vacations are fake, even the sex tape was fake."

"Sadie that's super weird," I said. "Your dad was okay with that?"

"It was his idea. All he thinks about now is how to keep me famous because he knows I'm famous for no reason. I can't sing, I can't act, I can't do anything."

She was fishing for a compliment that I wasn't about to give. Instead I asked, "Sadie, why did you call me?"

"I called you because you're my friend, Edwin, and I'm worried about you."

"Sadie, we're not friends. I haven't spoken to you in a year. You send these weird, rambling emails like every six weeks, but you never respond to anything I say. No one would confuse that for a friendship."

"Edwin you don't understand what it's like out here. I know I haven't been nice to you, but ..."

"But what?"

"I don't know. It's like I've been waiting for all this to end, because there's no way it can last. No matter how hard Dad or my publicists try, people will stop caring about me and there will be nothing left to do but go back home to Hornby and …"

"Sadie, what are you trying to say?"

"Just that you've always been there Edwin. When life was crazy I knew I could email you and you'd listen and write back. That's why I kept this old phone. I never use it, but I knew if I really needed you I could call and you'd answer. Or I could watch your YouTube videos and know that you still loved me."

"Wait, you watched my videos?"

"Every day. They were so sad, but somehow, I don't know, comforting. But then I saw you on the news, kissing that red-haired girl, and, I don't know, I was jealous I guess. It's just, I've just always thought when this was over I could go back home and you'd be …"

"I'd be what?"

"Still waiting for me."

I heard Parker close the door through the wall and panicked. "Shit, Sadie, I've got to go."

"Wait, Edwin … I love you."

And there they were, the words I'd waited twelve long months, risked my future, and broken countless laws to hear. But by then I knew Parker was right. Sadie was the girlfriend equivalent of a serial killer, and she'd only called because when she checked her shoebox my heart was no longer there. So in that moment I tried to think about the meanest thing I could say to my egomaniacal ex-girlfriend. Something a person who only thinks about others when she's wondering what they are thinking about her would least like to hear. On short notice this was the best I could come up with.

"Sadie?"

"Yes."

"Don't. Care."

Chapter Fifty-Eight

In which parting is such sweet sorrow.

Garland read my mind, pointed toward the door, and said, "Son, you'd better hurry." I burst into the hallway just as Parker was stepping on the elevator and I shouted, "Wait!"

She stepped back into the hallway and smiled. "Edwin Green, I've got to go. Switzerland is calling, or maybe Denmark, or Spain."

"I know," I said, walking across the faded green hotel carpet toward her. "I thought I'd missed you."

Parker pointed at the phone in my hand and said, "So you finally got your call from Sadie Evans."

I slid it into my pocket and said, "Yeah."

"And was it everything you dreamed it would be?"

"She told me she still loved me," I said, and Parker raised an eyebrow, "and I told her I didn't care."

Parker squealed and hugged me and said, "Good for you, Edwin Green. Oh my God how do you feel? Like a new man? I wish I'd heard you say it."

"I...I thought you'd be mad at me," I said. "I screwed up your second good deed."

Parker held me by the shoulders again and smiled. "Getting you over Sadie Evans was my second good deed."

"Wait, what?"

"When I moved to Hornby all anyone ever talked about was the great Sadie Evans, and I don't know why, but I was much more interested in you, the depressed boyfriend she left behind. I found your YouTube videos and—"

"Wait, you watched my videos too?" It was weird, I'd made those videos hoping they'd make me famous, but now that I knew people had actually seen them I sort of regretted their existence. I suspect the Germans have a word for this.

"I did, and they made me sad because I could tell you were still hung up on this girl who'd treated you worse than shit. And even though there are only like seven people in history worse than Sadie, and they were all dictators with weird little mustaches, no one in Hornby ever bothered to tell you you're better off without her because they're all morons who'd line up and pay good money just to have Sadie Evans treat them like shit too. I have a theory—"

"Sadie is a serial killer. You already told me."

"No, another theory," Parker said. "That you weren't even in love with Sadie, just the idea of her. The idea of having a girlfriend."

Fitz actually suggested this early on before I placed a moratorium on all Black Saturday talk, and looking back, I suspect he and Parker were probably right.

"So I had to get Sadie's attention," Parker said. "That's why I kissed you in the hall under the security camera. That's why I Instagrammed that picture of us in bed."

"So that's why everyone thinks we had sex."

"Vulgar details, Edwin Green," Parker said with a wink. "The thing is, I knew Sadie was terrible, and I knew seeing you with someone else would send her into a jealous rage. I just hoped when she finally called you'd realize how awful she is too."

This was a lot to process in the twenty seconds I had to process it, and while I tried I stood there in slack-jawed disbelief.

"I thought you liked me," I finally said.

"I do like you, Edwin Green. I wouldn't go through this much trouble for someone I didn't like. But look, I've got to go——"

"Don't," I blurted out.

"Well, I'm not staying and turning myself in."

"No, I think we can still find Madeleine. We just need to get out of Saint-Lô, keep quiet for a few weeks, then come back."

"We're not going to find——"

"And after we find her I could come with you. I'd get a job or something, you wouldn't have to support me. We could drift around Europe and, I don't know, it would be …"

Parker closed her eyes and sighed. "Edwin Green," she said, and shook her head and smiled. "You don't want to do that."

"But I do. I'm … I can't stop thinking about you. You …"

Parker touched my cheek and said, "I'm just the first girl you happened to notice after you finally stopped obsessing over Sadie Evans. I promise, whatever feelings you think you have for me will be gone by the time your plane lands in Atlanta." She pulled her hand back and said with a wink, "Besides, I refuse to be your rebound girl."

Since that day I've replayed this moment a few thousand times in my head, and I like to think if given the chance to do it over again I would have found a way to eloquently express my feelings to Parker. But instead I said something like, "No, you're not … I'm … I think I … It's just that you …" and there my brain and mouth stopped cooperating and a sad smile crossed Parker's face.

"Oh, Edwin Green," she said. "I've already read the last page. We don't end up together."

"But——" I began, but she put a finger to my lips, then leaned in and kissed me on the cheek.

"*Au revoir Edwin Green,*" she said, backing away. "Until we meet again."

"*Au revoir mademoiselle,*" I whispered, and she stepped into the elevator as I turned back to the room. I told myself not to look back. To be cool and just walk away. But at the last moment I spun around to say something stupid about keeping up through email and I caught a glimpse of Parker in the closing elevator doors.

She was crying.

Chapter Fifty-Nine

In which our hero throws a Hail Mary.

"Is she gone?"

I ignored Garland and walked across the room to the window where I watched Parker cross the street below. She climbed on a red Vespa and looked up and down the intersection, then she was gone.

"Son, is she gone?" Garland asked again.

"Yeah," I said, "she's gone," and when I turned around the old man must have seen the heartbreak smeared across my face because he said, "Son, I'm sorry."

"Me too," I said, and sat next to him on the bed. "What the hell just happened?"

"We helped a troubled girl start a new life," Garland said.

"She told me," I said, "but I thought that she … that she and I might … I told Sadie … Sadie called me and I told her … because I thought …"

Garland patted my back and walked over to the window. The sirens still blared and from the sound of things another helicopter or two had joined the fray. "She told me why she wanted to bring you," he said and sat down in the corner chair. "I told her you'd get hurt, but she said even if you did you'd be better off in the end. And I know you don't believe it now, but she was right. Parker gave you a gift, son."

I wiped my eyes and said, "I don't want it."

The old man smiled. "Oh cheer up, son, we're about to be arrested."

"Shit," I said, and fell back on the bed. "What have I done?"

"You've had an adventure," Garland said. "And you've broken whatever spell that preacher's daughter had on you. All things considered, it's been a productive week. Plus, you're famous now. Famous for being a hopeless romantic at that. When we get back home you'll be fighting off the girls with a stick."

This may have been true, but it wasn't exactly what I wanted to hear moments after having my heart shoveled through a wood chipper. "Yeah," I said, "maybe."

A siren grew louder as a police car sped past our hotel, and Garland stood up and said, "Son, I think it's best if I call and surrender now. I'd rather do things in an orderly fashion and not give some hothead an opportunity to crash through that door and put us both in chokeholds."

"Okay," I said, then jumped to my feet and said, "No. Not yet. I'm going back to the church. We never spoke to anyone at the church. Before you call, let me walk over there, and if they don't know anything about Madeleine we can turn ourselves in and go home."

"Son, I don't think—" Garland said, but changed his mind midsentence. "Go on," he said, "knock yourself out. Just be careful."

I left the Hotel Vue de la Rivière and walked toward the church. A low-flying helicopter shook the ground as it hovered nearby and I stopped to watch it before accidentally making eye contact with a man passing on the sidewalk. Glancing up I shrugged and he said, "Les fugitifs Américains." I nodded and hurried on my way, hoping he hadn't recognized me.

There was a small crowd gathered at the intersection where the road gave way to the cobblestoned cathedral square, and when I joined them I saw why. There were a dozen police cruisers parked in the square, along with at least fifty police officers, a few soldiers, and what looked like a small tank. I wondered why the hell they would need a tank. Despite all this people were still going about their business and moving through the square, so I pushed my way through the gawkers and walked toward Notre Dame church with my head down.

Inside the church was quiet, apart from a couple pigeons cooing in the rafters, and the massive bronze door squeaked as I gently closed it behind me. Light streamed in through ancient stained glass, and the towering concrete pillars cast long shadows across the floor. My footsteps echoed as I made my way across the black and white tiled floor toward the front of the church, and I wondered how a building could be all but blown away and yet the windows survived. I wanted it to be a miracle, because I needed to believe in miracles. I read later the church removed the windows a year before the bombing.

"Hello," I said, in what I guess you'd describe as a loud whisper. It's funny, I never thought twice about making out with Sadie in her dad's church, mainly because it was inside an old movie theater, but this church felt sacred somehow, and I didn't want to shout. No one answered though, so I sat on the front pew and considered praying, but just closed my eyes and missed Parker instead.

"*Bonjour,*" said a voice from behind and I jumped and cursed and spun around to see a nun standing in the shadows. I began apologizing, mostly for the cursing, but also for being inside the church if I wasn't supposed to be there, and at some point in my incoherent rambling she stopped me and said, "You are Monsieur Green, no?"

"Uh … yes ma'am," I said, not sure if you're supposed to call nuns ma'am or something else.

The nun stepped forward into the light and smiled. She was old, older than Garland maybe, and in that moment I let myself believe she was Madeleine, and she'd been right here, in this church, waiting for him the whole time. "I have been expecting you," the nun said. "My name is Sister Ava, I belong to the congregation of Bon Sauveur, here in Saint-Lô."

"Sister Ava," I repeated. "I thought maybe you were …"

"Madeleine?" Sister Ava asked. "No, but I was her friend. Speaking of friends, your friend, Monsieur Lenox, is he safe? The news said there was an incident, at La Matin vue Tonnelle."

"Oh he's fine," I said. "He just beat up an old man named Thibaut."

A hint of a smile crossed Sister Ava's face and she said, "Ah, Thibaut Larue, the peeping Tom. I have known him a lifetime. A punch in the nose might do him good."

I dared to laugh and said, "Wait, so you were friends with Madeleine?"

"We were," Sister Ava said, sitting on the front pew and motioning for me to join her. "She was a few years younger than me, but after the war we became close friends. We even lived together for some months, in the wooden barracks the Americans built, because Bon Sauveur was destroyed on D-Day. When I arrived Madeleine was very sick, but soon she recovered, and for a while we worked together, in the Irish hospital. Always she talked of her Garland, her G.I. Joe who would return. Of course the young girls, they all spoke of soldiers who would return, but Madeleine, she truly believed."

The door in the back of the church creaked open and we watched a man enter and take a seat on the last pew to pray. Sister Ava watched him for a moment, then looked back at me and in a softer voice said, "I remember the day well, it was early April, the year after the war ended, so … 1946. Madeleine spent many months writing letters, trying to find her Garland. She wrote letters to your Army, and your Air Force, and even to your President Truman, but she received no reply. Then one day an American engineer visited Saint-Lô, to observe the recovery, and Madeleine begged him for help. He promised to help find her Garland, and weeks later his letter arrived with the news that Garland was shot down over northern France and killed in action.

"No," I said, louder than I'd meant to. "They listed him as killed in action after he crashed in Saint-Lô. He said it took years to straighten out all the paperwork. I'm sure that officer thought … and Garland thought Madeleine was …"

"When I saw this man Garland on the news, looking for his lost Madeleine, I knew. I knew it was the same man," Sister Ava said, then put her arm around me because I'd started to cry. "Do not be ashamed of your tears," she said. "I have shed many this week."

After a moment I asked, "What did Madeleine do, when she thought Garland was dead?"

"She did not want to live," Sister Ava said. "She had already lost so much, and now she'd lost even more. She would come to me and we would pray, and cry, and sometimes laugh if we could cry no longer. Madeleine had a beautiful voice. She would sing to the soldiers in the hospital. She told me once, 'I sing to them and pretend they are my Garland.' One day, maybe a year later, I told her about the Benedictine Sisters of Sacré-Cœur. They had only just returned from exile in England. Madeleine laughed and said no, she could not, but three days later she came to me and said yes, that is where God wanted her. She joined the sisters in 1948. Then the sisters were here, in the north, but later they moved back to Sacré-Cœur, on Montmartre, in Paris."

I stared at Sister Ava in disbelief. "Madeleine was a nun? A singing nun at Sacré-Cœur?"

"For the rest of her life," Sister Ava said. "Sister Madeleine and I, we remained close friends, but she never returned to Saint-Lô. It was too painful I think. But I would see her when I visited Paris, and we shared many letters. The basilica on Montmartre, it has many tourists at every service, and Sister Madeleine once told me when she sings she sometimes imagines her Garland, sitting among the parishioners, listening to her again."

"You ... you said for the rest of her life."

Sister Ava frowned and touched my hand. "My friend Madeleine died six years ago. I am so sorry."

I hung my head and Sister Ava put her arm around me again and we both cried a little more. A helicopter passed low over the church and the walls seemed to shake and I raised my head and said, "I have to get back to Garland. We need to turn ourselves in now. I'm sorry for all the commotion. I'm sure the helicopters and police will be gone by morning."

Sister Ava smiled. "It is quite alright. Sleepy towns need excitement now and then." I smiled back and Sister Ava said, "Edwin, this thing you have done, for Monsieur Lenox, it is a very good thing. Please tell him ... tell him his Madeleine loved him ... all of her life."

"I will," I said, and I stood up and walked toward the back of the church where a bald man sat praying on the back pew. When I passed him Martin Blair said, "Edwin Green, I've been looking for you."

Chapter Sixty

In which everyone's favorite bureaucratic asshat returns.

"Edwin, please don't run," Martin Blair said after I glanced at the door. "I promise you it would not end well." Then, noticing the terror smeared across my face, he smiled and added, "It's okay, son, I promise. Here, take a seat."

There were pigeon feathers on the pew and I wiped them off and sat down and Martin Blair said, "First, Edwin, what the hell are you wearing?"

"Parker picked it out," I said, trying to smile. "She said it would help me blend in."

Martin Blair laughed and said, "Maybe in Milan … on Halloween." I forced a laugh and he asked, "So where is Miss Parker now?"

I stared at my feet and Martin Blair said, "Do you still not trust me Edwin, even after I let the three of you out of Charles de Gaulle?"

I looked up at Martin Blair and noticed someone had carved "Punk's not dead" on the column behind him. "So you did let us go?" I asked. "Why?"

"Because it was the right thing to do," Martin Blair said, "and because I retire in three months. What are they going to do, fire me? Now where is Parker?"

I hung my head again and Martin Blair said, "I don't want any of you getting hurt."

"She's gone," I said, without looking up. "She left about an hour ago. She has a lot of money, and who knows how many passports, and she's going to disappear. They'll never find her."

Martin Blair leaned back against the pew and said, "Good for her."

"Wait, you're happy she got away?" I asked.

"Life has been terribly unkind to that poor girl," he said. "She deserves a chance to start over."

"So you're not going to go look for her?"

"Me? No. I suspect the French police have a few questions for her since she shot at one of their comrades in a canola field, but if she makes it out of France I think she'll be fine. Why the hell did she shoot at a policeman anyway?"

"It was an accident," I said. "She was rapping, and she didn't know the gun was loaded, and … he thought we'd stolen a car."

"You did steal a car."

"No, we stole a van. Garland bought that car from a guy named Rémy."

"I don't understand why you didn't just take a train."

"That's what I said, but Garland was all, 'They'll arrest us the minute we step on a damn train, son.'"

"Who'd arrest you? We couldn't chase you and the French didn't care about you until you blew up that police car," Martin Blair said and shook his head.

"I told Garland the fireball was completely unnecessary," I said. "They never listened to me."

"Well," Martin Blair said with a sigh, "what's done is done. Now tell me what you found out."

"About what?"

"What do you think Edwin? About Garland's long lost love."

"Oh, right. An old man at the nursing home said she became a prostitute and Garland body slammed him."

Martin Blair chuckled. "Yeah, we heard. That's how we knew to come to Saint-Lô."

"Garland wanted us to turn ourselves in, but I had to talk to someone in this church first. He and Madeleine hid here, during the bombing, and I hoped someone would remember her. And that nun I just spoke to, Sister Ava, she did. She was friends with Madeleine after the liberation."

Martin Blair raised an eyebrow. "Did she know what became of her?"

"She … she was waiting for Garland to come back when she heard he'd been killed in action," I said, my voice cracking. "She joined a convent and … and died six years ago."

Martin Blair closed his eyes and rubbed his temples. A moment later he said, "I hate it for Garland … even if he did suggest I stick my fat head up my ass."

"He suggests that to a lot of people," I said, and Martin smiled.

"So what's your plan from here?"

"I told Garland we could turn ourselves in if I didn't learn anything at the church, so I guess you can arrest me now if you like."

"I work for the United States embassy, Edwin. I can't arrest you. But it would be much better for you and Garland if you were in American custody. You guys shot at a cop and blew up his car and stole two other cars."

"One car," I corrected him, "and Parker shot the cop, and Garland blew up his car."

"All the same," Martin said, "the French police don't necessarily consider you heroes like the rest of the world."

"The rest of the world thinks we're heroes?"

Martin Blair smiled and said, "Something like that. Listen. Where is Garland now? We need to act fast."

The never-ending roar of sirens still filled the air and I said, "He's back in his room." Then for reasons I can't explain I lied, "At the Hotel Mercure."

"Okay. Hurry back to him, and in fifteen minutes a blue van with the US embassy logo will pull up outside the hotel. Come down one at a time and get in the van, and we'll take you back to the embassy in Paris and this will all be over. Okay?"

"Okay," I said, and standing up added, "Thank you, Mr. Blair."

He smiled and said, "Don't thank me yet."

Chapter Sixty-One

In which Garland Lenox disparages French television
before undergoing a dramatic transformation.

"I don't think I'd even own a television if I lived in France," Garland said as I burst into his hotel room.

"What?" I asked, more confused than interested in what he was talking about.

"Sixty channels of the weirdest shit you've ever seen," the old man said. "Eight channels of nothing but soccer, and at least a dozen channels showing aerial views of Saint-Lô. I watched you walk across the church square. Hard to miss those pants."

I checked the hallway to make sure I wasn't followed, and as I shut the door behind me Garland added, "I was worried about you, son. Did you find religion?"

"What?" I asked again, now more preoccupied by the French game show he'd found in which most of the contestants appeared to be nude.

"I said what took you so long?" Garland repeated, and I said, "Martin Blair. I found him. Well, he found me."

"And he let you go?" Garland asked, sitting up on the bed.

"Sort of," I said. "He thinks we'd be better off in US custody. He's sending a van to pick us up in five minutes, but I told him the wrong hotel."

"Why'd you do that, son?"

"I'm not sure," I said, and Garland smiled.

"So what'd you find out at the church? Anyone remember Maddie?"

I started to speak but hesitated for a second and Garland asked, "Son, are you okay?"

"Yeah," I said, and composed myself. "I spoke with an old nun, Sister Ava. She … she knew Madeleine."

Garland was off the bed and standing right in front of me. "And?"

"And … Madeleine was waiting for you to come back, when she heard you'd been …"

"Been what, son?"

"Been killed in action."

"Son of a bitch," Garland said and sat back down on the bed. He was quiet for a long time, then said, "So'd this Sister Ava know what happened to Maddie, after she thought I was dead. She get married?"

"No," I said. "She joined the Benedictine—"

"Sisters of the Sacré-Cœur de Montmartre," Garland said, finishing my sentence. "Well I'll be damned." The old man hung his head while I thought of a way to tell him Madeleine died six years ago. But before I could say anything he smiled up at me with glistening tears in both eyes and said, "Son, we're going back to Paris."

"Paris? No. I don't think that's a great idea Garland."

"Noted," the old man said, and walked into the bathroom.

I continued my protest through the wall. "Garland, the police are everywhere. And soldiers. They even have a tank. It's a small tank, but it's still a tank and they could use it to shoot us or run over us or both."

"Pack up and be ready to go," Garland shouted through the door, ignoring everything I'd said about the tank.

"The tank isn't that small," I added. "It's bigger than most SUVs, and besides, Martin Blair already knows we are here. We'll never make it out of Saint-Lô, and even if we did—"

I shut up at the sight of an old woman stepping out of the bathroom.

"Laugh and I will kill you with my bare hands," Garland said, but I fell back on the bed and burst out laughing in spite of myself.

"Why?" I finally asked between laughs. "Why are you wearing a dress?"

Garland glared at me and growled, "I asked Parker to buy the wig and dress back in Bayeux. Thought they might come in handy."

I laughed some more. "Why did you think dressing like a woman would come in handy?"

"Son, in 1969 they had me in Cuba spying on the Castro brothers. I spent the better part of a year in drag. Fidel even asked me on a date, but I had to break his commie heart."

I began to reply but only laughed again and Garland said, "You can doubt me if you want to son, but you can't make this shit up. Now come here."

Still laughing, I followed the old man over to the window and he pointed across the street.

"Préfecture de la Manche," I said, reading the name of the building.

"Not the building son, the parking lot. We need a new car, so when you see me wave, you run like hell and be ready to drive fast."

"No Garland," I said, but he was already walking toward the door. "Seriously?" I asked. "We're not seriously going to—" But he was out the door and gone. I watched from the window, and minutes later saw the old man dressed as an old woman shuffle across the parking lot and walk up to a Porsche roadster.

"No," I said out loud. "Pick another car Garland. It will have an alarm."

But it didn't, or Garland somehow got in without setting it off, and then he waved at me. I cursed and ran across the street to meet him.

Chapter Sixty-Two

In which damning allegations are made against a six-time Wimbledon champion.

"Where'd your half pants go?" Garland said as I climbed into the driver's seat of—depending on who you ask—our second or third stolen car.

"Left them in the room," I said, a bit overwhelmed at the amount of buttons and knobs on the car's dash.

"Good call," he said, and I turned and raised an eyebrow at his less than flattering dress. "If you enjoy having a full set of teeth you might wanna keep your comments to yourself," Garland growled and I raised my hands in surrender. "Good," he said, "now drive. Drive casual. We don't need any added attention."

"What does driving casual look like?" I asked, backing out of the parking space.

"I don't know, son, just don't squeal the tires or anything else stupid. Now drive, I'll tell you when to turn."

Garland kept us on back roads because there'd be road blocks on the main roads in and out of Saint-Lô, and after thirty minutes we reached the A84 motorway south of town. I put the pedal down.

"Whoa, whoa, whoa, Steve McQueen," Garland shouted. "They've got traffic cameras all over these highways. Go the damn speed limit."

"Why'd you steal a Porsche if we weren't going to drive fast?" I asked.

"Because I had a Porsche once but lost it to Billy Jean King in a charity tennis match." He must have seen me roll my eyes because he said, "You can watch it on your YouTube, son, and I've got proof she paid off the chair umpire. Hell, I can't even hear 'Philadelphia Freedom' anymore without wanting to puke."

The old man spent the next ten minutes cursing Billy Jean King before presenting me with an exhaustive list of all the professional tennis players he'd had romantic entanglements with and/or lost cars to. It wasn't exactly what I wanted to hear—I'll never look at Maria Sharapova the same way again—but as long as he kept talking I could put off telling him that Madeleine was dead. Thankfully, the rhythmic bump of the motorway put him to sleep just after he regaled me with an overly detailed account of his weekend in Cabo with the Williams sisters.

I took the Caen bypass to the A13 motorway back to Paris, and for an hour I was alone with my thoughts. In particular, thoughts about (1) Parker and how she'd broken my heart under the guise of performing a karmic good deed. I mean sure, I wasn't necessarily happy before this trip, but I did have an idea of Sadie to hold on to. It wasn't the real Sadie, but at least it gave me reason for hope because (2) now when I thought of Sadie, I could only think about how Parker was right about her all along, which somehow made me pissed off at both of them. Luckily, when I'd get almost too angry to drive straight I could always think about (3) Garland and how he was still wearing a floral dress and how I needed to snap a picture of him before he woke up.

The old man stirred when I stopped for gas at a service area outside of Paris, and while I filled up the car and bought him a cup of coffee, Garland took the opportunity to change out of his dress. We pulled back onto the motorway and I asked, "Can you tell me what happened to Saint-Lô after D-Day? How'd you and Madeleine get separated?"

Garland took a sip of his coffee and said, "The Allies didn't reach Saint-Lô until six weeks after D-Day. They had a hell of a fight in those damned hedgerows. The Nazis pulled back but kept hitting the Americans and the town with their big guns. Thankfully by then there wasn't a soul left in Saint-Lô. Finally, on July 17th, the 29th Infantry Division rolled into town and the men from Saint-Lô trudged back from the fields and farms to meet their liberators and inspect the ruins. I hobbled back with them, but Maddie stayed behind. She hadn't been the same since the bombing. There'd been moments of lucidity, but then she'd go right back to staring at the walls. It was shock of course, but what could we do for her on a damn farm? 'I'm going back to town,' I told her, but she didn't say anything, so I kissed her head and walked away."

"Was that the last time you saw her?" I asked.

"Son, who's telling the damn story?" Garland snapped and I laughed and apologized.

"We walked back to Saint-Lô, but Saint-Lô wasn't there. The quiet little town I'd snuck into three months before was gone. Bombed off the map. A few empty shells of buildings were still standing, and there were some with only one or two walls, but most of the town was piles of rock and dust. Only Notre Dame church resembled itself. One tower had fallen, and the roof was gone, but compared to the rest of the city it looked okay. They'd placed an American officer killed in the hedgerows underneath a flag atop the rubble outside the church, and many of the men from town stopped to pay their respects.

"I made my way to where Maddie's house had been—it was just a pile of rocks and wood. I kicked some of the rubble around, not really looking for anything in particular, just something I could take back to Maddie, and I found that ugly ass painting she'd hung in the hidden bedroom. I stuck it in my backpack and stumbled over to where a couple of American soldiers were standing. When I walked up I overhead one say to the other, 'We sure liberated the hell out of this place.' I punched him in the jaw and knocked him out cold, then turned to his buddy and said, 'I need to speak to your commanding officer.' He looked down at his friend, then back at me, and pointed toward some tents on the banks of the Vire. I limped over and stepped inside the tent and an officer said, 'Can I help you, son?'

"Now you gotta remember, son, I'm wearing Maddie's dad's old clothes, and I'd been wearing them for weeks, so you can imagine how rough I looked."

"I can imagine you in just about anything now," I said, and Garland stuck his middle finger in my face.

"I told 'em, 'My name is Lt. Garland Lenox. A German Focke-Wulf 190 shot me down over Saint-Lô on April 24th, and I've been in hiding with …' and then the pain in my leg and the smell of the burning buildings and the sight of the rubble finally took their toll. I passed out right there in the tent.

"I woke up three days later in England. Turns out my leg needed surgery, so they sedated me and put me on a boat full of injured soldiers crossing back over the Channel. I came to a few hours after surgery, and when they told me where I was I went insane. Pulled out my IV and knocked over every table I could reach and screamed at anyone who'd listen that I had to get back to Saint-Lô, back to Maddie. It took the four biggest men I'd ever seen to hold me down and sedate me again, and when I woke up the next day the process repeated itself. The next time I woke up I tried a little tact, but they weren't letting me go back to Saint-Lô. Hell, they'd never let me fly again. There were rules for evaders—pilots shot down but not captured by the enemy.

We couldn't enter enemy territory again because if the Germans ever did capture us we'd put resistance groups at risk. So I asked for some paper, to write Maddie a letter, and this young doctor came in and sat down next to my bed and told me she'd died. I don't know if he just assumed she'd died because she was in Saint-Lô, or if it was mistaken identity, or if they just told me that so I wouldn't try and sneak out and swim the Channel back to France. Hell, I don't guess I'll ever know now. But that's what they told me, and I had no reason not to believe it. I spent a couple weeks recovering in England, then they put me on a boat home. For a while I thought they'd send me to fight in the Pacific, but they never did. I spent the rest of the war in Montgomery at Maxwell Field."

"Garland, I'm so sorry."

"It's alright, son. And hell, I can't say I didn't live an interesting life. They only wanted single men for my job, guys with no attachments. If I hadn't met Maddie, I might have married someone else and lived that picket-fenced American dream. But when you meet the one, you know it, and you know there ain't no use looking anymore."

We were quiet for a few minutes after that, and then my phone rang. It was Fitz. "I better answer this," I said.

Chapter Sixty-Three

In which our hero adds Failure to Signal Lane Change (a €135 fine),
to his ever-growing list of misdeeds.

"Green! I want to congratulate you in person, so don't get killed okay?"

"Uh … I'm not planning on it," I said.

"Yeah," Fitz said, "but there are like six hundred cops and a mini-tank outside your hotel and they're about to raid—wait, you're in a car, aren't you? You sneaky bastard."

"Yes, we're in a car. Congratulate me for what?"

"For telling Sadie Evans what you should have told her twelve months ago."

"Wait, how'd you know about—"

"Sadie. She had you on speakerphone and live streamed your entire call on Facebook. Four million people were watching. Green, it was amazing, at the end, when she told you she loved you and you told her you didn't care, Sadie dropped her phone and kicked over her computer and you could see her creepy-ass dad and that Paul dude chasing after her. They'd been there the whole time, probably telling her what to say. It was beautiful."

"Dude, why didn't you ever tell me you hated Sadie so much."

"Because you told me you didn't want to talk about her, and I'm a good friend, so I didn't talk about her."

"Fair enough," I said.

"So I'm guessing you and Ice-T are a thing now since you basically made a sex tape."

"Who the hell is Ice-T?"

"Parker. Everyone at school started calling her Ice-T because she's a cop killer."

"She's not a cop killer," I said. "She shot at one cop, just one, on accident, and he's fine. And a picture in bed is not a sex tape."

Garland looked my way and I preemptively told him to mind his own business.

"Whatever," Fitz said. "I'm happy for you, Green. Now don't get killed because the OPPs say they're going to protest your funeral if you do."

I didn't have it in me to tell Fitz that Parker Haddaway and I were not, in fact, a thing, and that she was currently en route to Belgium with what was left of my heart, so I just said, "I'll try not to," and hung up.

Garland and I drove a few minutes before the silence got to me and I snapped, "Parker and I didn't make a sex tape, okay? She posted a picture of us in bed to make Sadie jealous."

"Oh I know," Garland said. "I saw the picture on the news while you were at the church."

I laughed and shook my head. This fame thing had definitely gotten out of control. "Besides," I said, "Parker didn't like me, not that way."

"Is that what she said?" Garland asked.

"In as many words," I said.

"Bullshit," the old man said.

I looked at Garland and he said, "Son, New Year's Eve 2006 I played poker with Tiger Woods, Lance Armstrong, and Bernie Madoff, and—"

"Garland, please."

"I'm just saying I know when someone is lying, and if that girl said she didn't have feelings for you, she was lying. Hell, you're all she's talked about for weeks. Now that don't mean you two are gonna live happily ever after. If my life story taught you anything it's that loving somebody don't guarantee a damn thing. But don't you for one second think that Parker doesn't have feelings for you, because she does."

Maybe Garland was right, but I didn't really want to talk about it with him, so I turned up the radio only to have a news bulletin interrupt the music—a news bulletin that mentioned our names.

"What the hell are they saying?" Garland said.

"Shhh."

I heard something about Saint-Lô, and Paris, and a Porsche, then we drove into a tunnel and the radio cut out.

"They know we're going to Paris," I said, "and they know we're in a Porsche."

"Not good," Garland said. "We've got to ditch the car."

"In a tunnel?"

"No, not in a tunnel."

"Okay, but where?" I asked, because the tunnel we'd entered was turning out to be the longest tunnel in the history of tunnels.

"Just drive, fast," Garland said, so I did, passing cars and weaving across three lanes like I was playing Grand Theft Auto. Then we saw the literal light at the end of the tunnel, and Garland said, "Now look for an exit," before he shouted, "There!" and grabbed the wheel and we cut across two lanes of slow merging traffic, skidding the wrong way down a one-way connector, and slid to a halt next to a tree on the edge of the River Seine.

"What. The. Hell!" I shouted, but the old man just laughed and said, "Who says you can't find a parking spot in Paris?" Then he slapped my knee and said, "Now come on, before some Good Samaritan calls the police thinking we're hurt." He was out of the car and moving, and I climbed out and tried to follow but my legs were wobbly after our most recent near death experience. "Metro's this way," Garland shouted back at me, and I hurried to catch up. We speed walked the two blocks to La Défense station, which housed a train station, a shopping mall, and our metro stop, and as we stepped into the station the all too familiar roar of European sirens filled the air. "We need two tickets, son," Garland said, as we stared at the huge map of the Paris Metro.

"Okay, but to where?

"Sacré-Cœur."

"I know that, but what metro stop?"

Garland stepped closer to examine the map and said, "Abbesses looks close. Get us there."

I stood in line at a ticket machine, and when it came my turn it took me several minutes to figure out exactly how to buy tickets, mostly because I'd selected Dutch as my language and couldn't figure out how to change it. And just as the annoyed sighing from the line behind me grew deafening, the machine spit out two tickets and we were off down the stairs to catch our train.

I picked up a metro map and read it as we descended the stairs. "Looks like we take Line 1 to Concorde, then switch to Line 12 and take that to Abbesses."

"I'll leave you in charge of that," Garland said, as we reached the platform packed with rush-hour Parisians trying to get home. "We shouldn't stand next to each other on the train," Garland whispered, "someone might recognize us."

"Okay, but we can't lose each other," I said. "Stay close enough to keep eye contact, and remember, it's Line 1 to Concorde, Line 12 to Abbesses."

Garland moved a few steps down the platform and a train arrived stuffed full of commuters. There was a push from in front as hundreds of people exited the train, and a push from behind as everyone on the platform tried to get onboard at once. I fought my way inside and the crowd pinned me against the far wall of the train where I couldn't see Garland or anything except the apparent vacationing sumo wrestler wedged in front of me. The train began to move, and at the next stop people poured on and off but I never caught a glimpse of the old man. Eleven stops later I exited at Concorde but Garland wasn't there. I pushed my way along the platform looking for him but was afraid to shout his name and draw attention. I was still looking for him when the next train arrived and more people flooded onto the platform and I gave up. Not knowing what else to do, I convinced myself Garland knew where to go and that he'd be waiting for me at Abbesses. I walked downstairs to Line 12 and boarded the next train.

That train wasn't as crowded, and I stumbled through the carriage looking for Garland but never finding him. However, I did find a heavy dose of paranoia after noticing our photographs on the front page of a newspaper on the floor. Soon I felt the focus of every eye on the train, so I slumped in a seat and kept my head down until we reached Abbesses seven stops later. Again I looked for Garland on the platform but he wasn't there, so I took the seemingly never-ending spiral staircase to the street and stepped out through an ornate glass-covered entrance into a lovely Parisian evening. Shouts of children and the lights of a merry-go-round drew my eyes across the square, and that's when I saw Garland sitting on a bench.

Sitting on a bench between two police officers.

Chapter Sixty-Four

*In which the ninth-fastest long-distance runner on the
J. P. Hornby track team runs for his life.*

"Garland Lenox? That crazy old man blowing up cop cars in Normandy? You've eaten too many bad snails Jacques. My name's Joe Anderson and I'm a Canadian citizen on vacation with my wife. I was supposed to meet her for dinner ten minutes ago. Check your little radios, I'm sure she's already reported me missing."

The old man seemed to think the louder he lied to the police the more likely they were to believe him. I was standing at least twenty feet away, pretending to talk on my phone, and could hear every word he said. I couldn't hear what the police said to Garland in reply, but when I caught his eye the old man shook his head to say they weren't buying Canadian Joe's story. It would all be over soon, if it weren't over already, but I didn't feel the relief I'd expected. Garland wanted to get to Sacré-Cœur, and though I knew he wouldn't find what he was looking for, I was willing to do whatever it took to get him there. The church was close, but I couldn't see it from the square, and I was so turned around

I wasn't even sure which way to look. Garland hung his head as one of the policemen said something into his radio. There wasn't much time now, and I had to do something, and though I'm not exactly proud of it, this is what I did.

Remember when I told you at almost any moment in France you can spot a little old man shuffling down the street carrying a baguette? Well, the one I found wasn't exactly a dead ringer for Garland Lenox, but in the fading sunlight he was close enough. "*Excusez-moi,*" I said, tapping the old man on the shoulder, "*Où est Sacré-Cœur?*"

The old man grunted and pointed behind me, and after he finished giving directions I didn't pay attention to I said, "*Merci,*" then handed him the Montblanc pen Garland bought me back in Atlanta. The old man looked at the pen, then back at me with confusion, and I said, "For your troubles," then before I had time to reconsider, I shouted across the square, "*Les fugitifs Américains!*"

The two policemen looked up, and channeling Garland I shouted across the square, "Catch us if you can, you cheese loving bastards," then I took off running, and the confused old man with the baguette began shuffling away, and thankfully, the police came after us, one chasing me, the other tackling that poor old man after perhaps the shortest pursuit of all-time. I heard the policeman behind me shouting stop, but I'd hit my stride, and in front of me frightened parents scooped up their children and leapt out of the way. I ran through the square, across the cobblestone street, and as I rounded the corner I glanced back to see the real Garland Lenox, ambling up the hill toward Sacré-Cœur.

Since that day I've tried to map my run on Google Maps, but when the police are chasing you it's hard to take note of landmarks. I hadn't run in days, and I was jet-lagged and sleep-deprived to the point that falling asleep during a dead sprint seemed entirely possible, but the adrenaline combined with the cool night air pumping through my lungs felt incredible, and I wasn't thinking about Parker, or Sadie, or even Garland anymore. My mind was unburdened, its only concern to convince my legs to move faster than they'd ever moved before, and not to boast, but I was flying. A security camera caught the moment I pulled away from the pursuing police officer like I was Usain Bolt, and this was apparently such a national embarrassment the Police Nationale instituted stricter physical fitness requirements the following month. I took streets at random, ran in and out of stores, and darted through an open air market, knocking over a cafe table in the process. Soon the air around Montmartre filled with distant sirens, and I ducked down an alleyway to catch my bearings, and when I looked up I saw Sacré-Cœur, sitting high atop the hill. I walked through the alley and across the street where exhaustion hit me square in the face. "Good lord there's a million steps," I muttered to no one in particular and tried to run up the hill to the cathedral, but now my legs felt like they belonged to someone else, and they responded to my requests for movement with varying degrees of disloyalty. My run slowed to a walk and near the top was little more than a trudge, but I finally made it to the last step, where the old man sat waiting for me.

"Son, what took you so long?" he said, and I tried to flip him a bird but instead fell beside him and waited for my heart to explode.

Chapter Sixty-Five

In which Garland Lenox finds what he's looking for.

"Damn son, I thought you said you were a runner."

"I am a——" I began to say, but my lungs weren't quite ready to do anything but gasp for air, so I held up a hand and tried to catch my breath.

"Take your time," Garland said, "but not too much of it." When I finally sat up next to the old man I noticed he was still panting from his own journey up Montmartre.

"You okay?" I asked.

"I'm just fine," he said, then pointed out at the city below and said, "Beautiful, ain't it?"

"Yeah," I said, too tired to actually look.

"I've probably come here a hundred times over the years. Hard to believe I never saw her ..."

I had to tell him. "Garland, Madeleine is dead. Sister Ava told me she died ... six years ago."

The old man put an arm around me and patted my back and said, "I know, son."

"Wait," I said, "you knew?"

271

"Well, I didn't know for sure," Garland said, "but even before we left home I knew odds were she wasn't still alive. Then when she didn't come forward, even after all the racket we've made since we've been here, I knew she was gone."

We watched a couple stragglers walk into Sacré-Cœur for evening Vespers, then I asked Garland, "So what now? Just wait here until they come and arrest us?"

"I suppose so," Garland said and laughed to himself.

"I don't get it," I said. "If you knew Madeleine wasn't going to be here why didn't we just turn ourselves in back in Saint-Lô?"

The old man smiled and said, "Son, I don't know if this'll make much sense to you, but Maddie and me, this was our place. This hill, this church, this view, it was ours. I didn't know it until today, I just knew coming here reminded me of her somehow, and that's why I came back, again and again."

"Sister Ava …," I said. "She wanted me to tell you that Madeleine prayed for you every day, and that when she sang, she would pretend you were there in the church, listening." Garland smiled and I said, "She wanted you to know Madeleine loved you, all her life."

We were both crying now and Garland said, "See son, this was our place, and I couldn't go back home without coming here one last time."

I wiped my eyes and said, "I'm glad you made it back here."

"Me too, son. Thank you for getting me here. Thank you for everything."

I waved off his thanks and we both watched another late parishioner jog up the steps and into Sacré-Cœur, and as they opened the door to the church the sixteen angelic voices of the Benedictine Sisters of the Sacré-Cœur de Montmartre filled the evening air.

Garland smiled and I wanted to ask him why he wasn't angry. Why he wasn't cursing God or the universe or whoever decided that some people get a lifetime with their true love and he and Madeleine only got two months. Because if love wasn't going to play fair I wasn't sure I wanted to play anymore. But before I could ask, the old man stood up, and as if reading my mind said, "Edwin, I know you're hurting now … I'm hurting too … but I want you to know I'd suffer for another seventy years just for five minutes more with my Madeleine. The pain is always worth it, son, so promise me, promise me you'll never give up on love."

"I won't," I said. "I promise."

The old man tousled my hair and said, "Now if you'll excuse me, son, I'd like to hear my angel sing, once more for the ages." And Garland Lenox turned and walked up the final steps and into Sacré-Cœur.

I never saw him again.

Chapter Sixty-Six

In which—oh hell, just read it and find out.

After Garland left I slid down a few steps and leaned back on my elbows to admire Paris from atop Montmartre. The sunset had left the city blanketed under darkening clouds of pink and purple, and it was beautiful and peaceful, minus the growing roar of a thousand sirens heading my way. The sirens were so loud I didn't even hear the red Vespa pull up a few feet behind me.

"Edwin Green," Parker Haddaway said, and I spun around in disbelief.

"What are you—why'd you—how?"

"Ever the wordsmith," Parker said with a wink, and offered her hand to help me to my feet. She was back in jeans and her old army jacket, and I noticed for the first time "Bloom" on the name tape. It was her dad's old jacket. "Where's Garland?" she asked.

"In the church," I said. "Wait, how'd you know we'd be here?"

Parker pointed at the radio in the dash of the Vespa. "The news said you guys were headed back to Paris."

"So you just drove around until you found us?"

"Yeah," Parker said, then held her phone up and added, "or I may have enabled your Find a Friend app. So why'd Garland want to come back here?"

I smiled and shook my head at her blatant disregard of my privacy and said, "After you left Saint-Lô, I went to the church, Notre Dame, and I spoke to this old nun who was friends with Madeleine. She was waiting for him, Parker. Madeleine was waiting for Garland to come back and ... remember when Garland told us the army listed him as killed in action after his crash, and how it took years to straighten out all the paperwork?" Parker knew where this was going. Her smile faded and she nodded and I said, "A soldier tried to help Madeleine find Garland, but he ... when he ... she thought he'd died."

"And ... he thought she'd died," Parker said, and I nodded. After a moment Parker asked, "Did you find out what became of her? Of Madeleine?"

"She became a nun," I said. "One of the singing nuns here, at Sacré-Cœur."

"The ones Garland would come listen to," Parker said, completing my sentence.

I nodded again and we were both quiet for a moment before I said, "She's dead ... she died six years ago."

Parker wiped a tear from her cheek and said, "That poor man ... I'm glad he at least made it back here."

"Me too," I said.

The police were getting close now, I could tell by the red lights bouncing off the white-washed cathedral behind Parker. "You've got to go," I said. "Why'd you even come back?"

Parker smiled. I never got used to her smiling at me. "Garland was afraid I'd hurt you," she said, "and I told him that was the plan. I didn't know how to save you without breaking you a little."

The first police car slid to a stop at the bottom of the hill, and the handful of tourists still sitting on the steps realized something was about to go down and they might not want to be around for it.

"I'd almost made it to Belgium."

"Huh," I said, turning back to Parker. She was sitting on her Vespa again with a hand held out.

"I'd almost made it to Belgium when I realized I didn't want to do this without you. I think ... I think I love you, Edwin Green. And I don't know where we will go or what we'll do, but we've got a small fortune and the rest of our lives to figure it out." She looked behind me down the hill as dozens more police cars arrived on the scene and she said, "Come on, we've got to go. Now!"

"Parker, I ..."

"Not the time for romantic proclamations, Edwin Green. You can tell me in Belgium. Now come on," she said, slapping the back of the Vespa.

We like to think we'll have ample time to make the big decisions in life. Where will I go to college? Who will I marry? But sometimes we're upside down on an emotional roller coaster, sleep deprived beyond all coherent thought, and we've got five seconds to make the call. I told you I was a cautious person. That I rarely made a decision, any decision, without thinking two or three steps ahead and considering all possible negative outcomes. And though I spent the last week making a lifetime of rash decisions, in that moment, when all I wanted to do was climb on the back of that Vespa and tell Parker Haddaway that I loved her too, my mind flooded with a thousand and one reasons not to run away and live a vagabond life in Europe.

"Edwin?"

"Parker," I said, "I—"

I didn't say it, but I didn't need to, she knew I wasn't going. And if this hurt Parker Haddaway, if it caused her even the slightest emotional discomfort, she did not show it. She just put on her helmet, cranked her Vespa, and was gone before I had a chance to say anything else.

My regret was instant. I watched her speed off around Sacré-Cœur and out of my life forever, then I sat back down atop Montmartre as dozens of machine-gun-toting men rushed up the hill toward me. They were shouting things I didn't understand, and I buried my head in my knees and begged them to take me home.

Epilogue

"Well," Fitz asked with a wry smile, "how was France?"

"Oh lovely," I said. "You've got to go sometime. I'd go with you, but technically I'm forbidden from entering the country."

"Wait, forever?"

"That's what they said, but Martin Blair thinks they'll reconsider after a few years."

Fitz laughed and slapped me on the back. "Green, you international-incident-causing bastard, it's good to have you back."

I smiled and said, "It's good to be back, bitchwhore."

It was three weeks later. I was back at J. P. Hornby for the first time since Parker lured me out of algebra with Sir Mix-a-Lot lyrics, and Fitz and I were circling the track during second period gym.

Ignoring vocal protests from a couple of school board members, Principal Denham decided to let me return for the last week of school and take my finals. I was going to pass half my classes, but it looked like a heavy dose of summer school was in my future. Which was fine, honestly. Mom and Carl, despite being overly nice since I returned, had followed through on their promise to ground me for the better part of eternity. At least now

I'd get to leave the house during the summer.

"I've been texting you," Fitz said, "but the messages all failed."

"Yeah," I said. "The French government kept my phone, and Mom and Carl said I can't have a new one. No TV or internet either."

"Ugh. So, what was French prison like?"

I laughed. "I wasn't in prison. They kept me in a hotel room at the airport. I didn't have a TV or anything, but they let me read *USA Today*."

"So you read about Garland's funeral?"

They found Garland slumped over in the back pew at Sacré-Cœur. Heart attack, probably from climbing Montmartre. And even though CNN reported this, I still meet people who insist that Garland died in a shootout with French Commandos, or that he escaped and is still wandering around France, but knowing the old man, that's probably how he'd want it.

"Yeah," I said, "Did you go?"

"Yes, it was amazing. Here," Fitz said, handing me his phone, "watch this."

In an obituary he'd written before the trip, Garland asked in lieu of flowers people bring water guns to his funeral, and it wasn't until the half dozen Omaha Prophetic Presbyterians on hand to protest began chanting, "God hates Garland Lenox" that everyone realized why. "There were like five thousand people at the funeral," Fitz said, "all of us chasing those assholes around the cemetery with Super Soakers. It was amazing. There are better videos than mine on YouTube, if your mom and Carl ever let you use the internet again."

I watched the video twice and handed Fitz his phone back. He asked, "And I guess you read where the CIA confirmed that Garland worked for them for like forty-five years after the war?"

"Yeah," I said, "but the article I read said they refused to comment on the validity of any specific claim Garland made on my videos."

"So do you think he was telling the truth?" Fitz asked.

"I think there was some truth in everything he told me," I said, thinking about the way the old man's eyes would twinkle whenever he'd dive into one of his crazy stories. "But then again, I think he was entirely capable of making some of that shit up."

We walked in silence for half a lap before Fitz finally asked, "So, Parker?"

I sighed and told him everything, from our kiss in the hallway to the last time I saw her on Montmartre, and when I finished Fitz said, "Shit, I'm sorry Green," because what else could he say? After another half lap he asked, "And you haven't heard anything from her?"

I shook my head and said, "Nope. Technically she's still wanted in France, so I imagine she'll keep a low profile for a while. But she did have a Swiss bank send me a check for $50,000."

"Wait, $50,000? For real?"

"Yeah," I said, "it barely covered my cell phone bill from last month. International data is expensive, man."

Fitz laughed and asked, "How'd you know it was from Parker?"

"There was an Oscar Wilde poem in the envelope."

"Hey Edwin, are you guys talking about Sadie Evans?"

It was the three senior girls, all wearing the same teal running shorts, and the T-shirt from the Christmas Dance, "Xmas in Mordor"—Yes, Tyler Godfrey was on the Christmas Dance committee.

"Why the hell would we be talking about Sadie Evans?" Fitz said.

"Well she's pregnant, right?" asked the tallest girl.

She was referring to the latest issue of *Celebrity Digest*, which featured Sadie, Trevor, and me on the cover below the headline, "Heartbroken Sadie Is Preggers. But Who Is the Father?"

I'd picked up a copy at Charles de Gaulle when the French government finally sent me home. It was too funny not to. But I didn't care about Sadie Evans. Not anymore. I got to school early that morning to check my LadiezzzLuvCoolE email account and there were twenty-seven emails from her. I deleted them all, then I deleted the account.

"She's not pregnant," I said. "But even if she is Trevor's not the father, and neither am I."

"I bet she reproduced asexually," the shortest girl said.

"Yeah, like a fern," the middle girl agreed.

"Are y'all talking about Parker Haddaway?"

The two sophomore guys had joined the conversation.

"Sadie Evans," the tallest girl said.

"I heard Sadie is going to play Parker in Ron Howard's movie about that old man, Garland Leonard."

"Lenox," I said, "and I don't think Ron Howard is—"

"Who's playing Edwin?" the shortest girl asked.

"Tom Hanks," one of the sophomore guys said.

"That doesn't make any—"

"No, Tom Hanks is playing Garland Leonard—"

"Lenox—"

"—and some nobody is playing Edwin."

"That sounds about right," Fitz said to me and I shrugged in agreement.

"Oh right," the other sophomore guy said, "and that creepy actor with the weird eye is going to play Lucian Figg."

We all hummed Lucian's jingle and the middle girl said, "Oh my God you guys, Lucian Figg is like my mom's brother—"

"So he's your uncle?" Fitz asked.

"I guess," the girl said. "Anyway, she said he's going to be like disbarred or something because he forged that Leonard man's signature and put him in Morningview Arbor against his will."

"You guys talking about Sadie Evans?"

Jeff Parker the weedhead had joined the circle.

"Parker Haddaway," said the shortest girl.

"So do you really think she got away with six million dollars?" Jeff asked.

After interviewing an endless procession of financial and fine art experts, the media concluded that if Garland did sell a Picasso in 1948 and put the money in a Swiss investment account, Parker got away with somewhere between one and twenty-five million dollars. There was no way to know though, and the Swiss bank wasn't talking, but one night Anderson Cooper said Parker made off with six million dollars, and now everyone took that number as gospel.

"I don't know," I said, "but she got it all."

Of course that hadn't stopped Garland's distant relatives from coming out of the woodwork and naming me in a civil suit. It looked like the judge would dismiss the case though, since Parker had all the money, and Garland's will contained the line, "Now I don't have any family, but if some distant cousins come forward looking for money after I die they are assholes and you'd better not give them a red cent."

Jeff said, "I heard she works for the Russian mafia, helping them swindle old dudes out of their fortunes."

"A month ago you said she was a cop," Fitz said.

"And cops don't work for the mafia," the middle girl said.

"Exactly," Jeff said. "Plus a lot of Russian women are tall and redheaded, and I bet if she——"

"Okay ladies," Coach Cowden bellowed from his office window, "I know we're all excited to have a celebrity grace us with his presence today. But unless you all want to fail gym, you'd better start moving. Now!"

Fitz and I walked away, leaving them to discuss Russian mobsters and the reproductive methods of asexual B-list celebrities without us, and another half lap passed in silence before he asked me, "So what's next Green?"

"Algebra," I said, and he laughed and said, "Not what I meant."

I smiled and said, "Yeah, I know."

I also knew I'd never sit in a classroom again without praying for Parker Haddaway to knock on the door and take me away. I knew as long as I lived she'd haunt my dreams. That every night I'd chase her through that field of yellow flowers, but I'd never catch her, and she'd never look back. But I also knew I had a plan. I could make more videos. I could write a book about everything that happened. I could shout from the rooftops that I loved Parker Haddaway and even a world away she'd hear it because I was still famous. And then she'd know, and then maybe, one day—

The clock is ticking, but my fifteen minutes aren't up yet.

THE END

L'église Notre-Dame de Saint-Lô, 1944
Photograph courtesy of U.S. National Archives

L'église Notre-Dame de Saint-Lô, 2011
Photograph courtesy of Harald Bischoff

Acknowledgements

The author would like to thank his wife, who never complained too loudly when he'd set a ridiculously early alarm to wake up and work on this book. Who never yelled at him too loudly when she'd be in the middle of telling him about her day, only to realize he'd been daydreaming about Garland, Edwin, and Parker, and hadn't heard a word she said. And who didn't sigh too loudly when he'd take his laptop on beach vacations, or roll her eyes too hard when he'd pull out his phone during the middle of a nice dinner to write himself a note because she understands that inspiration strikes when it will.

The author would like to thank his two young sons, who were both still taking naps while he wrote most of this book.

The author would like to thank Becky Philpott, for believing in this book, more than the author at times, and for whipping it (the book, not the author) into shape.

The author would like to thank those who read, critiqued, and edited various early drafts of this book, including Amanda Bast, Shay Baugh, Kelsey Beckman, Brian Brown, Jeremy Burns, Jessie Buttram, Alicia and Russell Clayton, Nancy Rives Cooper, Joseph and Ellie Craven, Karen Day, Lori and Johnny Dorminey, Jordan Green, JT and Whitney Hornbuckle, Laura McClellan, Nick Mielke, Knox McCoy, Cherri Randall, Tyler Stanton, and Anne Victory.

The author would like to thank Laura Eby and Emerson Freybler, for making sure the few lines of French throughout this book were much more accurate than if the author had just run them through Google translate.

The author would like to thank Billy Dee Williams, obviously.

The author would like to thank Jihad Abbasi at World Cup Coffee, Toni Holt at Ross House Coffee, the Auburn Public Library, and Auburn University's Ralph Brown Draughon Library for books, caffiene, and quiet places to write.

The author would like to thank Andrew Stanley, JD Lloyd, and Robert Pitman, for applying their legal expertise to a very random email the author sent them about the consequences of busting an old man out of a nursing home.

The author would like to thank Catherine and Michael Doherty at Le Manoir de Hérouville in Normandy, France, for a wonderful weekend and the best yogurt and butter the author or his wife have ever tasted. Book your own visit at www.manoirdeherouville.com

The author would not like to thank the French Republic, nor its several traffic cameras, for the speeding ticket he received three weeks after what was an otherwise lovely visit.

Also by Chad Alan Gibbs

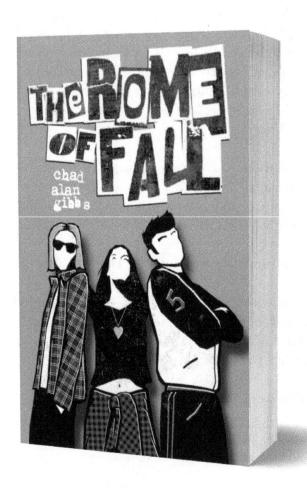

The Rome of Fall

A mixtape of Friday Night Lights, Shakespeare's Julius Caesasr, and early '90s nostalgia blasting through fifteen-inch speakers.

Available everywhere March 15, 2o2o

CPSIA information can be obtained
at www.ICGtesting.com
Printed in the USA
LVHW041653061120
670968LV00005B/848